The Revelation

The Descendants Series
Book Three

Susan Bushell

Violet,

Be Well,

Dedication

Many thanks to all who encouraged, pushed and supported me in writing this book. Special thanks to my wonderful family.

CHAPTER ONE

Gillian lay awake, her mind filled with thoughts of earth angels, disciples, and miracles. *Isn't this what everyone thinks about at three o'clock in the morning?*

Tomorrow, make that today, will be busy, I'll regret waking up this early. Banks scheduled an appointment for me with the attorney for Auntie Mary's estate. I still can't believe she never mentioned she owned a home in Glastonbury.

Banks said Auntie Mary also gave other items to the attorney with instructions to present them to Gillian once she learned of the Glastonbury property. What would she learn next? She was eager to discover more.

Frustration welled up within her. *So many secrets were kept from me. It's been several years since Auntie Mary passed away. The more I learn, the less I know.*

Banks said it was not secrecy but necessity, all in the "plan." An intricate plan to reveal only the knowledge she would understand and be equipped to use, for each new revelation. She could not learn of these things until she learned and accepted her true destiny. Only then would she understand what to do with the information. Each step revealed yet another secret.

We were so close. It's incomprehensible that Auntie Mary said nothing, not even a faint hint of all this.

Her mind drifted back to that day, just a few months ago, when she first met Samantha and Banks. She and her best friend and business partner, Maggie, received an invitation to a magnificent estate sale. It was a huge estate. When they arrived, Banks greeted them, manservant to the elderly heiress, Samantha Blythe. They soon realized they were the only ones invited, the invitation a ploy to get Gillian there.

Samantha, a dear sweet lady, proceeded over the course of a week to tell Gillian of her destiny. Gillian is a Chosen One, one of the twelve descendants, seventh generation. Descendant of whom? The original disciples, the twelve apostles of Christ. Among the numerous descendants, only seventh-generation descendants belonged to the group of twelve. Seventh generation descendants age slower and live longer, though she still had no clue how long; no one ever mentioned Samantha's age. Upon the death of one of the twelve, the next seventh generation in their line fills their role. At least that was Gillian's understanding. Samantha passed away soon after they met, so Gillian relied on Banks for guidance and answers to her many questions.

Where do they begin counting the seventh generation? Does that mean one of my descendants, seven generations from now, will take over from me? That must mean I will marry and have children. Or does it? Did Samantha marry? Did she have children? As far as I know, I'm not related to Samantha, so maybe I took the place of the child Samantha never had? My head is spinning. To add to this unbelievable story, there's Banks, the friendly, loyal manservant of Samantha. He's not your normal manservant, he's an earth angel. Unbelievable, but true. No surprise I can't sleep.

So much information has been given to me in the past few months. If I try to apply logical thought to what has taken place, I'll drive myself mad. It's too much to absorb, yet my heart accepts what it recognizes to be true. Many things on this earth cannot be explained, but through faith, I have learned to submit to what I know in my heart to be true. It's working so far. Well, somewhat.

Throwing back the covers and switching on the lamp, Gillian picked up her journal from the nightstand and wrote the questions disturbing her now.

I need clarification. Samantha told me to write my concerns in this journal, and a response would be given. Response was accurate, answer not always. Sometimes the responses are precise, other times I'm directed to another source to discover the answers on my own. Sometimes the answer appeared cryptic, a puzzle I need to complete before getting the full picture.

When Samantha first told Gillian the journal would help provide answers to her questions, composed by an unseen hand,

3

she thought Samantha to be suffering from dementia. She considered that many times in the initial days before she accepted that miracles and wonders still occur and she was part of them.

This trip being organized is important, no doubt. There is something in Glastonbury to learn, to experience before traveling back to Iona. I need to go back to Iona; at least that is what I'm led to believe. My acceptance increases daily, and my determination to accomplish the task before me is stronger after the frightful experience at Maggie's wedding. I want no one to endure the emotions I had that day.

Writing in her journal helped relax her. As she finished writing, her eyes grew heavy, and she drifted back to sleep.

"You must be cautious; there is more going on than you are aware. Do not doubt, understand what is true in your heart, and accept it."

Gillian jerked awake at the sound of the voice. Glancing around the room, she saw no one. Daylight poured in through the open curtain; it was morning. Searching around the room once again for the origin of the voice, she remained alone. *Must have been a dream.*

She entered the kitchen to find Banks alone. "Where is everyone?"

"Sam is assisting Mr. Somerhurst with further research before we leave for Glastonbury. They rose bright and early." Banks poured her a cup of coffee.

"Do you expect it will take long at the attorney's this morning?"

"No, I have communicated with him, and he will have things ready when we arrive. A few documents for you to sign as a formality, which shouldn't take long."

"Good, I'm eager to get it completed before our trip. Are we still leaving in the morning?"

"I believe it would be best if we leave this evening. You can rest on the plane and be ready for what you need to accomplish when we arrive in Glastonbury. If that meets your approval?"

"If you feel it's best we leave this evening, I'm in complete agreement. The sooner, the better." Gillian helped herself to an omelet and toast.

CHAPTER TWO

The attorney had everything ready for Gillian to sign. He then gave her a leather satchel with the instructions not to open it until she arrived in Glastonbury. She also received an envelope containing the key to Auntie Mary's house in Glastonbury.

As they left the attorney's office and made their way back to the car, Gillian felt the earth shake under her feet, so much so she stumbled toward Banks. He steadied her as they struggled to remain standing. She looked to see if everyone else on the street was okay.

An elderly man fell to the ground, she ran to help him.

"Are you all right?"

"Yes, nothing broken. What on earth was that? We don't have earthquakes here. Did something explode?" The old gentleman spoke with a shaking voice and fear in his eyes.

"I don't know, but it's stopped now. Will you be all right or can we help you get where you need to go?" Gillian asked, looking around for Banks, who was helping someone else up.

"Thank you for your kindness, but I'm all right," he said, brushing the dirt from his jacket sleeve.

Banks appeared at Gillian's side as the old gentleman walked away.

"Was he hurt?" Banks asked.

"No, just shaken. What happened?"

"Resistance. You are one step closer to foiling their cause. Despite their feeble attempt to scare you, you are shaken, but not scared."

"They will have to do better than that to scare us." Gillian laughed in an attempt to take the edge off her nervousness. She was not worried for herself but for so many innocents. She knew in her heart the darkness would now work harder to take as many souls as possible. *With help and guidance from God, I will do everything in my power to stop them.*

"Come, we must go home and prepare for our trip." Banks steered her toward the car, where the driver was waiting with the door open for Gillian to enter. She slid into the back seat while Banks sat in front with the driver. They were silent on the drive back.

Sam paced in the driveway as they pulled up to the house.

He jerked open Gillian's door. "Are you okay?"

Gillian gazed into his blue eyes and instantly relaxed. "Yes, we're fine. Did you feel it here, too?"

"Yes. I was worried." He ran his hand through his thick brown hair. His concern evident.

"I will leave you two to talk whilst I check on lunch," Banks said.

"I should have gone into town with you. When the shaking began, I feared something might happen to you."

"Sam, don't fuss, I'm fine. Banks was with me, and I don't think they would try to get near me when I have an earth angel in my company." But Gillian knew Sam had reason to worry.

"How did your visit with the attorney go?"

"It went well. I signed the prepared papers, and the attorney gave me a leather satchel with instructions not to open yet. I'm to wait until we reach Glastonbury. He also gave me the key to Auntie Mary's property. I don't understand why I can't look in the satchel until then. All the mystery still bothers me. If they would give me the facts, I could plan better."

"Hmm, seems like a little of the logical Gillian surfacing."

Gillian stopped, ready to give a curt reply. When she saw the mischievous look in his eyes, she relaxed. "Yes, I fight it, but it's still there. I know in my heart everything has a purpose, a reason, and a time, but when you've spent your entire life using logic, it's hard to stop. I'm not used to relying on my feelings and emotions."

"You're doing fine, you're adjusting better than you realize. Banks and Mr. Somerhurst spoke of it earlier. We're all proud of your progress."

"Thank you, Sam, that means a lot. Having your support and confidence helps more than I can say."

"Let's have lunch and then finish our preparations. Mr. Somerhurst and I have a few things to go over with you before we leave. He's excited about the opportunity to continue his research in Glastonbury."

They entered through the kitchen. Papers surrounded uncle Joe at the kitchen table. He looked up as they entered and began gathering his research papers together. "Gillian, I praise God no harm came to you during that unnerving event. Banks and I were just discussing the need to finish our preparations and leave this evening."

"Mr. Somerhurst, sorry, Uncle Joe, I agree. I'm not sure why, but I feel anxious, and as Sam just reminded me, I need to go with my feelings, not logic."

"I'm glad you remembered to call me Uncle Joe. I think it would be easier for you if Sam and Banks called me that as well. This Mr. Somerhurst is just too formal."

"As I am considerably older than you, I would prefer to call you Joseph," Banks said.

Uncle Joe laughed. "I see your point, Banks. Joseph will be fine. I think Sam will be comfortable calling me Uncle Joe, as I have known him since he was a boy."

Sam nodded. "Yes, you have, Uncle Joe is fine with me."

9

Uncle Joe patted Sam's shoulder. "Good, now all this research I've been going over has made me hungry. Is it time to eat?"

"Yes. The food is on the buffet in the dining room; we can talk more while we eat." Banks led the way.

Gillian helped herself to salad, soup, and bread. She was about to sit when Banks stopped her.

"Gillian, I must remind you, your place is at the head of the table. I will concede to many things, but the mistress of the house must sit at the head of the table."

"It's not Victorian times, Banks, but I'll do as you request."

"After lunch, we will adjourn to the sunroom for discussion. Joseph and Sam found new information they wish to share with us," Banks said.

"I spoke with Abe this morning; the newlyweds are enjoying themselves, and all is well," Uncle Joe said.

A wave a relief rushed through Gillian upon hearing of her best friend's safety on Iona. "I'm glad they are there. I wouldn't feel comfortable leaving if they were anywhere else."

Banks nodded. "I have made arrangements for them to stay here upon their return. They will have the place to themselves, and the driver will take them into town, so they will always be guarded."

"Good, I should have known you had everything covered." Gillian stood to take her plate into the kitchen.

"Gillian, you don't have to do that. Leave it here; it will be taken care of," Banks said.

"No. I need normal activity to keep me calm. I'll do the dishes and clear the buffet."

"I'll help." Sam gathered the other dishes and followed Gillian into the kitchen where they loaded the dishwasher and put the remaining food in the refrigerator.

"What happens to the leftover food? They have never served us leftovers, so I hope it's not thrown away."

"No, when they come to prepare the next meal, they take the leftovers to Pastor John's church, and he feeds the poor and homeless."

"Good. I like Pastor John. He is a true minister and uses everything given to his church to help others."

While they finished, Banks came in to prepare a tea tray to take into the sunroom.

"Joseph is waiting in the sunroom. I will join you there momentarily. Sam, can you stay and help me with the tea tray?"

Gillian looked at Banks and Sam, there was that unspoken communication between them again. *Banks doesn't need help with the tray. He wants to speak to Sam without me in the room.*

She opened her mouth to say something but thought better of it and went to join Uncle Joe.

Uncle Joe had a laptop on his knee and papers at his feet when she joined him in the sun room.

He looked up at Gillian. "I have an organized mess."

Gillian laughed, "At least it's organized." She watched as he made more notes before putting the laptop down and scooping up the papers.

He was like Maggie's Joe. Same brown eyes and dark hair, though his hair showed silver threads intermingled amongst the dark brown. Similar build, but slightly shorter than Joe. He shared his son's cheerful disposition. Maggie and Joe had been good friends long before they admitted their feelings for one another. When it happened, it happened quick. They went from first date to engagement to marriage in just a few months. They made a beautiful couple and Gillian couldn't be happier for her best friend.

Banks carried in a tea tray, and Sam followed with a plate of pastries.

"Now I understand why you needed Sam's help."

"We can't think clearly without dessert, can we?" Sam's mock indignation brought a smile to Gillian's lips.

Uncle Joe helped himself to a pastry and tea. "You are quite right, Sam, and if Joe were here, he would agree."

"Let's go over your information before we pack." Gillian took a bite of a chocolate éclair.

After wiping his hands on a napkin, Uncle Joe took a sip of tea before beginning. "Sam and I found some intriguing information regarding the early Christians in Glastonbury. While the Romans were in Britain, they sometimes tolerated and turned a blind eye to Christians; other times they executed them, depending upon the mood of the Emperor. It was a dangerous time, but that did not stop the faithful from getting out and spreading The Word. I kept thinking they must have had a safe place to hide during the turbulent times, but where was it? Until this morning I could find no evidence. While Sam was reading through a copy of an early communication between the followers, he found a strange mention of 'the winding hole' where someone took refuge. Neither of us knew what it might be until we looked at an old survey of the area from the third century, not a public map, it belongs to a helper. It included an area marked with a cross and two letters, WH. That was it. As we looked closer it appeared, not definite but almost certain, they identify a tunnel between the house of worship and another property. We think the winding hole is a tunnel."

"Wouldn't they have called it a tunnel?" Gillian asked. "A winding hole sounds rather odd."

"There was always the risk of being betrayed. We think it was code for a tunnel. It may not be as we think; though Sam and I feel we're on the right track."

Banks remained quiet.

"What do you think, Banks?" Gillian asked.

"It could be as they say, or it could be something different. We will have to wait and see."

"Ever cryptic Banks, you're not giving up anything, are you?" She sensed he knew precisely what they were talking about but could not confirm. As her eyes met Banks', he nodded and smiled. *So, he's acknowledging he knows more than he's saying. There must be a reason he can't say, or he would, I am confident of that.*

Uncle Joe continued. "We need to access more survey maps when we get there. We'll check if this notation is on any others, if so, when it was first noted. I have a list of every early building in the Glastonbury area and I've marked the location on a map, regardless of whether it's still standing. What I can't find, and it frustrates me, is the history of the twelve hides granted to Joseph of Arimathea and the disciples. There is little factual documentation. Though long considered folklore, it is more than that. We need to find the source. We know there is a reference to

King Arvirargus bequeathing the land to Joseph of Arimathea and his group, tax-free for life. We know it also came under the ownership of the Abbey. The history between the two is unknown. Tracing documentation back to the first century is more than difficult, some would say impossible, but I believe we are on the right track. I would like to continue my research while we're there, if that meets your approval."

"It's fine with me. Whatever documentation we can find of the early Christians the better. We know so little of their lives. I don't think it has any direct bearing on my work. But from a historical point of view, I'm interested in what you find. Banks, do you agree? Gillian asked.

"I think you are correct in your assumption. He should proceed."

"I agree. Any factual documentation of the early centuries will help us and the world," Sam said.

"Good, we're all in agreement. On that note, I will take a nap and prepare for our journey. What time did you plan on leaving this evening?" Uncle Joe asked Banks.

"Nine o'clock. It would be a good idea if you all rest and make ready for our trip. We can discuss any final concerns or questions over dinner." Banks collected the trays and left for the kitchen.

"Sam, did you download the pictures we took of the cave writings and the rocks on Iona?"

"Yes, I did. I was waiting until you returned to view them." Sam opened his laptop and clicked on a file.

Gillian moved closer to get a better view the pictures. "Can you enlarge them?"

Sam zoomed in on the writing in the first picture.

"Not much there, go on to the next one."

One by one they went through the pictures. When they came to the photo with what appeared to be a map of the cave, something caught Gillian's attention.

"Zoom in here." Gillian pointed to an area on the picture.

Gillian read the writing three times. It was a message to her in Ancient Greek. She read it two more times. *Sam can't read this. It's for my eyes only. I wish I could share this with him, tell him we're on the right track. Maybe one day, but not now.*

"Does this have meaning for you?" Sam asked.

"Yes, yes it does. You weren't able to read it, were you?"

"No, I could read most of the other writings but not this one. It was because it's only for you."

"I wish I could share it with you, but I can't, at least not right now. Though I can tell you, the news is good."

"That's a relief. Don't worry about not being able to share with me. I understand. We each have our role to play. I will

16

receive information I need to complete my work, as you will yours. Sometimes we will both receive the same information, sometimes not."

"Is that all the pictures?"

"Yes, except the one you took on Iona of the rocks. Did you want to view that too?"

"No, not right now. I think I'll go prepare for our trip and then I would like to take a walk before dinner."

"I'll do the same. When you're ready, knock on my door, and I'll go with you."

CHAPTER THREE

It was after five o'clock by the time she had showered and packed. Leaving her room, she walked down the hall and knocked on Sam's door.

Sam opened the door. "Perfect timing, I just finished getting everything ready."

They made their way downstairs and exited through the kitchen.

"Where would you like to walk?" Sam asked.

"Let's go along the path into the woods. Last time I came this way I saw a mother rabbit and her babies. I want to see if they're still there."

"There's a lot of wildlife around here. No one has ever hunted on this property, so it's a haven for the animals. A young deer once came up to me, not at all afraid. I remained still, not wanting to scare him away. He seemed curious about me. Once he satisfied his curiosity, he left. It was a nice experience."

"With all the negative feelings you deal with, I imagine experiencing nature at its best is a welcome occurrence."

"Yes, very much so." Sam hesitated.

"What is it, Sam? You can be open and honest with me. Tell me."

Gillian remained quiet, allowing him time.

18

"I dreamt of Samantha last night."

Gillian stopped. *She must have revealed something important to him.* Conflicting emotions showed on his face.

"Please, go on."

"She told me my gift of sensing the darkness will diminish and will be replaced with another gift. I will only sense the darkness when it concerns you." He hesitated.

She nodded.

"She said I will soon be relieved of this burden, and my main concern will be to protect and help you."

"Sam, that's wonderful! Before her death, Samantha told me she had requested this. She thought it an unfair burden for you. I'm happy you're my protector and helper, and I hope you are too."

Without thinking, she hugged him, then pulled back in embarrassment. "I'm sorry. I shouldn't have done that, but I'm happy at the news."

Sam beamed. "Don't apologize. I'm glad you think enough of me to hug me."

"I don't want you to think me too familiar," she muttered looking down at the ground.

"Oh my, you are an old-fashioned girl. I like that."

Gillian laughed. "I am. I often feel I belong in an earlier time. I'm not comfortable with the direction of our society."

"I wouldn't change anything about you. You're perfect just the way you are."

Gillian's stomach tightened, her heart rate increased, and her legs shook. *I've never felt this way about anyone. Could it be?* Her face grew warm.

"Oh look, there are the baby bunnies." Thankful for the distraction, she pointed.

They watched the rabbits play, tumbling over one another.

"Aren't they amazing? So innocent and carefree. I could watch them all day." Gillian whispered to avoid scaring the rabbits.

"So could I, but we should head back, so we are on time for dinner. Banks likes to keep everything on schedule." Sam took Gillian's hand, and they headed back to the house in silence.

The relaxed, cheerful expression on Banks' face when they returned to the kitchen prompted Gillian to ask, "You seem happy Banks, any particular reason?"

"I am delighted when things work out as they should. Dinner is ready. Joseph will be down soon."

"I need to run a comb through my hair, and wash my hands, then I'll be ready," Gillian said as she hurried to her room. *It feels so comfortable being with Sam. So many confusing emotions hitting me. Maybe I'm reading more into this than I should.* She washed her hands and sprayed water on her unruly curls. The water was enough to tame the mass of curls, so she could pull it back into a clip.

Looking happy and relaxed, Banks, Uncle Joe, and Sam waited at the dining table when Gillian entered. "I'm glad everyone is in good spirits and ready for our journey."

"I'm as excited as a child on Christmas Eve," Uncle Joe said.

She felt his excitement. She knew how much he loved history. Joe often talked of the trips he and his father took. While she was excited from a historical point of view, the importance of their journey did not escape her.

After an uneventful dinner, Sam helped Gillian clear the table and load the dishwasher. Uncle Joe wrapped the leftover food and put it in the refrigerator for the helpers to take to Pastor John.

With perfect timing, Banks entered the kitchen just as they finished. "The car will be ready to take us to the plane soon, please gather your things and make sure you have all you need. We will exit through the back into the stable yard."

Gillian checked items off her list. At least this trip she wouldn't have to borrow clothes. *I haven't over-packed, but I have sufficient clothes to last two weeks if needed.* Placing the leather satchel from the attorney on top of her clothes, she closed the suitcase. Her small bag contained her journal, toiletries, and a waterproof camera. *Although I have no idea why, my dream said to take a waterproof camera with me, so I bought one. Though all my dreams don't have meaning, I want to be as prepared as possible.*

Only the contents of the document belt remained. She double-checked its contents. The old map from the safe deposit box, the old keys and scroll from the trunk, and the key to Auntie Mary's house in Glastonbury. With everything on her list checked off, a final look around the bedroom verified she did not forget anything. Sliding the small bag over her shoulder and picking up her suitcase, she made her way downstairs.

CHAPTER FOUR

The short car ride to the plane took them to a different landing strip than they flew from the first time. The dark night prevented viewing its size or if there were other planes. Sam, Uncle Joe, and the driver took the luggage out of the car while Banks talked to the pilot. After they were settled, and the luggage stowed away, the driver spoke with Banks before leaving the plane. Gillian sensed the driver said something of importance to Banks and wondered what it might be. She decided not to ask. *He'll tell me if I need to know.*

Once they were in the air and the seatbelt sign went off, Uncle Joe surrounded himself with his notes and maps.

She glanced over at Banks, his eyes were closed, yet he didn't have the relaxed features of someone asleep. *Perhaps he's praying?*

"Do you mind if I sit here with you, or would you rather rest?"

"No, I'd love your company, Sam."

"So, what are your instincts regarding this trip? Any idea what we'll be doing?"

"Some, the rest will be revealed as we proceed. I do know, after we visit Glastonbury, we'll return to Iona. But there are things I need to experience, something I need to learn, and

23

people I need to meet first. What about you? Any instincts or feelings?"

"I'm not sure. Something of great importance will come of this trip. Other than that, I'm like you, waiting for instruction, guidance."

"I would like to look at the cave pictures again. Did you bring the thumb drive with you?"

"I did. If you want to look at them now, I can ask Uncle Joe if we can use his computer."

"Not right now. It can wait a day or two. But I do want to make sure I didn't miss something."

"You stress too much. I understand why, but you need to relax. We're here to help; it's not all on you."

"Thank you for reminding me." She paused. "Sam, I hope you don't mind me asking; if you do, just tell me. What of your family? Your parents, siblings? I never hear you mention anyone."

A flicker of pain crossed his face. "My parents are deceased, and I have no siblings."

"I'm sorry. I didn't mean to pry. Not only did I go through the loss of my adoptive parents, when I learned of my birth parents, they were already dead. So, I know the feeling well. I guess we are two orphans."

"Gillian, no need to feel sorry for me. I miss them, but I've been surrounded by a group that has nurtured and cared for me. After my parents passed, Samantha took me under her wing. I've had a good life. She was a loving and kind lady. The best anyone could know."

"Yes, she was. It was so strange, I felt an instant bond with her, and even though our time together was short, her passing resulted in a feeling of tremendous loss." Emotions arose, and she struggled not to cry, hating that she wore them so close to the surface.

Changing the subject, Sam told her funny stories of Joe, Abe, and himself when they were at college. Gillian laughed so hard Banks and Uncle Joe looked at them.

"Sorry for the disturbance. Sam's telling me funny stories about their college days." Gillian struggled to compose herself.

"Oh, I remember a few that were not so funny." Uncle Joe winked at Sam.

"Yes, well we won't go into those memories now," Sam said.

Gillian leaned forward. "Do tell. Were the boys up to mischief?"

"Well, not actual mischief, but they managed to get themselves into some, let's just call them, situations."

"I'm intrigued." Gillian raised her brows and looked at Sam.

"All right, I can tell I'm in trouble with you two talking, so on that note, I'll get some rest. I suggest everyone do the same; we have a busy time ahead of us." Sam moved to another row of seats and stretched out.

"You're not off the hook. I won't forget to remind Uncle Joe to share the stories."

Sam pretended not to hear her, stretched out with eyes closed feigning sleep. A hint of a smile playing on his lips said otherwise.

It's hard to imagine Sam as mischievous. He was so serious when we first met and only started to relax on Iona. No need to keep his guard up, Iona is the most peaceful place on earth. Gillian reclined her seat and closed her eyes. She woke with a start. *Something happened. No, no, not here on the plane. Something terrible has happened somewhere. But where?* Heart racing, she looked around. Sam and Uncle Joe looked at her with concern.

Sam moved to the seat next to her. "What's wrong?"

"I don't know. I was dreaming when a horrible feeling of catastrophe came over me, and I woke up."

Sam's brow furrowed. "Do you remember any details?"

Images flashed through her mind, all in a blur. "I need coffee to focus."

Uncle Joe stood. "I'll get it. We could all use some."

Gillian looked across the isle at Banks. His face expressionless, but his eyes said he knew what had happened. He returned her gaze, and as their eyes locked, a clear scene appeared before her.

A large group of people sang in a church. Everyone looked so happy. Some swayed in rhythm with the music. Then bodies and carnage everywhere. An explosion had brought the church walls down on the congregation. Men, women, children, babies, they were all....

"Oh no!" Tears fell hot against her cheeks. She looked at Sam. "How could anyone do that? Such evil."

Sam took her hand. "Tell me, Gillian, what happened?"

She placed her coffee in the cup holder. "It was horrible, a church full of worshipers, there was an explosion, bodies and blood everywhere, the walls fell on them. I don't think anyone survived."

"Was it a dream? Or a vision?"

"I'm certain it was a vision of something that happened or is to happen, but I'm not sure which. Banks, do you know?"

"It happened, Gillian, just as you said. There are those on this earth who want to wipe out Christianity." His voice trembled with emotion.

Gillian saw it was as hard on him as it was on her. "They will not win; we're stronger. They will be consumed by their own darkness." Gillian's voice shook, but her strengthening conviction grew stronger.

Banks nodded, his eyes still filled with sadness. "You are correct, Gillian. Since the beginning of time, the war of good and evil has been fought. The time has come to bring about a final end. God is providing his soldiers with the tools and miracles they will need. The line has been crossed."

"I promise to do everything in my power to help. I'll learn all I need to. I'll fight until my last breath. No one has the right to kill innocents." Gillian's emotions reflected in her words and on her face.

The four joined hands and prayed for all those who died and for the loved ones left behind.

To learn all she needed to, Gillian needed to remain clear-headed and focused. She spent much of the rest of the flight in a meditative state, sending prayers out to the world.

Banks sat next to her. "Once we land, a car will take us to the property. I feel confident you will receive direction there. Use your faith to help you, and be on your guard."

"Have you ever been to this property before?"

"Many times. It was under the ownership of one of your earlier ancestors when I first visited."

"Which one?"

"That story is for another time. We will prepare for landing in about ten minutes."

Sam's silence and the pain in his eyes concerned Gillian.

"I can handle it. I should be used to it by now, but when children are involved, it's always harder to recover." Sam attempted a smile to put her at ease; it didn't work.

"Perhaps you should check on Uncle Joe; he seemed upset," Gillian said.

"Good idea. Are you all right?"

Gillian summoned all her courage and conviction before answering. "Yes. I'm horrified and disgusted there can be such hate, but they will not win."

Sam nodded and headed for the back of the plane. Her words seemed to take the edge off his tension. His shoulders appeared less rigid as she watched him walk away.

CHAPTER FIVE

The sun was just coming up as they exited the plane. The air was cold, not freezing cold, but Gillian was glad of her jacket. Banks led her to a waiting car while Sam and Uncle Joe got their luggage.

"Banks, how far is it to the property?"

"About twenty minutes from here. Glastonbury is about ten minutes away, and we will drive through the town first. You can get an idea of the area as we drive through."

Gillian watched the scenery go by past the car window as they drove through the countryside. The hedgerows and stone walls lined the fields and properties. The English countryside always looked so organized. The driver slowed down as they entered the town center. Quaint little shops lined the narrow streets. *I would love to take a walk through the town if time permits while we're here.*

Banks was correct in his time estimation. Ten minutes after leaving town the driver turned off the road onto an unpaved lane. They drove for a few more minutes along a winding, tree-covered lane. *Looks like we're driving through a forest.* When they came to a clearing, the driver stopped in front of a manor house. Gillian gasped.

"Were you not expecting anything like this, Gillian?" Uncle Joe asked.

"No, not at all. I was expecting a small cottage. I had no idea it would be like this." Gillian stepped out of the car as she studied the house. It was big, not as big as Samantha's house, but much bigger than Auntie Mary's house she had been living in until the fire. There was little ornamentation, but the size and structure was very impressive. The front was flat with arched windows. Looking up she counted three stories. She took in every detail of the large, arched wooden door, with old fashioned wrought iron hinges. *The door looks ancient, I wonder how old this house is.* The sudden opening of the door made her jump.

"Oh, I didn't mean to startle you, dear," said a petite woman.

Banks stepped forward, greeting the lady. "Not your fault Enid, we are all a little on edge. Gillian, this is Enid, she has been the caretaker here for…, let's just say, a long time."

Gillian extended her hand, but the small lady swept her into a hug.

"I'm so happy to meet you at last. Mary spoke of you often on her visits here." Enid released Gillian from her tight hold.

"I'm pleased to meet you as well. You have me at a disadvantage though; Auntie Mary never mentioned this place or anyone she knew here."

31

"There's a reason and a time for everything, so don't you fret. We'll get to know each other soon enough. Now come in and make yourselves comfortable while I get a pot of tea and some food for you. I'm sure you're weary and hungry after your journey." Enid motioned them through the door and into the hall.

Gillian took in her surroundings. The hall was large but simple. A long table graced the wall nearest the door. A wooden bench, resembling a church pew, sat against the opposite wall. Several over-sized upholstered chairs were strategically placed throughout the hall. There were no stairs leading off the hall, which was odd as most homes had the main staircase in the hall. Wainscoting covered the wall to about the height of six feet, with rough plaster from the top of the wainscoting to the ceiling. It was an old home. Enid led them through a door into a narrow hallway. Further down the hall, they were directed into a bright, cheerful room. A seating area filled the center in front of the fireplace. On one side of the room, a desk and chair occupied the space near a window.

Gillian sat near the fireplace, while Banks took the chair opposite her, and Sam and Uncle Joe positioned themselves on the sofa. Gillian absorbed the details of the room. *Yes, this style reflects Auntie Mary. I can imagine her at the desk writing letters or perhaps recording in her journal. This room has a nice feeling of comfort.*

Enid returned with a rolling cart which held a tray with a teapot, cups, and saucers.

"Now, enjoy a cup of tea while I finish preparing breakfast. Tom, my husband, will come for you when it's ready." Enid placed the tea tray on the table and bustled out of the room.

Banks poured the tea. "Gillian, after breakfast we will leave you with Enid to tour the house and gardens. I am sure you are interested in seeing the rest."

"If you're going into town, I want to go too."

"No, we are not going anywhere. We want to give you the opportunity to get to explore the house. I am sure you have many questions about Mary's time here, and all those answers will come."

"We have so much to do. I'm uncomfortable wasting time touring the house with so many important issues at stake."

"Today is for planning and getting your bearings. The more comfortable you feel, the easier it will be for you to do what you need to do."

"Sam, what do you think?" Gillian needed his reassurance too.

"I agree with Banks. if you're feeling unsettled, your attention will not be where needed. Tour the house and garden, get to know Enid, and we'll discuss our plans over lunch."

"If you're both sure." Gillian's excitement over the opportunity to get to know this side of Auntie Mary produced a swirl of thoughts. *I'm learning more and more that I didn't really know the person I was closest to. Yet, I know she loved me. It must have hurt her not to share all of this with me. Even the fact we were related by blood. Not through my adopted parents as I had always been led to believe. If she hadn't been forbidden to tell me, I'm sure she would have.* She was so deep in thought she didn't realize a man had entered the room until he spoke.

"Enid has your breakfast ready."

Gillian recognized him as the driver who brought them here.

"You must be Tom."

"That I am."

They followed him to the kitchen where Enid had everything set up.

Sam held a chair out for Gillian as she took in the contents of the plates on the table. A variety of egg dishes, bacon and fruit.

Gillian enjoyed the vegetable omelet and a bowl of fruit. As soon as they finished eating the men departed to another room, leaving Gillian with Enid.

"Are you ready for the tour?"

"Yes. Thank you for taking the time to show me around."

"No bother at all. It will give us the opportunity to get to know one another." Enid led her back into the hall where they first entered when they arrived.

"This room is an entry, not so much a hall. As you can tell, only two doors lead from the entry and it includes no stairs." Enid opened the door on the opposite side. They entered a large room with a piano and a harp in the center; chairs flanked the walls.

I can imagine elegant ladies playing the harp and piano. I wonder who they performed for.

"This is the music room. The door on the far side leads into the main hall."

Gillian followed Enid into a large hall with a grand staircase going up the center of the hall. A hallway on each side of the staircase led toward the back of the house. Other than the door through which they had just entered, there were no other doors in this area of the hall.

"Forgive me for saying so, but it's rather an odd layout."

Enid chuckled. "That it is, I will explain later. Would you like to go upstairs first or tour the rest of downstairs?"

"Upstairs, please. Then we can finish downstairs and the garden if we have time."

Enid nodded. At the first landing, the stairs split with a stairway going up on either side of the landing. "We will go this way first." Enid motioned to the left. "This is the wing with your room. I have put you in the room Mary used when she was here."

Turning to the left at the top of the stairs Gillian was surprised to see how long the hall was. She counted the doors, five on each side.

"This hall has nine bedrooms," Enid said as they walked to the end.

"I count ten doors."

"That you do. The last door on the left is the back stairs, leading down to the kitchen. The door across from it is your room." Enid opened the door to Gillian's room and motioned for her to enter.

An elegant room greeted her. Rich draperies hung from two long windows, and a canopied, four poster bed graced the far wall. Floor to ceiling bookcases flanked the fireplace. Not a bare space remained in the bookcases, each row brimming with books.

She controlled the urge to look at the books. *Later.*

Enid opened the door to a large modern bathroom and another to a large walk-in closet-dressing room.

Auntie Mary's comforts here far exceeded those in her little home.

"I'll have time to explore this room later. Can you show me the other rooms?"

"Of course."

Enid led her to the room next to hers. It was not as large as her room but still very nice, with beautiful, vintage furniture. All the other rooms in this wing and the wing to the right of the landing were similar, each with a private bath.

Taking in the rich antique furnishings, Gillian's mystification grew regarding why Auntie Mary lived in her little cottage with simple furnishings. Though very nice before the fire destroyed it, curiosity still plagued her. Auntie Mary never mentioned this home, which again reminded her how those she loved had kept so many secrets from her.

"The last door on the right leads down to a walled patio, would you like to see that now?"

"No, I will explore that later. What's up there?" Gillian pointed to the stairs going up on either side of the central landing.

"The third floor has a large room which was used as a schoolroom, another library, and other guest rooms, much smaller than the ones on this floor. I'll show you that later. Would you like to go to the conservatory now? It was one of

Mary's favorite places to sit. We'll go down the back stairs through the kitchen."

Gillian followed Enid back to the door opposite her room, down the narrow stairs into the kitchen. She hadn't taken time to examine the kitchen when they ate breakfast. It reminded her of the kitchen at Samantha's house, similar in size and layout with the same homey, warm feeling.

"Did Auntie Mary spend a lot of time in the kitchen when she visited?"

Enid nodded. "Yes, this was her favorite room. She insisted on doing most of her own cooking and loved to experiment with herbs from the herb garden."

"That sounds like her. Did she visit often?"

"In her earlier years, yes, but not so much in her last years. She didn't want to be far from you." Enid led her through another door into a long, narrow hallway. Halfway down the hall, Enid opened a door on the left, and they entered the conservatory, a bright, sunny, calming room.

"Do you mind if we finish the tour later? I would like to relax and spend time in this comfortable room."

"I don't mind at all, Mary spent a lot of time in here. She would sit in here for hours reading and writing."

"I can imagine her in here; it feels so nice."

"I will leave you to enjoy. There's a button under the mantle of the fireplace. If you need anything, just give it a push and I will return."

Gillian wandered around the room, taking it all in. The sun shone on the view of the beautiful garden, creating warmth, despite the chill in the air. She eased into an oversized chair placed perfectly for relaxing and looking outside. Lost in her own thoughts and enjoying the tranquility, she dozed off.

The river was beautiful. She sat on the bank watching the water flow. A man approached her, dressed in a long flowing robe with sandals on his feet. "Come, I have something to show you."

"Who are you?" Gillian asked as she rose to go with him. She did not fear him and followed without reservation.

"Who I am is not important, what I show you is. Come with me."

Following him along a path, they came to an area with wooden dwellings. *This looks primitive. Where am I?* After a few minutes they came upon a large crowd. People as far back as she could see, all focused on someone in the center. The man guided her to an area enabling her to see and hear the speaker.

A man, dressed in a long robe, his dark hair and beard streaked with silver. Lines around his eyes showed his years, but his expression spoke of joy and peace. "We have much to celebrate. Our numbers grow daily. Our brothers to the north spread the word and have brought many to the Lord. As we rejoice, our work must continue. We cannot rest. We must seek the lost, the forgotten. Share the promise of our Lord and give hope. Let your light guide them."

Another man stepped forward. "There are still those near us who practice the old ways. We must stop them. Let them know of their eternal damnation if they do not repent and accept the Lord."

The first man looked down. He shook his head. "That is not the way we were directed. We are to tell them of our Lord and encourage them, but we must not judge them, lest we be judged. Christ did not win over the lost by fear; he won them over with love, as we must do."

The second man looked angry. "How can we let them go on with their wicked ways? They must be told!"

"Brother, I sense your pain. We want to bring them all into The Way, but it can only be of their free will. Instilling fear in them is not free will. We will win them over through the promise. Come with me. I have writings that tell of our Lord's teaching and love. They will enlighten you. This I know."

She followed the men into one of the dwellings.

The speaker pointed at a vessel containing scrolls. "You will find many writings of our Lord's teachings. You are welcome to stay here and read them."

The second man sat on a stool and withdrew a scroll.

Gillian watched; one by one, he read all the vessel contained.

When he finished, he turned to the speaker. "Do you have more of these writings?"

"We have many throughout this land and other lands."

"I want to read them all. I understand now why you teach as you do. I question our abilities. Christ could teach love because He is love, pure love. We are not pure; how can we teach only through love?"

"Did you not read where He said, 'Timeless truth, I tell you: whoever believes in me, those works which I have done he will also do, and he will do greater works than these.'"

"It is true then? He has empowered us?"

"Yes, believe with all your heart, and know the miracles you will see and be part of."

She woke at the call of her name. Enid stood before her.

"I'm sorry, Enid; I must have dozed off."

"Are you all right? That must have been quite a dream. I watched, not sure if I should wake you. Would you like to talk about it?"

"I dreamed I witnessed some of the early Christians. Though I didn't know him, their leader almost glowed with love and light. Confident in his mission, so calm. I wish I could be like him." Gillian told her of the dream in detail, still vivid in her mind.

"I think it was more than a dream, Gillian; it's a message to you. The man who guided you knew you needed to hear the words spoken. I came to tell you lunch is ready. Would you like to join us, or should I bring you a tray?"

"If it's not too much trouble, I would like to be alone; a tray would be nice."

"It's no problem at all. You need time to reflect on your dream."

I wonder who the leader was? Was it his words I needed to hear? He had the early writings of the disciples. Where was he? Was it here?

Enid interrupted her thoughts when she returned with a tray.

"I've told everyone to leave you alone, so you won't be bothered. I'll bring you a cup of tea after you've had time to eat, just relax."

When Enid returned with the tea, Gillian said, "Thank you, Enid. I think I'm ready to speak to the others. I'm sure they're wondering why I needed to be alone."

"I'll let them know. Sam will be relieved. He's been pacing the floor waiting to come in."

Sam rushed in. "Gillian, are you all right? Enid told us you needed alone time. For such a small lady, she's very bossy. I've been trying to get in here to check on you, but she wouldn't let anyone in."

"She did what she thought best. She thinks there's a message for me within the dream. I've been trying to clear my head and process it all. I don't know if I'm supposed to do anything with the information, or if I was just supposed to witness it."

"Is there anything I can do to help?"

"I'm not sure, let's wait until Banks comes in and I will share what I saw and heard."

"Might I come in?" Banks spoke from the doorway.

"Please do."

Banks chose a chair near her. "Tell me what happened."

She told them every detail. Her emotions rising to the surface as she spoke.

"The question is, was it a dream?" Gillian asked.

"No, Gillian, it wasn't a dream. You were blessed with a vision."

"Banks, were the scrolls what I think they were?"

"What do you think they were?"

"The writings of the disciples, our Bible."

43

"Then you would be correct. The early Christians had many groups around the world. Each group had a leader, a teacher, the one who taught them the Word. The writings from the disciples were copied and distributed to all the groups. In the early years, they were all on scrolls and usually kept in clay vessels to keep them safe from the elements. Eventually, they were all put together into what is now known as the Bible."

"It was amazing. Their leader was calm and emanated love and peace."

"Did anyone call him by name?" Sam asked.

"No, the only one who spoke to him was the angry man. It's not fair for me to call him the angry man as he really wasn't. That was just my first impression of him."

"Banks, do you know anything about him that might give some clarity?" Sam asked.

"It was Gillian's vision, not mine. If she is meant to learn of his identity, she will receive another vision."

"But what about the message Enid thinks the dream holds? Why am I not seeing it?"

"You are worrying too much. Why don't you and Sam take a walk? That will help clear your head and relax you. Not every answer comes when you wish. If you are to learn more, you will."

"You're right. I'm over-thinking again. Maybe it was just for me to see, no message, just a blessing. You might be right about a walk. I do want to see the gardens and it will relax me. I'd like to unpack first."

"I'll go up with you Gillian," Sam said. "I need to unpack too. When you're ready, we'll go for a walk."

CHAPTER SIX

She opened the suitcase and stared at the satchel laying on top. She knew she should open it but not now, she was still processing her dream. *I don't want to deal with it right now.* Laying it to one side, she concentrated on putting her clothes away. Taking her toiletry bag into the bathroom, she set everything out in an organized manner.

I need to write the dream in my journal. I understand what Banks said, but I still think there's something I need, something I'm not seeing. Sitting on the bed, she wrote every detail and then asked her questions. *I hope I get straightforward answers and not vague ones.* Satisfied she had documented everything, she put the journal away. *Time for a walk.*

Sam's door was open, he walked toward her as she approached. "Are you sure you want to go for a walk?"

"I need to walk, it energizes me. I get sluggish when I sit around too much."

"How do we get to the garden?"

"Enid said there's a walled patio down the stairs at the other end of this floor. I think it will lead out to the garden."

"Let's find out."

Gillian led the way to the end of the opposite hall and opened the door; the stairs were identical to the ones leading to the kitchen. At the bottom of the stairs, a long hall led to what she assumed was the kitchen. In the opposite direction, they went through a small entryway with a door leading outside.

"I want to explore the rooms down the hall, but that will have to wait. Let's go see the garden," Gillian said.

Sam opened the door, and they stepped out onto a large flagstone patio. Wooden benches flanked the walls of the patio, and a large fountain graced the center. Steps led to the garden.

"Oh, this is lovely," Gillian said, taking in the beautiful landscaped garden. The lawn extended as far as she could see. Shrubs and flowers grew along both sides of the lawn with ornamental circular flower beds down the center. Various fruit trees grew in amongst the flowers.

"I agree. Look over here; they have vegetables growing amongst the flowers. That's different."

"Auntie Mary used to do the same thing at home. She said certain plants were meant to grow near one another. I can't remember the reason. She did tell me, but unfortunately I didn't pay attention."

"You were young Gillian; don't be so hard on yourself."

"But so much of what she knew is now lost. I wish I'd been more attentive."

"I'm sure you took in more than you realize. Look how quick you were to remember she grew her flowers and vegetables like this."

"True."

They walked until Sam spotted a path between the shrubs. "Let's find out where this leads to."

They ducked under a low branch and stepped through the shrubs into a natural garden.

"Oh, I know what this is, it's a natural garden, all the plants are native to the area. Weeds, flowers, herbs, all the ones that grow wild, and you let them grow how naturally."

"How do you know that?" Sam asked.

Gillian laughed. "Because Auntie Mary had one."

"See, I told you."

"It feels good to be outside, enjoying nature's beauty. In my dream, or vision if you will, I felt such joy and happiness coming from the people. A sense of peace and calm emanated from the leader. Sam, what if I don't know what to do? What if we can't reach all those we are meant to? I can't stand thinking others will go through the experience I had at Maggie's wedding."

"What do you remember most about that?"

"A feeling of hopelessness, that there was no purpose in life, and I was all alone. A void inside me, darkness. It was horrible."

"Then remember that. Everything we do will offer hope to each person we come in contact with. Whether they take the offer is up to them. I've seen horrors you cannot imagine. There is evil in the world, Gillian, always has been. At some point, each person makes the choice."

"What of the ones who aren't aware they have a choice?"

"A choice is always there. Sometimes people find it hard to see, and I think that's where we come in. People today are jaded, few believe in miracles. Just as souls were won over in the time of Christ by his miracles, so will it be again. Not everyone believes on faith alone; some believe only when they see a miracle, others refuse to see the miracle for what it is."

"I understand what you're saying. I've seen miracles that others don't believe are miracles. That makes me sad, but you're right, we can't save everyone. I'm committed to do my part, whatever it may be."

"I know you are, as am I. Going off topic here, but I saw some pies in Enid's kitchen. Would it be rude if we asked for some?"

"In most cases, I would say yes, but Enid is different, and I don't think she would mind."

49

They entered the house the way they had left, and neither had any idea how to get to the kitchen without going back upstairs.

"Perhaps this hall leads down there. We know it's on the opposite side of the house from the patio, so let's see." Sam led the way.

Gillian wanted to open all the doors they passed but didn't want to get lost. *I'll wait and continue the tour with Enid.*

At the end of the hall, Sam opened the door to the back stairs leading up to the second floor. This led to the kitchen.

Enid was busy preparing food when they entered.

"We almost got lost coming back from the garden. I've never seen a house designed like this."

Nodding, Enid smiled. "It's odd to be sure, but there was a reason. You will learn soon enough. Now, if you two are hungry, I have fruit pies and a fresh pot of tea brewing."

Gillian laughed. "Sam was just talking about how delicious your pies looked."

"I cook for it to be enjoyed, feel free to help yourselves to anything you want. Now, would you like apple, rhubarb, or blackberry?"

"Rhubarb for me please, I haven't had rhubarb in a long time. We can get it though, no need to wait on us."

"They all sound good. I'll try blackberry this time and another kind after dinner," Sam said.

Banks entered the kitchen while Gillian was cutting the pie. "Good, I am just in time to indulge in Enid's tasty pies."

"Yes, and you need to be quick. Sam is plotting how many he can eat."

"I'm not that bad, but you have to admit they smell good."

"I have something to take care of," Enid said. "If you want anything, please help yourself. Tea is brewing, and the cups are on the table." She left them to enjoy the pie.

"Banks, what's the story on the layout of this house? Gillian and I nearly got lost coming back from the garden."

"It's quite a story, the full history that is, but I will give a summary. The original house was wooden. When that was no longer adequate, a sturdier house was built with a cellar. That house was destroyed, but the cellar remained intact. A small house was built over the entrance to the cellar, and then over the years, the house was expanded. Not wishing to disturb the foundation of the old house that held the entrance to the cellar, for reasons you will later learn, they got creative and did this. It served several purposes. Having such a strange design, anyone coming in to harm the occupants would get lost trying to find their way, thus giving the occupants time to hide or prepare to defend. Also, the original entrance to the cellar was maintained, but known to only a few."

"Why keep the entrance to the cellar a secret?" Gillian asked.

"You will learn the reason when the time is right."

"Mystery, always a mystery. It drives me crazy, but all right, if it's a secret today I will not push, as long as I find out before we leave."

Sam changed the subject. "What's our plan for tomorrow?"

"Gillian, would you like to share with us what you have in mind?" Banks asked.

"What? I've never been here before, and I know little of what needs to be done. I don't have a clue where to start." Gillian's voice grew louder as she spoke.

Sam gave Banks a confused look.

Banks met his gaze and sat back in his chair. "Sam, we are here to support Gillian. This is her journey, not ours. We follow, she leads. Now I need to visit with Tom. Gillian, if it makes you feel better, I can assure you, before tomorrow morning you will have direction."

"Wait, Banks. I'm sorry, I shouldn't get upset. You're right; I know I'll receive direction. I'm just a little overwhelmed."

Banks patted her shoulder as he left the room.

"I think I'll go explore my room and prepare for whatever I am to do. Thank you for helping me today, Sam. I feel much better."

"Anytime. If you need us, Enid will know where we are."

CHAPTER SEVEN

Gillian climbed the back stairs from the kitchen to her room. She was angry. No, not angry, frustrated. *They expect too much from me. How on earth am I supposed to know what we need to do? Banks is the earth angel, shouldn't he know? I can't even sleep without a strange dream or vision.* Her mind's rant continued until she closed her bedroom door. *Breathe, Gillian, just breathe.* As she calmed down, she thought of going back downstairs to talk to Banks, but knew it would be pointless. *Somehow, I'm supposed to know things. Samantha told me I would receive guidance. I need to have faith and relax. It will come.*

The bookcases caught her eye. *Nothing better to relax me than books. Some of these books look ancient. Uncle Joe will enjoy these.*

She ran her hand along the books at eye level, revealing time-honored classics, some she had read, several she had not. Moving to the bookcase on the other side of the fireplace, she viewed the rows of books and ran her hand along the spines. Jerking her hand back, she looked at her fingers, expecting to see an injury, a pinprick. Nothing. She pulled the offending book from the shelf. Touching it, she once again experienced a shock, burn, pain, something she couldn't describe. Grasping it with both hands, the sensation left her.

Gillian sat in the nearest chair and looked at the book. No title on the exterior of the book. Opening to the first page, she gasped. The title page read, Samantha. Gillian's thoughts raced. *How odd. Could it be about our Samantha?* Turning the page, she began to read. Lost in the book, she didn't realize how much time had passed and jumped when a knock came at the door.

She opened the door, Sam greeted her with a concerned look. "Are you okay?"

"Yes, I am. You look worried. Has something happened?"

"No, you've been up here for hours, we were a little concerned."

Gillian glanced at her watch. "Oh, my. I lost track of time. I'm so sorry. Have I delayed dinner?"

"Enid seemed to sense you needed extra time."

"Come in. I need to wash my hands and then we can go down together." Gillian motioned for him to have a seat and placed the book on the bed.

Sam was scanning the books when she came out of the bathroom.

"Uncle Joe will want to see these. There are all kinds of books on the early history of this area. Did you see these?" Sam asked.

"Yes. I thought the same thing when I saw them. I'm ready now. Sorry again for being up here so long."

"No problem. We've kept busy going over the maps of the area. Tom is an expert on the area and Uncle Joe is in his element. He keeps asking questions and taking notes. It's fun to watch him, and I'm learning a lot. If you don't mind me asking, what had your attention?"

"I'll share that later. I learned a lot too."

Banks, Uncle Joe and Tom were deep in conversation and only Banks noticed Gillian and Sam enter the dining room. Banks nodded at Gillian.

He knows what has kept my attention this long and that it helped me.

Tom stood. "I apologize, Miss, I'll be out of your way. Just having an interesting conversation with Joseph."

"No, Tom, please stay. I would like both you and Enid to dine with us this evening. If you would?" Gillian asked.

Before Tom could reply, Enid entered and answered for him. "If that's what you wish for us to do, then we will. You're so like your Auntie Mary. She always insisted we have the evening meal with her. I need Tom's help to bring in the rest of the food, and then we'll be ready."

"Can I help?" Gillian asked.

"No dear, you've had an enlightening day. Tom needs to work; he's been yacking like an old woman all afternoon." Enid chuckled as Tom followed her to the kitchen.

"What is it Banks? You look concerned."

"I worry for the ones who are not strong in their faith. The weaker ones who have endured loss are vulnerable. The darkness knows the time is limited and is targeting the weak and vulnerable. We face a difficult time. Faith will be tested, and some faithful may weaken."

Gillian felt her stomach tighten. "Is there something I should do to help?"

"We all need to do more, reaching out to those at risk, showing comfort and care to everyone we encounter. Our entire group is aware, and we have people working on this worldwide. They put themselves in danger in doing so, but they know any sacrifices made will be rewarded."

"But is there more I need to do?"

"Gillian, there are far more important things for you to worry about. We have a large group focusing on this. The other descendants are doing their part. Rest assured they are doing everything they can."

His words reassured Gillian. *Oh no, I got so distracted earlier I forgot about the satchel.* Her face showed her anguish and drew an immediate response from Sam.

"What's wrong, Gillian?"

"I just remembered something. I was engrossed in a book I found in my room and forgot about the satchel. The attorney told me to look in it once we arrived."

"I am sure there was something in the book you needed. Am I correct?" Banks asked.

Gillian smiled, remembering all she learned from the book, making her lose track of time. "Yes, Banks. I will excuse myself after dinner, though, to go through the satchel in case there's information we may need tomorrow. Uncle Joe, I think you might enjoy perusing the books in my room. They are ancient, and some are about this area."

"Thank you. I would love to. Let me know when it's convenient for me to look at them."

"Gillian, what did you find that held your interest?" Enid asked as she passed her the platter of roast chicken.

Gillian took a slice of chicken from the platter before replying. "I found a book that intrigued me. Actually, it made sure to get my attention." She paused and noticed Banks smiling and Sam's questioning look. "I'll tell you about it later, but for now I want to know more about this house. It's amazing and different from any house I've ever been in. I know they built it over the cellar of the original structure and then added onto over the years, but from the outside, it doesn't look to have additions."

"Looks can be deceiving," Enid said. "The original structure was built many, many years ago. The core of this house is the third house built on this site. That home was larger than the first two but not big enough to handle what was needed, so another house was built around the first and then another house built around that. There are a total of four additions around the original house. This house holds many secrets; some I know, and some I don't."

They all joined hands, and Banks said a prayer for all who were suffering and gave thanks for the many blessings bestowed on those around the table.

After everyone finished eating, Gillian helped Enid bring in the coffee and dessert while Sam, Uncle Joe, and Tom discussed local history.

"Unless anyone needs anything from me, I will go to my room. I have things to go over and prepare for tomorrow. I look forward to exploring the local area." Gillian stood to leave, saying goodnight to everyone.

Upstairs, the book still lay on the bed. Gillian wanted to read more but knew she should look at what the satchel held. Sitting down on the floor in front of the fireplace, she released the strap on the satchel. Taking care, she slid the contents onto the carpet in front of her. There were four envelopes, a large pouch secured with a ribbon, and another key.

She focused on the contents, willing the items to tell her which to examine first. Picking up the largest of the envelopes, she pulled out old documents, some in Latin and some in Old English script. She read the documents with ease. *So, that's why it was so important to keep the cellar.* Many thoughts ran through her mind as she learned the history of this property. The next envelope contained photographs of a group of children dressed in nineteenth century attire, two girls and four boys. The girls were seated, and the boys stood behind them. Flipping the picture over, she found names printed in neat handwriting on the back. It read, "Left to right standing, James, Joseph, Paul, and Thomas. Left to right seated, Samantha and Elizabeth, date July 21, 1838.

One name caught Gillian's attention. *Could it be? Could this be our Samantha? No, it couldn't be. The picture is too old; it must be a coincidence. Then why is the picture included in the satchel? Who were the boys? Were they all family? Siblings, cousins? What, if anything, does it have to do with what I need to do?*

Next, she picked up the pouch. Untying the ribbon, she pulled out an ancient scroll. Worn, fragile with faint writing, but

60

still readable. It measured about eight inches in length when opened and five inches wide. Handling it with care, she ran her fingers over the ancient script. Warmth shot into her fingers and up her arms, the scroll appeared to shimmer.

As she stared at the scroll, a bright light surrounded her and a scene appeared in front of her. A man sat at a small wooden table. His room was dim, lit only by an oil lamp. He wore a simple robe and sandals on his feet. Another man stood near him, it appeared the sitting man was writing what the standing man was saying. He was a scribe. *Who is the standing man?* She concentrated, focusing on his face, but shadows surrounded him, hiding his features. She heard and understood his words. Her gift of inherited memory coming easier. He spoke Aramaic. Listening to the words spoken, she felt transported to one of the most sacred times in Christian history. The light dimmed as the man finished speaking.

She looked at the scroll and began to read. She was pleased she had no difficulty in translating it. There was a difference in what she read and what she heard. *Why? Why were part of his words omitted?*

Jumping up, she grabbed paper and pen off the desk and wrote the words excluded on the scroll. *I don't understand. The words don't seem important. Are they important? The scribe omitted, "hope must never die."*

Reaching into the pouch again, she pulled out a silver locket and matching cuff bracelet, both with an intricate design. The locket wouldn't open, and she feared forcing it. In time she would learn what everything in the satchel meant, the picture, the documents, the key and the scroll. The envelopes she did not look in were not important at this moment, at least that was what her intuition was telling her, and she would follow it. Placing everything back in the satchel, she put it on a closet shelf.

I'm certain it will reveal more information next time I look at it. Everything has been set up to provide me with the guidance I need for the task before me. It would be impossible and detrimental to my conscious mind to learn everything at once. So much has been revealed over the past few months, and I will continue to learn on this journey. The inherited memory of my ancestors provides me with many of the tools I will need. I must keep a clear head, follow the guidance given, and stop getting cranky.

Sinking into a warm bath, she reflected on all she had learned today. *All of this put in place centuries ago, to be used when the time came. Little by little I'm guided in finding and learning what is needed. In doing so, it is setting in motion a time of miracles. Miracles which will help bring light to the darkness that has settled over the world.* Scared but confident, her faith remained steadfast, those who guided her would not fail her, nor she them.

Dressed in yoga pants and a t-shirt, she climbed into the large, old bed. *Auntie Mary slept here, in this bed. I so wish we could have talked about all this when you were alive Auntie Mary*. Memories flooded her mind, comforting her as she fell asleep with a smile on her face.

"You wouldn't have believed me then, my dear, and you know it, Little Miss I need only facts."

"Auntie Mary, I hoped you would visit me in my dreams tonight."

"You are doing well. You have many angels and helpers guarding and guiding you. Don't despair and never think you are alone. No human is ever alone. Once they open their minds, they will feel it too. It's a gift God gave us all at birth, the way to communicate with him directly."

"You mean prayer?"

"No, it's more than prayer. Prayer starts it, opens the door, it equips each and every human to converse with God and hear his words."

"Why aren't we taught that?"

"Because at some point it was made to seem insane, demonic, wrong for normal men to say God spoke with them. Those who did, were labeled fanatics, crazy, and so on. No one wants to be thought crazy. One by one, they shut their minds to it. They say their prayers, and never realize He is there waiting, waiting to talk to them too." Auntie Mary's smile dimmed at her words.

"I understand. I closed my mind to all my gifts until Samantha came into my life. I miss our talks, Auntie Mary. I miss you so." A tear slid down her cheek, and Auntie Mary brushed it away.

"I am always here, watching over you. You will have a busy day tomorrow. Be aware of the darkness though, Gillian. Pay attention to your instinct and keep your faith; you will be fine. Now rest, my child."

CHAPTER EIGHT

Her first thought was her dream when she woke. *Whether it was a dream or something else, it brings me comfort.*

She prepared for the day, curls secured in a ponytail, dressed in jeans, a sweater, and boots for comfort. One last look around the room verified nothing was forgotten.

The journal, I need to look in the journal. Sitting on the edge of the bed, she read the answers to her questions. "What was laid in stone by the blood of Christ will not be forgotten or undone. The legends of history are remembered by the faithful. Generations of the faithful kept written records waiting to be revealed. Miracles will increase, giving proof to what the faithful have believed. Seek and you will find."

Closing the journal, she reflected on the words written. *Time to prove all the doubters wrong.* Grabbing her jacket, she made her way to the kitchen.

In the kitchen, Enid greeted her. "Good morning, Gillian."

"Good morning, Enid. Is everyone else still upstairs?"

"You are the first one I've seen this morning. I'm sure they will be down soon enough. Would you like coffee or tea?"

"Coffee, please." Gillian sat at the table, and Enid handed her a mug filled with dark, steaming hot liquid. "Hmm, smells delicious." She tilted her head to one side and smiled at Enid.

"This is the same coffee Auntie Mary used to make."

"Yes, it is. She paid me a visit in my dreams last night. She said she had a nice conversation with you, and I was to tell you whatever you ask. That you are ready."

Gillian gaped. "I should be used to the visits and dreams by now, but I still find it unusual. Yes, the dream comforted me. I miss her so. You and she must have been close."

"Yes. She loved her time here, but her visits grew less and less frequent over the years. As you got older, you needed her more. She sensed you were questioning things, and she didn't want anyone filling your head with nonsense, so she spent more time in her cottage and less time here." Enid gazed off in the distance, as if remembering conversations from long ago.

"She was my rock; whenever anything was wrong, I would go to her. She never gave me the answer though. She guided me to find my own. She always said I had the power within me to tackle anything."

Enid grasped Gillian's hand. "She loved you. It bothered her she could not be honest with you, but she had no choice. You understand that, don't you?"

"Yes, I do, now. I was angry at first, and I still get a little frustrated by it all, but I understand. She knew how logical I am. If I had learned any of this before meeting Samantha, I would never have believed it. I've learned a lot during the past few months, and I'm still learning. You knew about the book in my room, didn't you?"

"Oh yes, the Samantha book. I was hoping it would call to you and it did. The knowledge within provided answers to at least some of your questions. It's been waiting on that shelf a long time for you to come and read it." Enid's chuckle amused Gillian.

"It's hard for me to grasp the number of things put in place over the centuries to help me and those like me find our strengths and do what is needed. It's all so…"

"Miraculous." Enid supplied the word Gillian struggled to find.

Gillian nodded. "Yes, that would be the word. Now, I need to visit the cellar before going to town. Will you take me?"

"I will show you the way, but it's a journey you must make on your own. You will understand why. No harm will come to you. Follow me, before anyone else comes down." Enid reached into the pantry and brought out a lantern. "You will need this."

Gillian took the lantern and followed Enid down a hall into another room. Enid pressed an area on the wall, and a door opened. After several minutes walking through a narrow passage, Enid stopped. Once again, she pressed on a wall, opening another door. Proceeding through a large room and again pushing on a wall, this door opened into another narrow hall which led to a dead end. Again, a push on an area of the wall opened a door.

"Now you're on your own. These stairs lead down to the original cellar. Careful how you go, they are worn and uneven." Enid turned the lantern on for Gillian and showed her how to operate it, full-ahead beam or multi-directional beam.

"Enid, I'll never find my way back."

"Yes, you will. You will know what to do and where to go. Have faith." Enid hugged Gillian and then watched her descend the stairs.

At the bottom of the stairs, a solid stone wall to her left and in front of her forced her to turn right. She walked down a narrow hallway, holding the lantern higher to illuminate the darkness ahead. At the end of the hallway an arched opening appeared. Cold, damp, quiet. Eerily quiet. Peering into the opening, the lantern provided insufficient light to see the entire room. Entering, she saw it was a chapel. An altar, carved from a rock, and benches also of rock. It looked as if they had taken large pieces of rock and placed them on other pieces of rock for support. *All very crude and uncomfortable but serving the purpose for which they were intended.* Sitting on a bench confirmed her thought. It was cold and hard, worn smooth by centuries of use.

Suddenly the room changed. Torches on the wall offered light and heat. The additional light revealed the room was larger than she had perceived, and full of worshippers: men, women, and children. A woman at the front caught her attention, dressed in a dark green, shapeless dress which flowed to her ankles, belted at the waist with a woven belt. A cloak was worn over the dress, held in place at the shoulder with a decorative brooch. The woman spoke to a man standing near the altar.

"Brother, when can we hold service again in our place of worship near the well?"

The man she spoke to wore a tunic, belted at the waist, over ill-fitting leg coverings, and sandals on his feet. The fabric looked worn but clean.

A tired smile appeared on his face. "Do you feel you cannot talk to the Lord in this chapel?"

The woman looked down at the floor, seeming uncomfortable with the question. "No, it would be nice to once again hear the birds sing while we worship, open to any new followers."

"I understand your concerns. The freedom to openly worship our Lord should be restored, but while those who would destroy

69

us watch, we cannot. They still worship the pagan ways and order death upon anyone who does not. Our time will come again, but we cannot spread the word when imprisoned or killed, so hide we must. Our ancestors sacrificed their lives. We have been directed otherwise. Count the number in this room; our fold continues to increase. Let us pray for that day." The man bowed his head, and the congregation followed.

Gillian watched the service. When it ended, everyone except a small group left the room. The remaining group of men spoke in whispers. She concentrated harder to hear all the words.

The tallest man spoke. "We have once again moved the sacred items to keep them safe. Are we to do more now? Or wait?"

The group turned as one to an elderly man. He looked old and frail, but a gentle smile accompanied a deep, strong voice. "As caretakers of the sacred Way, we must continue to pray and seek guidance. One day, one will seek what we protect, which must remain safe until that time. It is not for us to question when or how, only to do as guided."

The vision ended. Gillian once again sat in the cold, dark chapel by herself, with only the light from the lantern. *I know there's a message within the vision. The meaning will come as and when I need it.*

Rising from the bench, she spoke to the empty room. "I have a feeling I will make more trips to this room before I leave, and you will provide what I need to know."

"As it is to be."

Gillian spun around. She heard the deep, strong voice of the older man, but she was alone. She remembered Auntie Mary's words, "You are never alone" and sighed. *It seems I have several companions.*

Looking around the room one more time. *What might be revealed on my next visit?*

As Enid foretold, she found her way back to the kitchen without getting lost.

CHAPTER NINE

Sam, Banks, Uncle Joe, and Tom were at the kitchen table when she entered. Enid placed platters of food on the table and turned toward Gillian. Studying Gillian's face, she nodded as though satisfied with what she saw.

"Come, Gillian, sit and eat before this lot takes it all." Enid turned back to the stove to pick up the kettle.

"Can I help with anything?"

"No dear, sit and enjoy. I'll just get the pot of tea."

Gillian greeted everyone. Banks had that mysterious smile he so liked to do. The one that said, "I know, but I'm not telling."

No one asked where she had been, and she offered no information. *What I observed was for me only, not to share, at least not now.*

"Good morning, Gillian. I thought perhaps you were still sleeping, but Enid said you were taking care of something important." Sam gave her a quizzical look

He's wondering what the "something important" is. I hope he understands. "Yes. I'm glad I made it before you ate all the food."

"What? You malign me. It may seem I eat all the time, but it's only when I'm blessed with such good food."

"I can't argue with that. Enid is talented."

Uncle Joe stood, taking his plate to the sink. "Thank you Enid, for a delightful breakfast. It provided me with sufficient energy for my day. Gillian, there is so much history here that I'm struggling where to start. Between my research and the information Tom has shared, I need more time than we have to take it all in."

"Uncle Joe, you're welcome to return and use the house anytime you wish. I'm sure Tom and Enid would not object," Gillian said.

"We love to have guests; it keeps us from getting lazy," Tom said.

"I would enjoy spending more time here. I'll take you up on the offer as soon as I am able." Uncle Joe's face lit up at the prospect of more time to learn and explore.

"Gillian, unless you need my presence, I will stay here, and Sam can accompany you. After they take you into town, Tom and Joseph wish to explore the area. I would like to enjoy our time here and take a nice, long walk," Banks said.

"That's not a problem. I want to get a feel for the place and visit a few sites, so if Sam can put up with me…"

"Difficult thing you task me with, but I think I'm up to it."

Gillian laughed. "Glad you feel you can handle it. I'll try not to be too difficult." She finished her breakfast and stood to take her plate to the sink.

Enid took the plate from her. "You will not do any kitchen duties here, you have enough to do. I prepared a picnic lunch for you and Sam. I hope that meets your approval. Or would you rather eat in town?"

"A picnic sounds wonderful." Gillian hugged her and whispered, "Thank you," in her ear.

Enid glanced at Gillian's feet. "I'm glad you have sensible boots on. You should have no difficulty in climbing Tor and walking the area."

"Not the most fashionable, but they help me stay on my feet. Do you think this jacket will be warm enough, or should I wear something heavier?" Gillian asked.

"It's mild today; your jacket should suffice."

"Gillian, enjoy your day, you are in good hands with Sam."

"Thank you, Banks. Today will be a good day. Enjoy your walk." She looked around. "I may need a guide to find the front door. I can't remember which direction it is."

Enid laughed. "It takes a bit of getting used to, but you need not find the front door. Tom has the car around back. I'll show you the way out."

Gillian followed Enid through a door into a small room with boots and coats, which led to a small hallway and a door leading outside.

Gillian shook her head. "I feel like Hansel and Gretel; perhaps I should leave breadcrumbs."

"You'll get used to it; we've not lost anyone yet. Enjoy your day."

Tom held the car door open as she climbed inside. Uncle Joe and Sam soon joined them.

When they were near the town, Tom caught her eye in the rearview mirror, "Gillian, where would you like me to drop you off?"

"Along the main street would be fine. On the way here, I noticed several quaint little shops I would like to explore, before we go to the Tor, if that's all right with Sam?"

"No objection from me. I'm a tourist."

"Joseph and I are going to a village near here. We should return around four o'clock. Will that be all right with you?" Tom asked.

"Yes, that sounds fine. I'm looking forward to exploring the area. Don't rush on our account. I'm sure Sam and I will find plenty to keep us busy."

At the edge of town, Tom pulled the car over to the side of the road. "If you need to return sooner, call me; I have my cell phone." Tom handed her a card with the numbers to the house and his cell phone.

"Enjoy your day. Uncle Joe, I'll be excited to hear about your discoveries."

"Same to you, Gillian."

Sam retrieved the picnic basket, and they walked toward the main street.

"I thought I wanted to see the shops first, but now I think I would rather stay outside longer. It's a beautiful day. Let's head toward Tor first. From what Tom said, we should pass the spring and the well on the way to Tor."

Sam placed his arm around her shoulder. "If that's what you want to do, it's fine with me. I want you to relax and enjoy today. No brooding on what you might miss or not understand. When you learn to relax, clarity will come."

"You're right. Let's enjoy the day, my fellow tourist."

Sam laughed. "That won't be hard in your company. Come on, the entrance to the well is over there."

They entered the Chalice Well gardens area. The Garden was designed to be relaxing. Walking paths intersecting with nature. The sight and sound of the water gently flowing over the rocks before entering the pool, captivated the visitors. The water took on a red color as it flowed over the rocks but was clear in the pool. Wild flowers and plants natural to the area, grew along the paths and around the water's edge. Designed to encourage visitors to connect with their spiritual self. There were other people visiting today, everyone respectful of the spiritual aspects of the area, remaining quiet and only whispering when they spoke.

Odd, I thought I might feel something here, since the history of the springs are steeped in spiritual legends. It's a beautiful place to visit and relax, but I don't feel drawn to anything.

On the path to the Tor, Sam spoke. "What did you think of the well and spring?"

"It gives off a peaceful feeling. I felt calm and relaxed in the garden, and even more so near the water sources. I'm not sure if it's because of the area legends or appreciation for the beauty of nature. I didn't feel, well, anything like what I felt on Iona. What about you?"

"I agree. It's calming and spiritual in the sense of enjoying what God placed here for us to enjoy. Legends are strong in this area. Some focus more on the Druid side and King Arthur, others on the connection to Christ. Did you notice how red the water looked running over the rocks?"

"I did. I can understand how some might think it represents Christ's blood. Yet, the water is clear; it only looks red where it flows over the rocks. Is it the minerals in the rocks that make it appear red?"

"Yes. Some believe Joseph of Arimathea brought the cup which held the blood of Christ with him. Legend says it is the blood of Christ that makes it red. The cup itself has spun many stories of legend, the most famous being King Arthur and the hunt for the holy grail." Sam breathed heavier as they climbed up the Tor.

"Sounds like you need to run more. A little out of shape, maybe?"

"Is that a challenge? I'll race you to the top; winner picks where we picnic."

Gillian accepted the challenge and took off at a faster pace. Running this incline would be foolish; she would give out before reaching the top. Sam took off at a run. When Gillian passed him, he was bent over with hands on knees trying to catch his breath.

"I should have known better than to run it. With the added burden of the picnic basket, I won't say you had an advantage, but you win and get to choose the picnic spot." Sam still gasped for breath.

Gillian was a little winded but had made uphill runs part of her routine. She knew how to pace herself. "The Abbey grounds would be a good place. One of the travel guides indicated there were several nice spots for picnics."

From the top of the Tor, she took in the magnificent view of the town and surrounding countryside. *I wonder if my ancestors came here. It would have looked much different then.*

The tower, the only remains of Saint Michael's Church, stood tall on Tor. The church was destroyed during the Dissolution of the Monasteries in the 16th century.

"Sad to think so many churches were ransacked and destroyed during that time. All because of one man."

"Gillian, it's never just one man. They need help and use their followers to fulfill their evil goals. A plentiful supply of weak, greedy people willing to do wrong for money and power. They will do anything he or she wants until another, more powerful one comes along who they can benefit from. Their followers are loyal only to themselves, they serve at the will of immoral and evil ones for their own gain. It occurs throughout history. Evil serves them well for a time, but in the end, they must pay the price. No one escapes the final reckoning."

"Do you think we will succeed? Will we be able to convince those who have lost their faith to change their ways?"

"Followers of Christ have worked to do this for over two thousand years. No one knows what others will choose. I do know, one day all wrongs will be put right. Time for me to pay my debt."

Gillian looked at him, puzzled.

Sam laughed. "Picnic, lunch, I was wrong to think I could get the better of you, so now I pay my debt. Guide me to the picnic place of your choice. We will take a slow walk, along the main street to the Abbey."

"A slow walk sounds good. I admit, I'm a little out of shape for running. I need to get back in my routine, or I will have to forgo dessert."

"I'll go for a morning run or walk with you anytime, Gillian. I would rather exercise than pass on dessert."

"Deal. Schedule permitting, we'll go for a morning run."

Gillian gazed over the landscape on the way back down. *What mysteries do you hold? Are the legends true? Is this the birthplace of Christianity in England?*

Walking along Main Street, they stopped to window shop.

"Do you want to go in?" Sam asked.

"No, I'm more of a window shopper than a real shopper. It seems there are a lot of new age, crystal shops."

They stopped in front of a bakery and the Pastries in the window caught their attention. Sam took her hand and pulled her inside.

"Hello, what can I help you with today?"

Gillian drew her attention away from the display of pastries and looked for the source of the voice. She could barely see the woman behind the big display case. The short, round woman possessed a bright smile and sparkling eyes.

"Hello. You have so many delicious choices; I can't decide," Gillian said.

"Well, maybe I can help. Is it sweet or savory you are looking for?"

"Sweet," Gillian and Sam said in unison.

The lady walked to the far end of the display case. "My Eccles cakes are my most popular, followed by the fruit tarts and the custard tarts."

Sam stepped closer to view the pastries she pointed to. "I would like an Eccles cake. Gillian?"

"Perfect, it's been a long time since I enjoyed an Eccles cake, but I remember them being delicious. Are they made with natural ingredients? I don't like to eat anything with preservatives or artificial flavorings."

"If God don't make it, we don't bake it. I'm glad you appreciate the natural things in life, as God intended." The woman put the pastries in a small box.

Gillian was pleased the woman was a believer. "We have a bakery in our town similar to yours, delicious and all natural. I have to curb myself, or I would visit them every day."

"That would be the Jacobs' bakery."

It was a statement not a question. Gillian struggled to speak, taken aback by the woman's comment. "How did you know?"

"Sharon is a distant cousin. Our family have been bakers since time began. My name is Theresa, and you must be Gillian. I have heard all good things about you, and knew your Auntie Mary well, good woman."

Gillian struggled for words. "So, you are one of the..."

Theresa helped Gillian finish her sentence. "Helpers, yes. Our family have been helpers for a very long time. There are a few of us in the area. Some bad blood comes in from time to time and tries to chase us out, but they never win."

Gillian relaxed and spoke without stumbling. "I'm pleased to meet you, Theresa. If your baking is half as good as the Jacobs', we'll return for more. How did you know it was me? No one knew we were coming here."

Theresa handed Sam the box. "You have a presence. One can't help but feel it. Besides, your Auntie Mary showed me a picture of you last time she visited. She knew you would come one day and wanted to make sure I kept an eye out for you."

Gillian absorbed Theresa's words. *It makes sense. Auntie Mary would let helpers know I would come one day. She would always want to ensure there were people looking after me.* "That sounds like Auntie Mary."

Sam listened to the interaction between the ladies, not intruding in their conversation.

"Oh, I'm sorry. How rude of me, this is Sam." Gillian gestured towards Sam.

Theresa smiled at him. "Pleased to meet you, Sam."

"I'm pleased to meet you too. I hope we'll see each other again while we're here," Sam said.

"I'm sure we will."

Sam pulled out his wallet.

"You can put your wallet away; this is my treat. Enjoy the day and take care of this girl." Theresa waved her hand.

"We appreciate your generosity. I can only agree if you let me pay next time." Sam put his wallet away.

Theresa chuckled. "I might let you pay and I might not."

Sam shook his head, sensing there was no point arguing with this little lady.

"Thank you, Theresa. I'll be sure and tell the Jacobs we met," Gillian said.

When they arrived at the Abbey, Sam set the picnic basket and pastry box down while he retrieved his wallet. "I'm paying for entry, so don't even try to argue with me."

Gillian smiled, "I'll let you this time."

They walked around the grounds of the Abbey. Sam pointed to a large old tree; its branches offering shade but not so dense as block out the sunlight, allowing grass to grow underneath. "What do you think of that spot?"

Gillian looked in the direction he pointed and liked what she saw. It was off the path of tourists, but still within sight of the Abbey. "Looks like the perfect spot for a picnic."

Removing their jackets, they spread them on the ground to sit on. Sam opened the picnic basket and took out the lunch Enid had prepared; small meat pies, strong cheese, and fresh fruit.

"I'm glad she didn't give us dessert, I would feel guilty eating the Eccles cake and neglecting Enid's hard work," Gillian said.

"I wouldn't have felt guilty. I would have eaten both." Sam replied, taking a bite of a meat pie.

They ate in silence, enjoying the view of the abbey and surrounding area; and watching the occasional tourist pass.

"I didn't expect to run into anyone who knew of me. Are there helpers everywhere?"

Sam took the last bite of his pastry before replying. "Almost everywhere. Everywhere I've traveled, and I've traveled the world, there have always been helpers. There are many. Most come from generations of helpers, some are the first in their family to be a helper."

"Who decides who the helpers are?"

"Gillian, do you have to ask? Think about it. Who would know the goodness in their hearts, their faithfulness, and commitment to God?"

"Oh, of course. Well, now I feel silly for asking. So, they are all chosen by God. That makes sense. Do helpers ever stray?"

"Yes, as you saw with the young girl at the dinner. With some, we can intervene and save, but some are lost to us. The more evil the world becomes, the harder it gets. Some people are strong in their faith and don't waver regardless of hardships. Others are not as strong and succumb to temptation. It does not end well for those who stray, and it's a huge jolt to the group when it happens. It is one thing to lose someone who has never known all the wonders, but to lose one who has benefited and experienced all the blessings hits everyone hard."

Gillian thought on Sam's words. "Yes, I can understand that. Have you ever met an evil person who has no good in them?

Sam's jaw clenched. "Yes, I have. I wish I hadn't. They spread destruction everywhere they go. Their souls are so dark it's painful to be around them."

"Are they born that way?"

"That I don't know. There are a few who are the darkest of darkness, evil personified." Sam's face and tone revealed his disgust.

Sam paused, seeing the brooding expression on Gillian's face. "Don't worry Gillian, you're stronger than they are, and I hope you never meet one, but you will know if you do. The other dark ones are lost souls consumed by greed, lust, jealousy, any or all of the destructive sins. They are weak in body and mind, consumed by the darkness. They live to destroy others. It's like they suck all the goodness and joy from those who succumb to them."

"Whatever my role is in awakening people to the world that God intended, I will do everything I'm directed to do. Speaking of Izzy, the young girl at the dinner, do we know what happened to her?"

"You will be happy to hear she has changed her ways and is staying somewhere she can be helped until she recovers. When this kind of thing happens, we send them where guidance can be given. They are monitored and supported, until we are sure all the darkness is gone. Now, get your mind off the darkness in the world, and try the Eccles cake. It's delicious, one of the best I've tried, if not the best. If you don't like it, I would be happy to take it."

"Oh no, you won't. I saw the look on your face when you were eating yours; you're not getting mine!" Gillian bit into it, then laughed at the forlorn expression on Sam's face. "Oh, my goodness, this is delicious."

"Told you so. I wonder if Enid knows how to make them."

"We need to ask her. I wouldn't be surprised if she does. She seems to have many talents. I've always wondered why they are called cakes. They consist of flaky pastry with currant filling so why not call them Eccles pies?"

"That's a mystery you need not solve, but if you do, let me know because I've wondered the same thing. I think I'll put this picnic basket behind the tree and we can collect it on our way out. Few people come close to here, so it should be safe."

"I agree, then you can enjoy walking without carrying it."

They found a waste bin and disposed of their trash.

Sam took Gillian's hand as they walked toward the ruins of the Abbey. "Do you know the history of the Abbey?"

"Some. I know the archaeological digs have revealed several foundations here but no evidence to support the legend of a first century church. These ruins are the remains of the Abbey destroyed by Henry VIII in 1539, during the Dissolution of the Monasteries. In the tenth century, they erected a monastery around the old church, but it burned in the twelfth century. This Abbey was built over the ruins of that one."

"Good, you did your homework. I'm impressed. This site has known Christianity since the first century. There are some who argue against that claim, but the locals will stand firm on the belief this is the birthplace of Christianity in England. The faithful from all over the world have made the pilgrimage here for centuries. There was also a strong Druid community here. It's said the original Christians converted many of the Druids to Christianity. You will find a mix, those who celebrate the Druid vision and those who celebrate Christianity."

"The history is interesting. The early Christians suffered for their faith, but they didn't waver. They worshipped God in even the hardest times. I admire their dedication and strength. It must have been difficult facing persecution and death for their faith."

"Gillian, there are places in the world where persecution continues. It seems ironic in this day and time, but it happens more than people are aware."

There was a tour guide giving the history of the ruins and Gillian and Sam joined the group. When they finished the tour, Gillian said, "Let's go back to the Lady Chapel, I want to explore that a little more."

"Did something catch your attention?"

"Just a feeling. I want to view the crypt."

Sam took her hand as they made their way back to the Lady Chapel. "I want to look at the Abbots kitchen afterward, if that's all right with you?"

"Yes, I wanted to see it too."

Sam led the way down the stairs to the crypt. At the bottom of the stairs was a small opening with a clear covering over a well. With no one near, they took their time looking at the well.

"They call this Joseph's well. Legend says the first church was built near this well. Some claim the Abbey created the legend to increase visitors. The problem with that theory is the legend was around long before they built the Abbey."

Gillian nodded. "I have found in studying history that every legend has some basis in fact."

They walked around the lower level, looking into openings which once served as burial places for the wealthy. An altar, known as Joseph's Altar, occupied one opening. Gillian sat on a nearby bench, and Sam followed.

Gillian closed her eyes, *Does this site hold secrets of the lives of the earliest Christians? What must it have been like for them to be empowered by Christ to spread the Word and The Way to all nations?* She remained quiet for several minutes, but nothing came to her, no visions or voices.

"Come on, let's go explore the Abbots kitchen. What interests you there? Are you going to learn to cook the old way?" Gillian teased.

"I might, and if the electric grid gets knocked out, you'll be glad I made the effort."

They laughed as they climbed the stairs. Gillian heard it first, singing and rejoicing. She stood outside the Lady Chapel looking for the source of the sound. A smoky swirl appeared before her. She saw a round church. Entering the building, she saw everyone dressed in robes of varying styles. The women wore long scarves over their heads, flowing down over their shoulders. A young woman at the back of the room caught her attention. She looked too young to be the mother of the infant she held, but Gillian's instincts told her otherwise. Gazing at the baby's beautiful chubby face and bright eyes brought a smile to Gillian. The baby seemed to see her; when their eyes met, the baby smiled. *Can the baby see me*? The image changed along with the clothing of the worshippers. These worshippers did not look as happy as the first group; their faces held expressions of fear.

Gillian sat on a stone bench and listened to the man speaking to the congregation.

"You know we are under attack, we have endured this before. There is no need for us to hide, not yet. We will go about our business and try not to draw attention. Do not be outspoken, now is not the time. The Romans outnumber us by thousands. This will pass as it always does. Every time an Emperor changes we endure persecution. One day soon, there will be a ruler of Rome who will believe in The Way."

Another man in the room stood. "So, you ask us to hide our light under a bushel. Is that not against the will of God? Are we not directed to spread the Word to all?"

"Yes, James, you are correct; we are to spread the Word of our Lord to all we meet. We may still minister, with caution. If we are too obvious, we will anger the pagans, and they will report us to the Romans. Have patience. A better time is coming."

The vision changed again, and Gillian saw an empty, neglected building. *Where is the congregation? What happened to them?*

Once again the vision changed. Men filled the room. They wore dark robes belted with rope, and all had short hair.

Monks? Did this little church belong to monks at one time? The vision faded.

"Gillian, are you all right? I have been talking to you, but you kept staring."

"I'm sorry, Sam. Was I distracted long?"

"A few minutes, enough for me to wonder if I needed to do something."

Gillian shook her head. "I had a vision. I don't want to talk about it right now. Can we go to Wearyall Hill?"

Sam did not press. "Of course. Do you want to look at the museum on the way out?"

Gillian felt edgy. Something about the visions remained out of her grasp. She started to say no to the museum but thought better of it. "Yes, that would be nice. It will help me clear my head before we go to Wearyall Hill. Will we have time before we are to meet Tom and Uncle Joe?"

Sam looked at his watch. "Yes, that shouldn't be a problem, we have over two hours. If we are a little late, I don't think they will leave us behind."

"I'm sure you're right, but I don't want to keep them waiting. Oh, I almost forgot, you wanted to go to the Abbott's kitchen. Let's go there first and then the museum."

"We can skip the Abbott's kitchen. It's not important."

"No, Sam. We have time, and I want to see it too."

They felt transported back to the fourteenth century when entering the kitchen. Laid out as it would have been then, the original structure had undergone restoration. It contained four fireplaces. One for meat, another included a bread oven set into the rear of the fireplace, and the other two for all other foods and vegetables. The kitchen spoke of the wealth of the Abbey. A kitchen of this size, with all the amenities of its time, was not the norm. They prepared food for residents of the Abbey, rich visitors and poor travelers. Staying true to their faith, they did not discriminate and served the rich and poor alike. The work here would have been hard, but it felt like a happy place.

"I wonder if they have a cookbook in town or the gift shop from this period? I would love to get one and learn what kind of food they prepared here."

Surprise lit Sam's face. "I didn't know you liked to cook."

"I do. I love to experiment. I don't cook as often as I used to, but I enjoy it. I like learning about regional foods and foods from different time periods."

"Something else we have in common."

"Now I'm the one who's surprised. You like to cook?"

Sam winked at her. "Guilty. In my travels, I learned to experiment with spices, herbs, and produce from the different regions. It relaxes me, and I do my best thinking when I'm cooking."

"When we get home perhaps you would like to cook for us?"

"Deal, as long as you cook for us too. I need to find out if you can cook."

Gillian nudged him with her shoulder. "Oh, I'll show you. I may be a bit rusty, but I love a challenge."

They left the kitchen sharing some of their favorite dishes and epic recipe failures. Sam was more adventurous in his cooking experiments than Gillian.

The museum was interesting. *I'm glad Sam loves history as much as I do. It means we have even more in common.* Walking around the exhibits and reading the information, she knew the museum had part of it wrong. A continual Christian church presence existed here since the first century. *My visions have confirmed that. One day all will know the truth, but not yet. It will reveal the true history and strengthen the faith of all, opening the eyes of those with no faith.*

The tour of the museum relaxed Gillian, leaving her appreciative of the blessing of the visions of the early Christians.

CHAPTER TEN

"All this walking and talking has my throat dry. Do you want to stop and get a cold drink on our way to Wearyall Hill? Sam asked.

"You're in tune with my thoughts, I was just thinking a refreshing cold drink would be nice."

"I am in tune with your needs."

Gillian gazed into his eyes. Her feelings for him grew stronger each day. "Yes, I think you are."

Sam went into a shop which sold cold drinks while Gillian waited outside. Voices yelling caught her attention. An elderly man walked toward her as a group of four young boys taunted him. They ran around him saying something she couldn't hear. When the elderly man stumbled, Gillian intervened.

"Sir, are you all right?"

"No worries, just trying to get to the church service."

He's trying to make light of the situation, but his eyes show fear.

The boys looked to be about ten or eleven years old. She walked up to the tallest boy, who seemed to be the instigator of their mischief.

"Why are you bothering this man?"

"What's it to ya? Get out of my way, or you'll be next."

"I don't think so." Gillian placed her hand on his shoulder. Shock showed on his face.

Gillian felt this boy's anger. Not a bad boy, more misguided and angry. She felt his pain at losing someone he respected and loved, his grandfather. Now he felt no one cared. He felt alone.

"Your grandfather would be ashamed of you for this behavior. He's probably looking down from Heaven wondering what happened to you."

The boy's face showed fear, and the other three backed away.

"You don't know my granddad, and there ain't no Heaven, so get lost."

"Hmm, you don't think there's a Heaven or God. You are so wrong." Leaning forward, she whispered a message he needed to hear in his ear. "Now, the choice is yours, Daniel; make good choices and be with your Grandfather again one day, or follow the path of destruction and risk never seeing him again. We all face choices. Your grandfather was a good man. He cared for others and worshipped our Lord. He is now reaping his rewards in Heaven."

The boy swiped tears from his eyes. She had touched a nerve.

The old man he had been harassing spoke. "You know, my grandson is grown now and has moved away. He used to go to church with me. I could never take your grandfather's place, but I would be happy if you would consider coming with me."

Daniel looked confused. The three other boys stood still, heads hung in shame.

"Mister, I've been mean to you. Why would you want me to go anywhere with you? I'm bad, not a nice person. Ask anybody who knows me. They'll tell you I'm a loser. You don't want to be seen with the likes of me."

"Daniel, you're not bad. You have made a few bad choices and acted on them. You can be whatever you want. Will you come?"

With his hands in his pockets, Daniel looked at Gillian and then at the old man. "Just this once. To make it up to you for being mean. I ain't making no promises though."

The old man smiled. "Daniel, I'm honored. My name is Nathaniel Bridges, but you may call me Uncle Nat if you like."

Sam came up behind Gillian. "What's going on?"

Before Gillian could speak, Nathaniel answered. "Your lady introduced me to my new friend Daniel." He turned to the other three boys who still showed faces of shame. "Now boys, if you would like to come with Daniel and me, you are welcome. If not today, maybe another day."

The three boys apologized to Gillian and Nathaniel for their behavior but declined the invitation for church. Daniel urged them to come, and after some persuasion, they agreed. Gillian and Sam watched the boys and Nathaniel walk away together.

"I can't leave you alone for a minute. What on earth was all that about?"

"Misguided youth being given a choice. I hope they always remember this day and make better choices. They are good kids, just misguided. I think Daniel was the instigator and leader; if he changes his ways, the others will follow."

"Can I ask how you showed them the way? I'm intrigued."

Gillian told him everything that happened as they sipped their drinks on their way to Wearyall Hill.

"I'm impressed. You're getting stronger, but Gillian, it could have ended badly."

"With those little guys? I could take all four with no problem."

"When I said you're getting stronger I meant spiritually, not physically."

Gillian laughed. "I know what you meant. Maggie and I took self-defense courses in college, and we were good students."

"I guess I need to be careful and not make you mad."

She noticed a bag under his arm. "What's in the bag?"

"I almost forgot, this is what took me so long in the shop." He handed the bag to her. "I asked about a cookbook from the time period relating to the Abbott's kitchen, and she remembered she had one in the back. It took a few minutes for her to find, but now we have one. Well, it's yours, but I thought maybe you could share with me."

"Sam, this is fantastic. I can't wait to look through it. Thank you so much, and yes, I'll share. We should have a cookoff when we get home. The kitchen at Samantha's is big enough."

"Sounds like fun." He studied her. "When are you going to quit calling your house Samantha's?"

"Probably never. it's so hard to get used to. I think in my mind it will always be Samantha's."

Taking her hand, Sam guided her to a path leading to Wearyall Hill. "Almost there."

Gillian looked at the hill in front of them, smaller than she had imagined. She thought it would be bigger.

"I asked the lady in the shop if they revived the vandalized thorn tree. They tried, but it didn't survive. They planted another graft from the original tree, and it was vandalized as well. She was very emotional when she talked about the tree. She said the people here were devastated when it happened. The tree represented a sacred monument to them. There is still the tree at the Abbey, and there are other grafts of the original around the country. The one on this hill meant the most to them because this is the site of the original, according to legend."

"I hate to see any tree destroyed, and I understand the locals' distress. People need the connection to history. Did she say if there were plans to plant another here?"

"No, she didn't say. If they do, I hope they install cameras so if it happens again, they can find who did it."

From the top of Wearyall Hill she took in the panoramic view.

The surrounding farm land, and the houses they had passed on their way here. The hill offered a good view of Glastonbury Tor. Gillian gazed around, seeing only land. "I thought this was close to the water?"

"Yes, in the first century. Most of the land you see over there was once under water. Waterways have changed and land drained; the landscape has changed quite a bit since then."

"Can we sit and enjoy the view or are we short on time?"

Sam looked at his watch. "We have about ten minutes before we need to start back. While you take in the view, I'll look at your cookbook."

"Help yourself, but it's our cookbook."

A beautiful day, with crisp, cool air, and a bright sun shining left Gillian trying to imagine what it would have been like arriving on this coast in the first century. As she lay on the soft grass and closed her eyes, another vision took form.

She stood on the hill watching a group of pilgrims make their way up the hill. *I'm viewing it through the eyes of another woman, a first century woman. How do I know that? I can't explain it, but I do. I feel her strength and her faith. I also feel her emotions and hear her thoughts.*

"Since I arrived here, many have followed. Word of the Lord spread throughout the area and we gain converts daily. It is a wonderful time. The Roman troops near here do not seem interested in us, as their concentration seems to be further north. Everyone is enjoying the peaceful life, and many locals have given up their pagan ways and joined us in worship. They have baptized many. Yes, a time to rejoice."

The vision ended. *Who was this woman?* Gillian opened her eyes. Though Sam appeared to be looking at the cookbook, she sensed he had been watching her.

"I thought perhaps you had fallen asleep; you looked so relaxed and peaceful."

Gillian sat up. "I almost did. Is it time for us to leave?"

Sam checked his watch "Yes, but we don't have to hurry. I'm sure they won't mind waiting for us." Sam stood and offered his hand to help Gillian up.

"I'm not sure why, but this is my favorite part of Glastonbury we have visited today. It speaks of peace, love, and hope."

Sam studied her face before he spoke. "You're opening up, Gillian. What you're meant to see and feel is coming easier for you. I'm glad you're starting to relax. It's been an adjustment for you, but believe me when I tell you that everything you see and hear is for a purpose."

"Are you saying you see what I see?"

"Sometimes, yes. Other times it is meant for only you."

Gillian bristled. The thought of Sam sharing her visions made her on edge. She knew she was being silly. She had always been a private person, and as much as she liked Sam....

Sam sensed her discomfort. "I'm not in your head Gillian. Sometimes it's a shared vision, one I need as well. I have no more control over it than you do."

"It's okay. I'm just being silly, still struggling with the old me, logical and private Gillian."

Sam put his arm around her shoulder. "You're not silly. If I hadn't grown up with all this, I would find it more difficult than you do. No one will criticize you. Samantha once shared with me what she was like in the beginning. She was a stubborn woman, and it took her longer to accept. Ask Banks sometime about the things she put him through."

Gillian laughed. "Oh, I know some things. You're right; she was a handful for Banks in the beginning. Does anyone know how old Banks is? Or how many chosen he has served?"

"Not that I know of. You will learn as time goes on those details are not important. He doesn't like to talk about it. I understand your curiosity though."

"Sam, you are the most patient and understanding person I've ever met. Do you ever get irritated with me?"

"Why would I? Little personality quirks are insignificant. It's the goodness I look for, and you have a good heart. Do I irritate you?"

Gillian stopped, "Hmm, let me think. There was one time or maybe two times."

Sam's face showed disappointment. "Oh."

"No, I'm teasing. You're the perfect companion."

Sam beamed at her words. They reached the main road just as Tom and Uncle Joe pulled over to the side. They increased their pace.

Gillian slid into the back seat with Sam right behind her. "Did you enjoy your day, Uncle Joe?"

"Enjoy would be an understatement. I have a notebook full of observations. I can't wait to share it with Joe. I'd love to call him now, but I don't think he and Maggie would appreciate his dad interrupting their honeymoon. Tom knows all the places to go for information, places regular tourists would never know about. How about you two?"

"We had a good day. I learned a lot too, and Sam took good care of me. I don't think Joe would mind you calling, you raised him well, but I can understand your reluctance."

Tom pulled the car around to the back entrance and let them out before putting the car away.

Enid looked up as they entered. "I'm just making a pot of tea."

They sat at the kitchen table drinking their tea when Banks and Tom came in.

"Banks, I hope you enjoyed your peaceful day. Sam and I had a good day, and Uncle Joe is on cloud nine. Tom is the tour guide every history lover should have."

"I had a good day. I want to hear more about your day. I am sure Joseph is eager to share."

They laughed. Everyone knew Uncle Joe could ramble for hours on subjects he found interesting.

"I'm eager to share but if I get carried away, feel free to stop me. If Joe were here, he would not hesitate to tell me." Uncle Joe laughed.

"Why don't you go freshen up while Enid prepares dinner. We can meet in the dining room when you are ready."

"Good idea, Banks. I'd like to take a shower. Will I have time?"

Enid turned from the stove. "Dinner will be ready in an hour; that should give you time."

Leaving everyone in the kitchen, Gillian went to her room. The wind and damp air had not been kind to her curls, and she needed to tame them before dinner. After spending longer than intended in the shower, she hurried through the rest of her ritual, securing her hair back and applying lip gloss. Dressed in a tan, calf length, knit dress, and brown pumps, a quick look in the mirror satisfied her.

Enid looked up as she entered. "Well, that didn't take you long. You look lovely. The men went up not long ago, so they may be awhile."

"Good, I can sit and visit with you then. When was the first house built here?

"The first wooden house was built in the late first century; the house with the cellar was built in the early second century. They needed a safe place, away from the eyes of the Romans. It served as a house of refuge for those being persecuted. There have always been groups who would rid the world of all Christian's if they could. There are houses like this all around the world, safe havens."

"I met a lady at the bakery in town who knew Auntie Mary and recognized me from a picture she had seen."

"That would be Theresa, a good woman and a wonderful baker. Did you try her Eccles cakes? She's famous for them. I have tried to make them like hers, but I can never seem to get them just right. She says she has a secret ingredient, but I can't figure out what it is."

"Yes, we did, and they were delicious. We were hoping you knew how to make them. Was the first church here near the Lady chapel and the well they call Joseph's well?"

Enid laughed, "Now why would you ask me that? Do I look that old?"

"Oh no, Enid, I'm sorry, I didn't mean…"

"Relax, I'm kidding with you. Mary said I must tell you what you ask so I will. Yes, the first church was near the Lady Chapel; there was also a church near Wearyall hill in the first century. They built the first church when Christianity was in its infancy before the Lord was crucified."

"Wait, what did you say? You mean there was Christianity here before Christ died?"

"All around the world, my love. I don't know why so many think Christianity was only in the east in the early years. They traveled all over during that time. The merchants traded in many countries, and they came to England for the metals. From the time Christ was born, word spread throughout the world of his birth. Before the crucifixion, He ministered outside of the east himself. He had followers from the beginning. You probably think the apostles brought Christianity to England and Europe after his death. There were people, followers, Christians, waiting to aid them in every land they went to."

"Enid, there is so much I don't know. How am I supposed to help reveal all that was meant to be if I'm ignorant of the history?"

"You will know what you need to know and reveal what you need to reveal. Your guidance does not come from this earth, so don't doubt the accuracy. When the time comes, you will be able to reveal what is true and what is false. Just keep doing what you're doing. What did you experience near the Lady chapel?"

"Oh, my goodness, it was amazing. I saw different time periods of Christians worshipping in an old round wooden church. Each time my vision changed, I had a glimpse into whether it was a time of rejoicing or fear. The final vision appeared to be monks worshipping there, all men with brown woolen robes and short hair. I sensed their joy and fear."

"What a blessing you've been given, to view the past. Use it wisely, and you won't fail. Now would you like to learn how to make perfect, no-fail gravy?"

Gillian jumped up, "Yes I would, gravy is always something I've struggled with to get the right consistency and flavor."

Watching Enid first, and then trying it herself, she mastered it in her first attempt.

"Don't teach her too much Enid; she will have the advantage. She has challenged me to a cooking competition when we return home."

Gillian turned toward the sound of Sam's voice.

Enid waved her spoon at him. "You may get her on some things, but you won't beat her gravy, the lass learns quick. Sam, if you will get the cart out of the pantry, I can put dinner on it. Then you can take it to the dining room."

Sam wheeled the cart in and helped Enid and Gillian place the dishes. The others arrived by the time they transferred the food to the table.

Uncle Joe talked through the entire meal, but no one minded. His excitement brought joy to everyone.

"Uncle Joe, the city of Wells sounds interesting. Are you going there tomorrow or somewhere else?"

"Tomorrow, I will stay here and organize my notes. I have learned so much in just one day. If you don't mind, I would like to look at the old books in your room."

"Be my guest. I was thinking of staying here tomorrow and reading more of a book I found. Maybe I will be enlightened as to what I need to do next."

"A nice relaxing day tomorrow would benefit everyone," Banks said. "There are some beautiful walking paths around the estate. I went for a long walk today and feel refreshed."

"Tom, I hear there are antique cars in one of the old barns. Would you mind showing them to me?" Sam asked.

Tom nodded, "I'll be happy to show you, there are some beauties in there."

"Old cars? Sounds interesting I would like to take a look myself, but I need some alone time. Enid, the meal was delicious, you have a gift."

"Why thank you, Gillian. I'm not a fancy cook, but I enjoy using herbs from my garden to add different flavors. Your Auntie Mary also enjoyed my herb garden. Did you see it yesterday when you went for a walk?"

"I saw your vegetables planted amongst the flowers. Auntie Mary used to do that, but I don't remember seeing an herb garden. I noticed the natural garden though."

"Ah yes, some of those herbs are my most treasured, but I do have a garden just for herbs. I also grow some in the greenhouse, which makes them available all year. I'll show you tomorrow if you like."

"I would love that. I told Sam earlier that Auntie Mary tried to teach me about the various herbs and their healing properties, but I didn't pay attention. I wish I had."

"I'll be glad to teach you what I know." Enid rose and cleared the table. "I have something you might like. After dinner, I will get it for you."

Gillian rose. "Enid, please let me help. I enjoy washing dishes."

"You're a strange one. I must admit washing dishes is not my favorite thing to do, so if it makes you happy, I'll let you help. Tom, if you will get the coffee tray ready, Gillian and I will take care of the rest."

Gillian enjoyed talking to Enid while she washed the dishes. *It's strange; I formed an instant bond with Mirabelle, Moyra, and now Enid. Everyone I've met has been loving and helpful. Well, except Elizabeth. I hope our next meeting will be better.*

"Do you want to have coffee with the men or would you like to have a cup of tea in here with me?"

"I would love to have a cup of tea with you and sit at the kitchen table. Auntie Mary and I used to sit in the kitchen and talk for hours."

"You miss her, don't you?"

"More than I can say."

"While the tea is brewing, I need to go fetch something; I'll be right back. If you check the pantry, you'll find some cakes. I'll let you choose one we can have with our tea."

The pantry contained a shelf with home-baked goods. *Decisions, decisions.* Picking up a cake drizzled in a glaze, she breathed in the aroma. *Ginger, oh yes, that smells good.*

Enid returned to the kitchen as Gillian put the plate on the table.

"Good choice. I'll get the plates and you pour the tea." Enid handed Gillian a book. "Look inside; I think you'll like it."

Gillian opened the book and recognized Auntie Mary's handwriting. She flipped through a few pages and saw descriptions of herbs and their uses, with drawings at the top of each page. "Enid, this is wonderful, thank you."

"Last time she came, she gave me that book and said I would find a use for it. I think she knew one day you would be happy to have it."

Gillian tried to fight the tears welling in her eyes, but decided it was a lost effort, she let them flow.

Enid held her while she sobbed. "It's all right, luv. Have a good cry, and then we'll take a look at the book."

So many emotions rose to the surface. No longer only the loss of Auntie Mary, but every vision seemed to leave a footprint of

111

emotions within her. Finally, she regained control, and Enid brought her a cold cloth.

"Hold this cloth over your eyes for a bit. The coldness will keep the swelling down. I'll make you an herb tea to relax you and help you sleep tonight. The recipe is in the book."

Gillian looked through the book while Enid made the tea.

They talked about the book and Auntie Mary. Gillian's eyes drooped as the tea took effect.

"Enid, thank you again. Though my tears may not have shown it, you made me very happy." Gillian picked up her book and hugged Enid. "Will you tell everyone good night for me?"

"That I will. Now go on and rest. Tomorrow I will show you the herb garden and greenhouse."

CHAPTER ELEVEN

The sun warmed her face. She glanced at the still-open curtains. *Wow, that tea works, I barely remember getting into bed.*

In the bathroom, she looked in the mirror. *Oh dear, this hair is another matter.* Spraying her hair with a mixture of water and conditioner, she pulled it into a tight ponytail. *There, that's better.*

Enid was in the kitchen washing dishes. "Good morning Enid. I slept like a baby last night. Whatever that tea was, it worked."

"I'll show you the recipe in the book. You look rested. The men rode to one of the barns to check out the old automobiles. Would you like to tour the garden after you've had your breakfast?"

"Yes, I would. It looks like another beautiful day. You said they rode to one of the barns; how big is this property?"

"It's just over 640 acres. There's this house and the surrounding gardens, a hayfield, two new barns, two old barns, numerous storage sheds, and two greenhouses. There is also a caretaker's cottage, which doesn't get used much, but now and then someone comes for solitude and likes to stay there."

Gillian's mouth fell open. "I had no idea. Who maintains it all? It can't be just Tom? It's far too much work for one person."

"Groups come from all around the world. They help with repairs, harvests, and any other needed tasks. In turn, they have a nice place to stay and get away from the world for a spell." Enid placed Gillian's breakfast in front of her and poured her a cup of tea.

"Thank you. Will I ever learn all this?"

"Oh Gillian, there is much more, but don't let it overwhelm you. You will learn what you need to as you need to."

"That's what everybody keeps telling me." Gillian buttered her toast and took a bite of egg. "Now, what about the cars? Who do they belong to, and how many are there?"

"They belong to you. I'm not sure of the exact number, but there are more than twenty."

"You're kidding me. Enid, tell me you're kidding me."

Enid laughed. "Why? I'm not kidding. They are all yours, and some are near a hundred years old."

"I've got to see them. Maybe I can get Sam to take me later. This morning, I want to spend time with you."

"When you're ready, we'll go to the greenhouse and then the herb garden. Then if you like, you can help me make lunch."

"Yes, yes, and yes!" Gillian clapped her hands in excitement.

After getting her boots, Gillian met Enid back in the kitchen. The greenhouse was huge and full of every type of herb imaginable. It also contained a lemon tree and other fruit trees that needed the controlled environment of the greenhouse.

"It's heated, and with automatic vents, we manage a constant temperature. There are also automatic sprinklers, which Tom set on a timer, to mist and water everything. There is another greenhouse on the other side of the barns. We use it for the grapevines and berries." She nodded toward the door. "Now we'll go to the herb garden."

Gillian was expecting a small area and was surprised at the size. "How do you keep up with all this, and what do you do with all the herbs?"

"Tom does most of the weeding, and the herbs grow themselves; they don't like a lot of fuss. It's a bit of work, but I don't mind. Some herbs we dry for later use, some I send to areas that can't grow them because of soil conditions and poverty, and some we give to a helper who makes oils from them. Tom also trades them for goods we aren't able to produce. Nothing gets wasted."

"I can tell."

"Come, I'll show you our storage shed."

The storage shed was a small barn. One area held racks where herbs were bundled and hung to dry. To her left was an area that had tall shelves. Each shelve held jars with canned vegetables and fruits. Toward the back was a large walk-in freezer and a walk-in refrigerator. "Enid, you could feed a village with all that's here."

"We sometimes feed more than a village. Helpers from all over come to collect food for the poor. We do most of the canning when a large group of helpers is here. We do what we can to help anyone in need."

"This is amazing! I had no idea. All the helpers I've met work hard to help those who are in need. I'm grateful to be part of a group like this. Is this the way it was intended to be? That those who have, share with those in need?"

"Yes, that was how we were designed. Those in need don't just take either. When they are able, they are expected to pass it on to someone less fortunate. It's a balanced system, all done with goodness of heart. It may seem the world has more bad than good, Gillian, but in truth, there is more good; we just don't make a fuss. With all the helpers and the other chosen you have multitudes of people working with you. Come, I will show you the hens, lambs, and pigs. The cows are out to pasture. Though you may see some, most are in the far field."

"You raise animals too?"

"Gillian, everything on our table is either grown or raised here. We only trade for things like flour and sugar. There is a helper further north who has a mill, and he gives us our flour. Tom keeps bees, which provide more honey than we need, so we trade the honey for the flour and other staples."

"I'm in awe, you do all this while staying low key, yet helping so many of the unfortunate. You amaze me, Enid; you and Tom work so hard. I have a question, I feel silly for not knowing. Do you and Tom get paid for doing all of this?"

Enid took a moment to respond. "Yes, we do and quite nicely too. Mary arranged for us to receive a set sum each month from the estate. There is also a fund for estate expenses. I'm surprised no one has gone over the finances with you. Would you like Tom to show you the financials for this estate?"

"Yes, I should learn what there is and what might be needed for the future. A place this size must be expensive to maintain and run."

"It doesn't take much, but Tom will show you. This estate has been in your family for a very long time, and there are more than enough funds to keep it going for many years."

"What do I do when you and Tom decide to retire? Will I have others to help me?"

"Retire? Why on earth would we want to retire? We are with you until we leave this earth. We do what we love and what we have been blessed to do. There is no other pleasure on this earth that could entice us from here. Sorry, Gillian, but you are stuck with us for a long time."

Relief flooded Gillian, "I'm delighted to hear that. When I realized the magnitude of this estate, my respect and admiration for you and Tom grew. Through your hard work and dedication, it runs so well. How would I ever find another couple as wonderful as you?"

"Get that worry out of your head. You have more important things to concern yourself with. We are here for you, and will be, 'till we go to meet our Lord."

They reached the stables, and a fenced in area with pigs, sheep, and chickens. The sheep lined up at the fence line as if wanting to meet this new human.

Leaning over the fence, she stroked the soft fleece of the smallest lamb near her. "They are adorable! Now I feel guilty for enjoying lamb. Perhaps I shouldn't meet the animals. If I get to know them, I would have to become a vegetarian."

"Most of these have been around a long time. We shear them for their wool, and we use only a few for meat. We fall in love with them too. Always remember, Gillian, God designed everything to provide man with what he would need to survive.

We are only to take what we need. It's a sin to waste or take more than we need."

"Who spins the wool? Is that done here too?"

Enid nodded. "We'll go to that area next. Follow me."

Upon entering a large, stone building, Gillian gazed in awe at the spinning wheels, looms, and vats. "Oh my, weaving is done here too?"

"Yes. I don't do any of this, but we have weavers and spinners who come. Their work is beautiful. They use the vats for cleaning the wool and coloring it. We only use basic colors, but once the weavers have worked their skills, the end product is better than anything you could buy."

"I'm overwhelmed by all the work done here. How can I ever thank you and Tom enough for managing all this? Do you ever rest?"

"When you love what you do, there is no need for rest. Now, we'll collect our eggs on the way back, and I will teach you how to make a quiche."

"I would love that. Auntie Mary sacrificed her time here to be near me. I wish I'd known; I would have enjoyed coming here with her."

"Don't wish for what might have been; it's a waste of energy and emotion. There's a time and a reason for everything. Yes, she enjoyed her time here and missed it, but she knew you were more important. She had a good life. You can be sure that."

Gillian knew Enid was right. No need to waste time dwelling on what might have been.

CHAPTER TWELVE

"Wait, let me find a pen and paper, so I can write each step in the process. I want this to be perfect."

"Over by the sink, there's a notebook for you to take notes."

Enid held out a bib front apron. "Here, put this apron on to keep you from getting flour all over your clothes."

Gillian slipped the loop over her head and tied the strings in back. "I feel professional now. This is exciting."

"Well, I'm not sure about exciting, but I do like to create good, nutritious food that looks appealing, and quiche fits that description. Here's the list of ingredients we'll need; you write them in your notebook while I gather them together."

Gillian copied all the ingredients and quantities. "Did you and Auntie Mary make quiche together?"

"Yes, we did. She enjoyed adding different herbs and vegetables to the basic recipe to get new tastes."

"I'll try to be a good student. Do you want to make it and I'll watch, or should I do it and you coach me?"

"Let's do it together. Watch what I do, and you can make one too."

Later, Sam found them enjoying a cup of tea. "What's going on here? You're wearing an apron, with flour on your cheek. Are you taking cooking lessons to compete with me?"

"I doubt I need cooking lessons to compete with you, but I couldn't pass on the opportunity to learn to make quiche. Enid has been teaching me some tips and tricks. Are you nervous I will win the cook-off?"

"Not at all. I am a master in the kitchen, but I don't think I can compete with Enid's special skills."

"No need to fear my skills, but you need to fear this one. She followed my instructions step-by-step, and I think it will surprise you. We're waiting for them to finish baking. If you're such a master in the kitchen, perhaps you can help with a meal while you're here?"

"I'll help in any way you wish, Enid. As I told Gillian yesterday, I've used cooking as a relaxation method for years, and I enjoy it. Anything you need me to do, I will try, but I can't make a quiche."

"Yes! I'm glad to hear that. I would feel bad if my quiche was better than yours, so I'm glad you can't make it." Gillian laughed.

Enid stood to check on the oven. "Are the others coming in?"

"They're right behind me and should be in any minute. I came to check if I could help with lunch. Would you like me to do anything?"

"Gillian, show Sam where the plates are, and he can set the table. The quiche are done, and the soup is ready; all we need to do is set it out, and everyone can help themselves."

The two quiche had been cut and placed in the center of the table, but neither Gillian nor Enid would say which one they made.

"Sample both. One is broccoli and cheese, and one is spinach and cheese. Let's see if you can guess which one is mine," Gillian said.

Sam took a bite of each. "I can't taste a difference. The pastry is tender and flaky in both, and the body of the quiche is firm as it should be. They are both delicious."

"I told you she was a good student. She copied everything I did and has a light hand with the pastry. You need to watch out, Sam, I think she'll win your competition," Enid said.

"What competition is this?" Uncle Joe asked.

"Sam and I are planning a cook-off when we return home. He seems to think he's a better cook than I. My goal is to prove him wrong."

"Sam, I think you have met your match, in more ways than one."

Sam nodded, "Uncle Joe, I think you're right."

"Tell me about the cars you went to see this morning while Enid and I slaved in the kitchen."

"Gillian, you must check them out before we leave. Some cars are from the early 1900s. I think the newest one was from the 1980s. They are all in perfect condition, a collector's dream," Uncle Joe said.

"I want to see them, maybe tomorrow. I have other things I want to do this afternoon."

"Tom has agreed to be my guide tomorrow. He's taking me to a place that houses ancient documents from the area. Anybody want to join us?" Uncle Joe asked.

Gillian shook her head. "I plan on going back to Wearyall Hill tomorrow, for at least part of the day. Banks, would you like to go with Uncle Joe? I'd like Sam to come with me if that's all right with him."

"I plan to stay at the estate tomorrow, but I look forward to hearing what you find, Joseph."

"You don't have to ask me, Gillian. I have no other plans than accompanying you. Can we visit Theresa while we're in town?"

"Sam, be honest, is it Theresa you wish to visit, or are her Eccles cakes calling you?"

Sam grinned. "Theresa is the main reason, but if we are in her shop, we have to buy something don't we?"

"All right then, tomorrow is settled. Enid, I'll help with the dishes. Don't say no; I have things I want to discuss with you."

"Gillian, while you're busy with Enid, do you mind if I look at the books in your room?" Uncle Joe asked.

"Be my guest; help yourself to any you wish to read."

Banks and Sam excused themselves, leaving Gillian alone with Enid.

"Enid, I need to go back to the cellar. Will you show me again how to get there?"

"I'll show you, but there's no need. You will find your way. Don't look worried. Now that you've been there, you will know how to get there again. Trust me." Enid laid the dishcloth down and went to get the lantern for Gillian.

"Are you sure I won't get lost?"

Enid handed her the lantern. "I'm sure; have faith."

To Gillian's surprise, Enid was correct. She remembered how to get to the entrance to the cellar. She navigated the old steps with care and used the lantern to find her way.

Why did I have a sudden desire, need, to visit this little chapel again? Am I to learn something else?

Sitting on a bench at the rear of the chapel, she prayed for guidance. The chill in the chapel made her shiver. *No wonder my ancestors wore layers of clothing. The cold and damp down here chills you to the bone.*

"Gillian, how can I aid you?"

Startled by the voice near her ear, she opened her eyes.
Looking to her left she saw the older man she had seen on her
first visit to the chapel.

"Who are you?"

"My name is Thomas."

"I'm not sure how you can aid me. I don't know what to ask.
I prayed for guidance, and you appeared. Is there something you
want to tell me?"

"There is much I could tell you. I don't know what you need,
but I will tell you of my life. Perhaps that will help. I was born
on this land in the year of our Lord 117. I knew not of hate or
evil until I became a young man. My early years were
surrounded by only the faithful. As a young man, I was charged
with protecting what the evil came to destroy. The truth. I am
part of a group that has protected that which is sacred to bring
about the promise. My descendants took up my role, and
through the centuries we have kept it safe. Waiting, waiting for
the time to reveal."

"But why didn't you reveal it? I don't understand why you
had to wait?"

"Child, those who come to the Lord of their free will with a
pure heart are blessed by all that is good. Those who turn to the
Lord when they know of the promise will be redeemed, but

never learn all God intended. Just as those who call themselves followers but lack a pure heart will never receive all that was intended. God wanted everyone to reap the rewards of all the gifts He offered, but only through their own free will, faith, and love. He has been waiting, giving as many as possible a chance. The time has come. The chance has been given. The wait is over and evil will soon be no more. The truth will never again be in danger of being destroyed. All will be revealed. The world as it is known will end."

"What do you mean? Are we going to be destroyed?"

"It has been written; the time has come for the final battle." He disappeared.

"No, come back. I have questions. Please, come back." She spoke to an empty room.

As she turned to leave, a woman stood in the doorway. *This is the woman whose eyes I saw through on Wearyall Hill. I don't understand how I know, but I do.*

"You seek answers?"

"Yes, yes I do. Can you help me?"

"Come to the hill where you knew of me. I will show you of my life." The woman disappeared.

Gillian sat back down on the bench. *I need to pray, pray for answers, pray for guidance. The visions are jumbled, a small insight into the lives of the faithful over different centuries. What am I missing?*

CHAPTER THIRTEEN

Enid waited for her in the kitchen. "Did you find what you needed?"

"No, yes, I'm not sure."

"You look confused; a walk always clears a confused mind. Sam is in the parlor. Sit, and I'll fetch him. I think he would enjoy taking a walk with you." Enid did not wait for Gillian to respond.

Sam entered and took her by the hand, leading her outside. He didn't ask questions.

Sam guided her onto a path through the woods. The trees blocking out the sun made her shiver.

"Are you cold? I can go back for your jacket if you are."

"No Sam, I'm fine. Chilly, but I'll warm up as we walk."

"I met him too."

"Who?"

"Thomas. Somehow, I can't explain it, but I was with you in the cellar, though not physically."

"How?"

"I wasn't sure where you were and didn't know if you were safe or if you needed me. I went to Banks, he assured me of your safety and said for me to share the vision with you. Our bond is now so strong, most of what you see, I will see. After the vision ended, Banks explained where you were and the history of the hidden chapel. Gillian, even for me, one who has experienced the miraculous my entire life, this is new and overwhelming. I can't imagine what you're feeling."

"Comfort. I was confused when I returned from the cellar. Learning that you experienced it with me, I feel comfort. I don't mind you sharing this. I'm not alone and I have you to turn to. I've seen so much alone, unable to share with anyone. Left with so many questions and no one to talk to about them. I know I have Banks, but it seems he can never answer my questions. I'm not criticizing him. He has his duties and has boundaries and parameters to follow. I must seek my own answers, but now with your help, I feel more confident. You're the answer to a prayer."

"Together, we can be stronger. I'm honored to share this with you. I wonder if this is one of my new gifts Samantha mentioned?"

"I hadn't thought about that. If it is, I'm grateful."

"What did you think of what Thomas told you?"

"I'm not sure. I felt fear when he said this is the end of the world we know. We need to reach as many as we can, Sam. Time is running out. Yet, I also felt hope. He said when the promise is revealed there will no longer be a danger of the truth being destroyed. He said it is written. Do you have any idea what he meant?"

"Well, it's written in the Bible about end times."

"Yes, but I felt he meant something else. Something with greater clarity, telling us what to do. I've never really understood the scriptures about end times. It seems everyone has their own interpretation, and the end of the world has been proclaimed for hundreds of years."

"Actually, since the time of Christ. Every anomaly in the weather, drought, flood, storms, has some who interpret it as a sign of end times. The first disciples thought it would come in their time. The truth is, no one will know until it happens, that is why it's written to be prepared. Perhaps tomorrow Rachel will clarify what he said."

"You saw her too?"

"Yes, I sensed you had met her before."

"Yes, well, I didn't actually meet her. On Wearyall Hill, I didn't see her, I saw her world through her eyes. When I saw her in the chapel doorway, I knew she was the one. On Wearyall Hill, I not only saw her world through her eyes, I felt her emotions, her strength. She was strong in her faith and brought many to the Lord. I knew her name when I saw her. I don't understand how, but I did. It seems you did too."

"Strange, isn't it? There are many wonders in the world, things that can't be explained. I've seen many miracles and horrors in my work, but I have to say experiencing this with you is amazing. I'm honored to have the opportunity to enter this new journey with you."

"Me too, together we can find clarity in some of these messages, visions."

"What's this?"

Gillian looked up at Sam's words. They had come to a clearing with an old stone building in the center.

"It looks old. Can we go in? It's still on my property, isn't it?" Gillian asked.

"I'm sure it is. Tom took us on a ride around a large part of the property this morning, and he said we had only covered a portion of it."

As they approached the front of the building, Gillian stopped to take a good look. It was rustic, made of stone, a slate roof and stained-glass windows on either side of the front door. They approached the large wooden door, darkened with age. A wrought iron circular handle was the only ornamentation.

Sam pulled the handle, but the door didn't give. He then twisted it, and the door opened. "Let me go in first, Gillian. I need to make sure it's safe to enter."

"If you insist; it looks safe to me, it's old but looks solid."

"I wasn't referring to the structure. Out here in the woods, there is a chance some wildlife might have made this their home."

"Oh, right, hadn't thought of that. By all means, you go first."

"Not a fan of wild animals?"

"Depends on what they are."

Sam came back out. "It's safe. No bats, no bears, we should be safe."

"Bats! No way. They have bats here?"

"Gillian, bats are almost everywhere. Come on; you will like this."

The smell of beeswax tickled her nose as she entered; rows of pews, polished to a shine, filled the room. Walking up the center isle she noticed cloth covered cushions placed on the floor in front of every pew. *Prayer cushions? I've only seen the cushions attached to a kneeling bar in church, but I've heard of only cushions used.*

The altar consisted of dark wood with a beautifully carved front. Closer examination showed the scene depicted Christ, a basket of fish, and a loaf of bread.

"Sam, come look at this."

Sam bent down to exam the carving. "This is from the scripture where Christ showed his disciples who he was by feeding the multitude."

Gillian walked around the altar, the side carving depicted Christ raising Lazarus from the dead. She continued to the other side and the carving depicted the blind man healed. *This is it; we are to help people see and understand His miracles, just as He showed His miracles to convince people He is the Son of God. We will be given the opportunity to reveal His miracles. Thank you, God.*

"Gillian, what is it? You're looking at the altar and smiling. Care to share?"

"Come here. This is Christ raising Lazarus from the dead." She moved around the altar. "This one depicts the blind man He healed, and the front shows Him feeding the multitude from five loaves of bread and two fish."

"Yes, I see that, but what has you so excited?"

"Don't you see? The miracles, they will be widespread again. Just as miracles were widespread then, they will be again. I'm not sure how I know this, but I feel it, and it's a strong feeling."

"I hope you're right. Just as the multitudes turned to Him then, they will again."

Gillian walked to the back center of the altar, where the Bible lay open; she read the scripture.

"In John 14:12, Jesus says, 'Truly, truly, I say to you, whoever believes in me will also do the works that I do; and greater works than these will he do, because I am going to the Father'."

"Sam, this is what the speaker said in one of my visions."

"It seems you're on the right track. I would like to say a prayer before we leave."

"Me too, I have so much to be thankful for."

CHAPTER FOURTEEN

They met Enid walking toward the vegetable garden when they returned.

"I trust you enjoyed your walk. I was just going to cut some cabbage. Would you like to help?"

"Yes, I would. Sam, do you want to help or are you going to the house?"

"I'll help. Not sure how to cut a cabbage, but if Enid tells me what to do, I'll do it."

"There's a knack to cutting the cabbage just right." Enid led them to the area where the cabbage grew amongst other vegetables and flowers.

"Enid, why do you grow these flowers in with the vegetables? Auntie Mary did the same thing, but I didn't know why."

"Some things are meant to be together. The flowers planted here keep insects away from the vegetables. They give off a scent the insects don't like, so they stay away. Even in a greenhouse, insects get in and can cause damage. If you remember, I told you God designed everything for a purpose. Once we learn how to use all He gave us, the impossible becomes possible."

Why do I feel she's talking about more than the plants? Is she telling me to keep learning or to use what I've learned? Or both?

"Now, pull the cabbage gently, just enough to slide the knife under it. Cut close to the base of the cabbage and leave as much of the stem as you can. If cut right, we'll have a few more cabbages from this plant."

Sam and Gillian did as Enid instructed.

"Sam, if you wouldn't mind taking these to the kitchen and wash them for me, we'll be along in a few minutes."

"Do you want me to cook them?"

"If you like, that would be a help. Remember to put a tablespoon of bicarbonate of soda in the pot."

Sam cocked his head to one side. "Bicarbonate of soda?"

"Cuts down on gas. I always put some in cabbage and Brussels sprouts."

Sam nodded. Loaded with cabbage, he headed for the house.

"Enid, I sense you sent Sam off for a reason. Is there something you want to talk to me about?"

"There is. How was your walk?"

"Very interesting. Is the church on the other side of the woods part of the estate?"

"Yes, it is. We have service there every Sunday. Did you like our little place of worship?"

"I did, it's simple but beautiful. I'm intrigued by the carvings on the altar. What can you tell me about them?"

"Thought you might ask me about them. The carpenter who built the altar wanted everyone to always be reminded of miracles. Even the faithful sometimes doubt miracles. Some are emphatic that only Christ performed miracles, and when He died, they ended. This is correct in one sense, it is through Christ the miracles happen, but He gave authority to His followers to perform them in His name."

"True, but why do they doubt?"

"Teaching. Some teach miracles are supernatural and therefore not from God. Have you noticed miracles seem to be happening and spoken of more often?"

"Yes, I have. The good deed contract I made with Nicholas is a miracle. It spread far and wide and is bringing out the good in so many. I see the miracle; others may not."

"You are correct. Miracles aren't just big things. Little miracles happen every day, and when people open their eyes to them, they will see God at work. As the time approaches, there will be increasingly obvious miracles that even the most skeptical cannot deny. They will see angels for who they are. Pain and sickness will be no more. You are fitting the pieces of the puzzle together. Once you have, you will know how to do what needs to be done."

"Enid, the vision I had in the cellar, Sam witnessed it too. He said it was like he was there with me. It was emotional for both of us. I'm thankful I've been given someone to walk this path with."

"As I said before, some things are meant to be together."

Sam was busy at the stove when they returned. Gillian watched him, his face relaxed, smiling as he tended to cabbage. *He looks like he's enjoying himself.*

Enid checked on his progress. "Looks like it's almost ready. Everything else is warming in the oven. Sam, could you fetch the cart for me?"

Sam came back with the cart, and the three of them put everything in serving dishes. "Banks was in here before you came back. He's gone to round up Uncle Joe and Tom. They should be waiting for us in the dining room."

Uncle Joe lead them in prayer before the meal. "Gillian, I found some very interesting books in your room. Tom said there is another room with a library I might be interested in."

"I thought you might find something of interest. I would need a decade here just to read all the books in my room. Where is the other room?"

"Upstairs, next to the room the tutor stayed in when they had children and lessons here," Enid said.

"That would be the floor we didn't cover on the tour?" Gillian asked.

"Yes, you can go look anytime you like. I can go with you if you have questions, or you can explore on your own," Enid said.

"I would like to see it. Maybe after dinner we can all go up?"

Sam tapped his glass with a spoon, "I am sure we'll all go up with you, Gillian, but there is something important we need to discuss."

Panic hit Gillian. "What? Has something happened?"

"No, but I slaved over the cabbage, and not one person has voiced their delight in my tasteful dish."

Gillian picked up her glass of water and stood. "Hear ye, hear ye. Please, let us take this opportunity to congratulate the cabbage chef. The taste surpasses any cabbage I've ever tasted. Let us all drink a toast to the world-renowned cabbage chef."

Everyone laughed, and Sam shook his head, "All right, I asked for that. Mock if you will, but it tastes good."

After they cleared away dinner and the dishes were washed, Tom and Enid led them to the third floor.

Gillian noticed it was similar to the second floor, but more doors lined the hallway to the left.

"I'll take you through all the rooms, and we will end in the library," Enid said, leading them to the left of the landing.

In stark contrast to the bedrooms on the second floor, these rooms were small and sparsely furnished. Not shabby but obvious they weren't the 'best' rooms. The student desks in the schoolroom were the old-fashioned, flat table type, two or three students would have sat at each table. The teacher's desk was similar but larger than the students. Behind the teacher's desk was a fireplace with a mesh guard fastened to the opening. Bookcases filled the alcoves on either side of the fireplace.

Gillian examined the bookcases. Besides the usual school books, books on etiquette, farming, horticulture, cookbooks, and religion filled the shelves.

"Were the children who lived here required to learn to farm and cook?"

"Yes. To the residents of the house, this knowledge was considered as important as the basics. To help people, they needed to learn how to manage, farm, and prepare the crops from this land," Tom said.

"That's interesting. Would the owner's children and servant's children attend school together?"

"Yes, it was important to educate all the children. But they weren't servants; they were other helpers who came here for refuge or to assist with the crops. They treated them no different from the children who lived here."

Enid moved toward the door. "Shall we move on to the next room?"

"You can all go on to the next room; I want to examine these books further." Gillian said.

Once alone, she went back to one of the student desks, pulling out a chair and sitting at the desk. *No little vandals lived here. Most old, school desks are scarred by names carved into them by a bored child. Other than wear from years of use, these desks are undamaged. I'm sure the teacher's desk is the same.*

She sat at the teacher's desk. It was the same as the students, worn but undamaged. The books on the corner of the desk caught her eye. *I wonder when this room was last used? No dust on the desks or books. It's either still in use, or they are diligent in their cleaning.* A stack of books remained on the teacher's desk as if waiting for the teacher to enter. Picking up one from the stack, she saw the subject was biblical history. *I wonder how old this is? No date or copyright, that's unusual.*

She remained at the teacher's desk for several minutes. *Okay, Gillian, you're thinking everything has meaning. Nothing in here to see or learn, just your imagination.*

She joined the others in the library next door. This room surprised her. It resembled a country home library; floor to ceiling bookcases on every wall, with comfortable reading chairs grouped in the center. Uncle Joe and Sam perused the books. Tom, Banks, and Enid relaxed in chairs.

"I'm impressed. Everything else on this floor is very basic, but this room is quite elegant. If Uncle Joe is missing during our stay, we'll know where to find him," Gillian said.

"Gillian, there are books in here that are unknown to the general public," Uncle Joe said. "Tom told us they were printed for only the chosen and helpers. I need more time, so much information."

"I wondered about that. When I looked at the books on the teacher's desk, I couldn't find a publisher, copyright, or date."

Enid nodded, "It was decided long ago the children of the faithful must be taught only the truth. Not interpreted truth, God's truth. These books are written and published by our group of faithful. We can be certain the readers will not be misled. The contents of these books were taken from the actual writing of the early followers. No variation, no interpretation. Even spelling and grammar errors were not corrected. In the 4th century, Rome's rulers decided they would be the judges of what was truth. They ordered the destruction of any writings they did not deem factual. Faithful followers hid many of these writings and passed them on through the generations. We were given free will for a reason; it is not up to any man or leader to dictate what to believe. Some of these writings have been revealed to the public through the years, and scholars argue and debate their authenticity. If you are faithful and learn with an open mind to all God's blessings, you will determine truth."

"I would love to read some of these, but not now. I'll leave you here. It's been a busy day, and I'm ready for bed. See everyone in the morning." Gillian left the library and started on her way downstairs to her room when she stopped.

Published by the group, that's what Enid said. I need to read the biblical history book on the teacher's desk. Maybe that's what made me think there was something in the room.

Turning back to the schoolroom, she tucked the biblical history book under her arm and headed to her room.

CHAPTER FIFTEEN

While getting ready for bed, her thoughts returned to the schoolroom and all the books used, written, and published by the group of faithful. *There are a lot of truthful books for education; I wonder why they didn't just monitor the contents to verify everything was factual? It seems like a lot of trouble to have your own publishing house. Why not just correct what was not factual in books already published? It seems the more I learn, the less I know.* Climbing into bed, she opened the book to the first chapter and began to read.

A pain in her neck woke her from a deep sleep. *Oh my, I must have fallen asleep reading. My poor neck.*

She checked the time, eight o'clock. *I can't believe I read as long as I did, but I couldn't put it down. So much history, more detailed than anything I've ever read.*

After a long, hot shower to ease her neck, she dressed in jeans and a sweater. *Thank you for leading me to where you need me to be.*

In the kitchen, she said, "Good morning everyone, are you ready for our next adventure?"

"Well, somebody is perky this morning. A good night's sleep served you well, or is it something else that has put a spring in your step this morning?" Enid asked.

"Something else. I learned a lot about my ancestors last night, and an educated mind is an enlightened mind. If you get my drift."

"Yes, I do. Would it be the biblical history book that enlightened you?"

Gillian smiled. "Yes, Enid, it was. I had no idea our early ancestors had access to writings of the Apostles. We are blessed."

Sam, Banks, and Uncle Joe remained silent, waiting for Gillian to continue.

"Oh, I know you all have questions about what I learned, but I'll tell you later. I'm eager to begin our day. Enid, do you think Tom would mind if Sam and I borrow one of the cars? I don't want to interfere with Tom's and Uncle Joe's plans."

"How could he mind? They are all yours. It seems I have to keep reminding you." Enid shook her head and smiled.

"I'm sorry, and yes, you do have to keep reminding me, because I forget."

Sam gently tapped Gillian's hand. "If I might interrupt, where are we going?"

"Wearyall Hill and wherever else we're led."

Gillian was almost giddy, even her sore neck could not disturb her mood.

"Enid, what herbs do you have for a stiff neck? I fell asleep reading, and the hot shower has not eased it. I don't want any distractions today."

"I have a salve for sore muscles. I'll get it for you."

Enid came back with a small container and rubbed the salve into her neck muscles.

"Oh, that feels good. Cool and warm at the same time. What's in it?"

"Camphor, peppermint, and lavender. It's a basic blend but works well on sore muscles. I'll mix a fresh batch to keep with you. It works well on my back when I've been bending over in the garden too much."

"Can I help you make it? I want to learn all these things."

"Don't you think you have enough on your plate? I will be glad to show you, but you might be trying to learn too much when your concentration is needed elsewhere."

"You're right, Enid, I need to slow down and concentrate on the important issues. Will you write your mixture in my recipe book, so I have it?"

"That I will be glad to do. It might even be in Mary's herbal book, but it won't hurt to have it in two places."

"Tom is taking me on a tour of Glastonbury this morning. Banks, are you sure you don't want to join us?" Uncle Joe asked.

"Thank you for asking, but I plan to stay here unless I am needed elsewhere."

"Sam and I are going to Wearyall Hill first and maybe some other places, not sure yet. I have a request of everyone, it may sound odd, and I'm not sure why I'm asking. We all need to visit the chapel on the other side of the woods before dinner this evening. Does the chapel have a pastor?"

Enid paused before answering. "Yes, we do. Would you like me to ask if he's available?"

"Yes, please, and invite those who attend church there on Sundays."

"Gillian, you know they will ask why. Is there a reason I might give them?"

Gillian smiled. "No, but they won't want to miss it. The pure in heart will attend without explanation and those who don't may need our prayers."

Enid seemed to search for words. Banks' laughter broke the silence, and all eyes turned to him.

"Glory be to God. Gillian, you lift my heart. Your will is strong, and your faith is even stronger."

"I can't describe it, but I feel like a different person this morning. I don't want to lean on my own understanding; I want to follow wherever my faith leads me."

"I can tell, and the result is joyous."

"I have to admit, I have read the same book you read many times," Enid said. "Although it enlightened me, I did not have the reaction you've had, Gillian."

"I can understand that, Enid. You were not privy to what I have seen and learned since my acceptance. I understand things that might seem insignificant to others. All will be revealed soon, and everyone will feel my joy."

"I don't doubt what you say, and I look forward to the times this new joy brings us." Enid turned away as she spoke, but not before Gillian saw tears welling up in her eyes.

Sam cleared his throat. Emotions were strong in everyone; the feeling of new beginnings and miracles was evident.

"What time will the service be?" Uncle Joe asked.

"I was thinking about five o'clock. Enid, would it be possible, with such short notice, to have a reception after? Sam and I can help you prepare."

"No need. I will ask the ladies attending to bring a dish; they will be happy to do so."

"Do all the helpers in the area attend service in the chapel on Sundays?"

"Yes, some come from other villages. All the helpers within driving distance attend."

"Good, I want to meet them all. But I don't want to put any more work on you than you already have. We'll help you. Sam, I remembered something. We forgot to go back and get Enid's picnic basket we left near the tree."

"Don't fret about that; I have others," Enid said.

"It's my fault," Sam said. "It was my idea to leave it there. We'll stop by the Abbey this morning, and if it's still there, we'll bring it back. If not, I'll buy you a new one. I'm sorry; we were enjoying the sites and talking about the Abbot's kitchen and forgot."

Enid took Sam's hand. "Come, let me show you something." She opened a tall cupboard which was full from top to bottom with picnic baskets.

"Now, do you still think you need to buy me another?"

"No, but I still feel bad. I don't like losing anything that belongs to someone else."

"If it makes you feel better, perhaps it was found by someone who needed it. You may have blessed someone by leaving it behind. Everything happens for a reason."

"Enid, if that were true I would feel better."

"I have prepared another basket for you today and one for Joseph and Tom."

"Everyone go and have an enlightening day," Banks said. "I will help Enid with making the calls and anything else she needs of me."

Sam spoke with Tom about a vehicle while Gillian gathered her jacket and boots. When she returned to the kitchen, Sam was waiting for her.

"Uncle Joe and Tom just left. We have the pleasure of using the 1942 Willys Jeep, the most indestructible vehicle known to man. I have always wanted to drive one. Come, it's parked out back." Sam led her through the back door.

"I can tell how excited you are, but what if I want to drive?"

Sam's face fell. "Okay, but if I drive, you're free to look around."

Gillian laughed. "I'm teasing, Sam. I would prefer you drive."

Relief showed on Sam's face. "Thank you."

She walked around the vehicle before getting in. There was no visible rust or dents, the body was in mint condition. "Is it really that old? It looks almost new."

"Yes, it is. All the vehicles look like new, with original parts and upholstery. It's amazing how they kept them so pristine. The barn they store them in is solid, and they keep a dehumidifier going to keep the moisture level down. Joe and Maggie need to come here; they both love old cars."

"I miss them, but I'm sure they are enjoying their time on Iona. We might get to see them there, though I'm not sure yet if Iona is our next destination."

"The book you read last night, can you tell me about it?"

"Yes. Transcribed from scrolls found of the writings of the early followers of Christ, the information is amazing. It gives insight into the personal lives of the Apostles, amongst other things. You will have the same reaction I did, because you have shared in the knowledge, well some of it, that I have received. Although miraculous, some things written in it would not impact those without our knowledge. It clarified many things and gave me a new insight into the miracles of their time."

"I'd like to read it before we leave Glastonbury."

"I'm almost finished, just a little more to read, then you can read it. I'm not sure what time I fell asleep, but it was after midnight."

"Where are we going first?" Sam asked.

"Wearyall Hill. We will be guided from there. I hope to learn more about Rachel; she intrigues me."

CHAPTER SIXTEEN

Sam parked the Jeep for their walk up Wearyall Hill. "Do you want to take the picnic basket with us now or come back for it?"

"We can take it with us. This is a peaceful place, and I would like to spend time here."

Gillian teased Sam while they walked. "I don't think I've ever seen you so excited as when you were driving the Jeep."

"It's a dream come true, I've heard many stories about the old Willys Jeep. Everyone who has ever had the pleasure of driving one from the World War II era has said no other driving machine can match them. They can go anywhere and have a powerful engine, almost indestructible. Now I've driven one, I understand what they mean. I feel guilty though, it's an earthly pleasure, and I have succumbed to it, but don't worry, I won't get too attached."

"You shouldn't feel guilty. Even the most devoted are entitled to some guilty pleasure, as long as the pleasure never interferes with devotion to God."

"That will not happen. Yes, I enjoy it, and it was a pleasure to drive, but it's an object, nothing more. I've witnessed many in my work who have let themselves become obsessed with possessions, willing to do anything to maintain the lifestyle of the rich and famous. You've heard the saying 'selling their

153

soul'? Well, it's true. Some go to the darkest place for money and possessions. I once dealt with a woman who sold her children as sex slaves for money to support her drug habit. They sent me to rescue the children. The woman had no soul. Her behavior was sickening."

"Sam, that's terrible. I'm sorry you experienced something so depraved. Were you able to rescue the children?"

"Yes, I'm thankful we were. They had been abused in the worst possible ways and the children will probably have nightmares for a long time. They are being cared for in a loving helper's home, monitored closely, surrounded in prayer and love. I only wish we could save all the children. They are innocents and should not suffer for the sin of others."

"I'll pray for their healing; this is a time of miracles. Here, on top of Wearyall Hill, a holy place where Christians from foreign lands stood centuries ago." Gillian said a silent prayer for all the children in the world.

When finished, she stood and walked around the hill, taking in the view from every angle. She gazed at the remains of the thorn tree. "I don't understand why someone would want to destroy a tree. The tree did them no harm."

"It's the symbol it represented: God, Christ, love, and hope. Evil can't bear to be around any of those things and wants to extinguish everything connected to God. You've heard, I'm sure, of the events in the Middle East. The radicals are destroying early history, especially religious statues and buildings. They even destroy ones not connected to Christianity, but they destroy because they want to eradicate any link."

"That reminds me of something I read or heard recently; I can't remember which. Something about, 'in order to know the future direction we must revisit the past.' Oh, I remember, it was a thought that popped into my head when we were heading back to Iona for the second time. I felt then it meant something. With your comments on the destruction of history being destroyed, it becomes clearer."

"In what way?"

"History is important; symbols, monuments, books, anything related to history must be preserved. Whether it's religious history or civilization's history. When we destroy history of any kind, we can re-write it. There is nothing left to dispute our rendition, so it can be rewritten for the benefit of the teller. Symbols of historical mistakes eradicated only to be repeated in another form. History not only reminds us of the good but of the mistakes made, so they are not made again. Does any of this make sense?"

"Yes, you make perfect sense. I see where you're going with this. If you remember your World War II history, Hitler destroyed the past, books which were not in line with his new world. He deceived people into thinking he was good, that he wanted what was best for them. This allowed him to manipulate and form his own version of what life should be. All for personal gain and the destruction of so many innocent lives."

"Yes, exactly. There are world leaders today who wish to eradicate history. There are so many wrongdoings in history that must never be repeated, but if we destroy the reminders, it will be. History is important and part of our humanity. Suppose, someday, someone comes along and says memories of the Holocaust should not be seen, the memories are too painful. Then they destroy the buildings, museums, and historical records. Any account of the event disappears. The history of the horrible time, can then be re-written. How will future generations learn of the true atrocities that took place? The physical history is not pretty, but we need to be reminded to prevent us from repeating the same mistakes. Nothing of any value can be built by destruction, and history is what it is. A lesson to us all."

"I understand everything you're saying, but there is only so much we can do to prevent this happening."

"You're right, Sam, but the important documents, books, and pictures need protection, just as our ancestors protected the writings of the earlier followers of Christ. Copies must be made and held in a safe place."

"If you feel so strongly about this, we should talk to Banks; he will know what to do."

"Sam, I feel it's all connected. Hate is what destroys the records and symbols of history, and hate is what we are fighting. Everywhere we stop the hate, we save the people."

"You came here to relax, and now you're all fired up. How did we get so off topic?"

"I'm sorry, my mind is going in so many directions. Sometimes, since my acceptance, words, ideas, and directions flow through my head. Some I dismiss, but some I feel in my heart I must listen to. I'm not sure what I'm to do with all this, but when the time comes, I will."

"The sun is shining, and the birds are singing. Sit down, relax, and enjoy."

"Thank you, Sam, I didn't mean to go off on a tangent. I need to focus and regroup."

"Yes, you do, and if you're a good girl, we will stop by the bakery for a treat."

"Hmm, for me or you?"

"For both of us, of course. Right now, you need to relax, then we'll have our picnic. When you're ready, we'll go into town or wherever you wish to go next."

Gillian spread her jacket on the grass and laid back, staring at the clouds. *I love the shape the clouds form. That one looks like a poodle, that one looks like an angel…* A vision appeared in her mind before she finished her thought.

The woman, Rachel, spoke. "Take my hand, Gillian. I will show you my home."

They walked down the hill together. It was different, the ground squished under her feet, like a wetland. They walked for a distance, remaining in sight of the hill, before arriving at a cluster of primitive round buildings.

"Are these all homes?"

"Yes, we are a small community, but we are growing. More and more come from other lands. It is safe here, and we are free to worship. The Romans are not interested in us; they think we are locals and don't bother us. Only a few in our group are locals; the rest are from other lands."

"Where did you come from, Rachel?"

"I was born in Jerusalem and came here with my family as a young girl."

Rachel motioned for Gillian to enter one of the buildings.

"This is the home I share with my father, mother, and grandfather."

It was primitive, but clean and functional. A fire glowed in the center, the smoke venting through the roof above. What looked to be pillows and blankets lay around the circular walls. The only furniture was a table and rustic stools.

"Where do you cook?"

"We have a kitchen building that all of us use. In our homeland, we had rooms in our homes; here we only have these small places, but they provide comfort. We are blessed."

"Tell me, Rachel. What do I seek?"

"Truth. You must return to the cleansing place. There you will receive the truth you need. All will know of our Lord. Once, all knew, then the darkness came and blocked it from the weak. They took our writings, but not all were lost. The more the darkness grew, the more people we lost to them. The light will once again cast out the darkness, and the heavens will rejoice. Many tried to do what you are doing, but the darkness stopped them. You have an army of spiritual and physical protectors and your pure heart. Keep your heart pure and you will not fail. The one who shares your light strengthens you."

She was gone. Gillian lay staring at the clouds. *What am I missing? She didn't tell me anything I didn't already know. No, there is something she did or said, but what was it?*

She glanced over at Sam. "Did you see her?"

"Yes."

"I don't understand, what was she trying to tell me? I'm missing something. Is there any paper in the picnic basket?"

Sam opened it and found a napkin. "Will this work?"

"Yes, but I need a pen."

Sam pulled a pen from his jacket pocket.

Gillian wrote every word Rachel said and everything she saw. *I will keep reading this until it comes to me.*

"Food helps me think clearer, so let's eat and think it over."

"I agree. I'm just confusing myself right now. What did Enid pack for us today?"

Sam reached into the basket, "We have pork pies, boiled eggs, and a cucumber-tomato salad for each of us. Hmm, she didn't pack any dessert."

"She knew you couldn't resist the bakery, and she was right."

"True, but I like her deserts as well."

"Do you still want to stop by the Abbey to check if the picnic basket is still there?" Gillian asked.

"Yes, I do. She said it was okay, but I still feel bad. You don't mind if we go, do you?"

"Not at all. I would like to have another look around while we're there."

They parked near the Abbey and made their way to the entrance.

"Let me pay this time, Sam." Gillian pulled money out of her pocket and paid the entrance fee.

"You are injuring my pride. The man is supposed to pay, not the lady."

"Now who's being old-fashioned?" Gillian raised her brows as she peered sideways at Sam.

They went first to the tree and the picnic basket was gone.

"Don't worry, Sam, remember what Enid said. You might have blessed someone who needed one."

"If they needed it, then I'm glad. Where did you want to go now?"

"I would like to take another look around the Abbot's kitchen and the area around the Lady Chapel."

Entering the Abbot's kitchen, she once again noticed the size and efficient design. "They must have fed thousands from this kitchen. It's hard to believe this building is over six hundred years old. It's a testimony to the builders and architects of the time. Professor Stratis was correct when he said we were smarter in ancient times than we are now."

"Ancient Rome enjoyed running water and central heating over two thousand years ago," Sam said. "A recent excavation discovered sewer pipes dating back to 800 BC, but I wouldn't be surprised if they find earlier evidence."

"After everything I've learned in the past few months, little surprises me."

"Careful, when you say something like that, it often proves you wrong. Are you ready to go to the Lady Chapel?"

"Not yet, this building emits a sense of peace and love. Those who worked in the kitchen enjoyed their labors. I can almost hear the noise. The number of dishes washed here must have been monumental. Would they have used metal plates or porcelain?"

"I can answer that for you."

Gillian turned in the direction of the voice. An elderly gentleman dressed in a three-piece suit, smiled at her. He looked too well dressed to be a tourist. "Do you work here?"

"No, but I am a historian. I have studied the activities in and around the Abbey through the centuries. In its earliest years, they served the poor and rich alike. During some periods they used pewter plates and cups, but as time went on and more things were donated, they used porcelain. The monks did not differentiate between the classes; they took in many stranded travelers and helped them on their way. Some will tell you the Abbey grew rich because of its claim to legends. That is not true; they became rich because of their compassion and good work. Those who made the pilgrimage here could not have done so without the generosity of the monks. Because of their good deeds, people from far and wide aided them when King Henry VIII pillaged and destroyed the Abbey. They moved many items belonging to the church for safekeeping. A network of faithful aided them in moving the items from the Abbey and distributed them throughout the land. I am told one day they will all come together again, and each church and abbey will be restored."

"Were manuscripts included in the items moved to safety?" Gillian asked.

"Yes, there were many early writings, as far back as the first century. So much history would have been lost if not for the faithful who aided the monks."

"I'm glad we ran into you, you've given us some valuable information to consider. My name is Gillian, and this is Sam."

"Pleased to meet you," Danial shook Sam's hand. "My name is Daniel Thorn."

"Thank you again. It's always nice to find an expert. So much is not told in guide books. I'm always curious about the little details," Gillian said.

"Glad to be of assistance. Here is my contact information if I can be of further help. I have studied the history of this area for many years and enjoy sharing my knowledge. I must be on my way now, but we will meet again."

Sam turned to Gillian after Daniel left them. "Now what was I saying about being surprised?"

Gillian laughed. "What a strange coincidence to bump into someone who seems to know more than most about the Abbey and its early Christian history. So, there were documents held here and taken to safety. He said they were distributed throughout the land. Interesting, we may need to visit with him again before we leave."

"If Uncle Joe had been with us, Daniel may never have gotten away. He would have a million questions for him."

"I'm sure he would. I wonder if Daniel knows the type or content of the early manuscripts?"

"You have his card, call him tomorrow. Speaking of tomorrow, do you have any idea yet how long we'll be here? Or where we go next?"

"Not yet, there is still something here. I'm not sure what, but I know I need to see, experience, or learn something. Let's walk around the grounds, then stop off near the Lady Chapel."

Despite the cool air, the sun shone bright, a beautiful day for walking. They walked around the ruins of the different buildings and stopped near the Lady Chapel.

"What is it about the Lady Chapel that intrigues you?" Sam asked.

"It draws me. I think they built the first church on grounds near here. Though they have found no real evidence in their archaeological digs, I'm sure it was here."

"A great deal of discussion on that subject has occurred amongst the experts. Some say it's possible. Others say there is no proof, therefore, it didn't happen."

It was busier today than last time they came; several tour groups passed them.

"I feel rather conspicuous standing here with so many coming this way. Let's go down here, and we can sit on one of the steps leading to the crypt."

Nothing, I'm not picking up on anything today. I had a vision on my first visit. Maybe I'm trying to force it. "Okay, I think we can walk to your new favorite place and check on what Theresa has for us."

"No need to tell me twice, I'm ready." Sam took Gillian's hand and helped her stand.

CHAPTER SEVENTEEN

The bakery was busy when they entered. They stood back and waited for the crowd to be served before going to the counter.

"I thought I would see you two again," Theresa said.

"Sam's raved about your Eccles cakes since we tried them, and I must admit, so have I."

"I'm thrilled to hear you enjoyed them. I have a secret ingredient that sets mine apart from the rest. Twice a year I take orders and ship them around the world. If I had time, I would do it more often."

"I understand their popularity. How many do you have today?" Gillian asked.

"Let me take a look." She returned soon. "I have seven in the case and a tray of twenty-four in the back."

"I'll take them all," Gillian said.

"All of them? My, you must be hungry or feeding a crowd. Let me box them for you. Will there be anything else you would like?"

"Yes. What are these small tarts?" Gillian pointed to another tray in the case.

"Those are blackberry, and the tray next to them are apple."

"I'll take a tray of each."

"Are you sure? You're not just buying them because I was a friend of Mary?"

Gillian shook her head. "No, I have plans for them. Did you receive a call today from Enid?"

"Why, yes, I did. She said we're having a meeting at the old church, followed by a potluck supper at the house. Is that what these are for?"

"Yes, I wanted to contribute, and everyone loves your pastries."

"I'm flattered. I'll bring whatever I have left in the shop when I close." Theresa boxed everything, tying the boxes with string.

Gillian opened her wallet. "How much do I owe you?"

"If it's all for the supper, I don't want to charge you."

"Theresa, I will not accept them unless you let me pay," Gillian said, handing her more than enough to pay for all the treats.

"This is too much; it doesn't come to that amount." Theresa paused, studying Gillian's face. "I see there's no sense arguing with you. You're a lovely girl; I look forward to spending time with you this evening."

"And I look forward to chatting with you. We'll see you this evening."

Gillian and Sam left the shop with their purchases.

"You were very quiet in there Sam."

"I didn't want to intrude, and you had it under control. I have two questions though. First one is, do I get one of these now? Second is, what is tonight about?"

"You're impossible! Yes, you can have one now. As for tonight, you'll have to wait and see."

"Now who's impossible? Not even a small clue? I thought we were partners."

"We are. Truth is, I'm not sure about tonight. I only know I need to do it. What is to happen? I have no idea. Maybe I just need to meet them. As I've told you before, I'm not in control of the things I'm directed to do."

"I understand, Gillian. I only pressed because I want to be as supportive as I can. I'm not trying to give you a hard time. I understand more than you realize. Sometimes you're directed to do something, and you're not sure of the reasoning. I do know, at some point, it all becomes clear."

"Thank you, Sam, I don't doubt your support, and I don't blame you for asking. I will always share with you what I can. Let's get these pastries in the jeep so we can head back and help Enid."

Sam went to untie a box and stopped. "I want to eat one of the Eccles cakes, but I'll use restraint, at least until we get them safely in the house."

"I commend your restraint, but I sense there might be an ulterior motive. Perhaps you want to try one of the other pastries too?"

Sam laughed. "Guilty as charged."

CHAPTER EIGHTEEN

Gillian and Sam arrived at the manor to find everything under control. Enid and Banks had contacted all who attended service in the little church.

"Did anyone question you about the purpose?" Gillian asked.

"Only one or two, which came as no surprise. They would question why the sun comes up in the morning if they could; it's just their nature. Everyone will be there; no one declined. What do you have?" Enid motioned to the boxes Sam carried.

"Gillian bought them from Theresa for tonight's supper. Can I tempt you to indulge in an Eccles cake with us?"

"I'm sure Theresa appreciated the purchase. Once we have everything finished, I'll have one with you. I only wish she would share the secret ingredient with me," Enid said.

"What can we do to help?" Gillian asked.

"The plates and cutlery are on that cart, cups and glasses on the other. I need them taken into the music room. That's where we'll have the supper."

"Good choice, I was wondering which room would be best. We'll take the carts in. Are Uncle Joe and Tom back yet?"

"Yes, they returned about an hour ago, and I put them to work. Everything is almost complete. I will put the kettle on and brew a pot of tea and go over the details with you."

They music room had been transformed. Two long tables now occupied the center where the harp had been. Small tables stood in front of the chairs lining the walls. The harp sat in a corner, out of the way of guests, but still in view. *I wonder if any of our guests can play the harp. I would love to hear how it sounds.*

"It looks like the long center tables will hold the food," Gillian said. "Let's put the carts at the end of the tables until we find out what else to do."

Under Enid's direction, the men were busy in the kitchen when they returned.

"We put the carts at the end of the long tables. Would you like us to set them out, or is everyone helping themselves from the carts?" Gillian asked.

"We'll leave the plates and bowls on a cart; the cutlery, glasses, and cups we will set on the end of a table. It will only take a minute or two if we all chip in. Everything else is ready. We can relax for a spell and enjoy a pastry with our tea."

"How many will attend?" Gillian asked.

Banks pulled a piece of paper from his pocket, "We have a tally of fifty-seven. Would you like to share with us the reason for this service and get together?"

Gillian paused before replying. "I would if I could. I can only tell you something compelled me to do it. Whether the intent is for me to meet everyone or if someone within the group has information I need, I don't know. Perhaps we will all be enlightened this evening."

"It should be a nice gathering regardless of reason," Enid said. "Those who are dropping off warm dishes will be here soon. We have chafing dishes ready to keep them warm. Follow me to the music room, and we will finish preparations."

Once set up was complete. Gillian excused herself to get ready. She took a quick shower, styled her hair, and chose a royal blue knit dress. *Shoes, we have to walk through the woods to get there, I'll need to wear flats. I'm excited for what tonight might bring. It should be interesting, regardless of reason.*

A knock on her door interrupted her thoughts.

Sam looked handsome in black slacks and a tweed wool jacket. "You look nice, very distinguished in the tweed. I'm ready, just let me slip into my shoes."

"No hurry. I may need to give up the jacket. You may need to borrow it."

"Thank you, Sam. I only brought a casual jacket, and I don't think it goes well with my dress. This dress is warm, so I should be fine. We'll be back at the house before the chill sets in."

"There seems to be an electric vibe of excitement in the air. Do you feel it?"

"Yes, I do. It's probably the helpers wondering what this is all about. I hope I don't disappoint them."

"Gillian, it might just be they are excited to meet you, and they won't be disappointed."

Banks was waiting for them in the kitchen. "Enid and Tom are tending to the chafing dishes. They said we should go ahead and they will be along soon. As soon as Joseph comes down, we will depart."

Uncle Joe came in as Banks finished speaking. "I hope I haven't kept you waiting."

"No, we just got here. I didn't get a chance earlier to ask how your day was?"

"Gillian, it was better than good, it was amazing. Tom arranged for a historian to meet with us. This man knows everything, and I do mean everything about the area."

The image of the historian they met today flashed in her mind. "Was his name Daniel?"

"Why yes, it was. Did Tom tell you about him?"

"No, we bumped into a gentleman at the Abbey; he answered many of our questions and gave me his card. Sam and I both thought you would love to speak with him. How ironic that you met him."

"Tom invited him to spend the day with us tomorrow. I'm looking forward to it," Uncle Joe said.

"That's fantastic. I planned to call him, but if he'll be here tomorrow, I can ask him then. Sam and I only spoke with him for a short time, but he seemed to have a great deal of knowledge."

The little church was almost full when they entered. Conversations stopped, and all eyes focused on Gillian. *Oh boy, now what do I do?*

Banks took control. "It's nice to see so many here for the service. You will have the opportunity to chat and get to know Gillian at the supper after the service; she is eager to meet all of you."

Gillian whispered, "Thank you Banks, I had no idea what to do."

"Don't be nervous; everything will be fine. Come, I will introduce you to Pastor Patrick Hall."

Gillian and Sam followed Banks to the front of the church where a tall, thin silver-haired man conversed with an older lady. When their group approached, the lady nodded and moved away, leaving them to talk to the pastor in private.

"Pastor Patrick, this is Gillian and Sam."

"Pleased to meet you. I was a little surprised when Enid called and asked if we could have a service this evening. Is there something special you wish me to speak on?"

Gillian paused before replying; one word popped into her head. "Yes, faith. I hope we haven't inconvenienced you with such short notice. I know you haven't had time to prepare, but I'm sure you have something to say on the subject."

Pastor Patrick's face lit up. "Oh, I most certainly do. I couldn't have picked a better topic myself. Will you wish to speak?"

"Please forgive me, I don't mean to sound vague, but I don't know yet."

Pastor Patrick studied Gillian before replying. "Is it direction from a higher power that will decide for you?"

Gillian nodded. "Yes, it is. I don't always know what I will do until I do it. I think you understand."

"That I do. We will play it by ear then. I must prepare for service, but I hope to have time to talk with you at the supper."

"I hope so too. Thank you, Pastor Patrick."

Banks led Gillian and Sam back to the first row of pews where Uncle Joe sat. Enid and Tom were just coming through the door.

Sam whispered in Gillian's ear. "Tell me if I need to do anything. If not, I will sit back and enjoy the service."

"Sam, I have no clue, what, if anything, I'm to do. I had no idea of the topic of the service until it popped into my head when Pastor Patrick asked."

Gillian looked around the room as she listened to Pastor Patrick's moving sermon on faith. A few of the facial expressions she witnessed, made her think he had hit a nerve. *Perhaps their faith is not as strong as it should be. If so, I hope this sermon renews it, for each and everyone one of us.*

Nothing came to Gillian during the service. She was relieved to just listen and take in the message.

He's good. I'm amazed he could produce such a powerful sermon at short notice. He doesn't have any notes; he must be preaching from his heart. He's covering all the points, loss of faith, lack of faith, and the importance of faith.

After the service, Gillian went up to Pastor Patrick. "I can't thank you enough. That is just what was needed. If you are this good with no notice, I must come to one of your prepared sermons while I'm here."

"Thank you, Gillian. It's a topic near and dear to my heart. Like you, I also receive guidance. I feel blessed to be asked to do this. I think they needed it. No matter how faithful we are, a little nudge every now and again to look deep within ourselves is needed."

"Now more than ever, Pastor. Our faith needs to be at its strongest."

Enid placed her hand on Pastor Patrick's arm. "Sorry to intrude, but I must take Gillian back to the house. She'll want to greet each guest as they arrive, so we must hurry. You can talk in a more relaxed fashion at the supper."

"By all means, I'll be along soon. Everyone is excited to meet Gillian."

"And I them, Pastor Patrick. Thank you again, and I will talk with you later," Gillian said, as Enid led her away.

CHAPTER NINETEEN

Gillian attempted to remember all the names and faces as she was introduced. Everyone was so friendly and warm, her anxiety disappeared. A familiar face brought a smile when she recognized Daniel, from the Abbey.

"We meet again. I knew who you were when we met at the Abbey, but I thought it would be presumptuous of me to say. It can be unnerving when a stranger knows who you are," Daniel said, taking Gillian's hand.

"It has happened, and I admit, it's a little unsettling, but I adjust. I'm looking forward to talking with all of you. Uncle Joe told us he met you. I hope you can spare time for me tomorrow when you visit, as I do have more questions."

"It will be my pleasure to answer your questions."

Daniel moved on and next inline was another familiar face, Theresa from the bakery.

"I dropped off some more pastries before I came to the church. I had some left over when I closed shop. What isn't eaten, Pastor Patrick will take for those in need."

"Thank you, Theresa, that was kind of you. I'm glad to hear Pastor Patrick helps provide for the needy in the area. Our local pastor at home does the same thing. Everyone gives him leftovers, and he distributes to the poor and sick. I am blessed to be surrounded by so many good, caring people."

"The world has more good than many realize. We don't make a fuss or look for glory." Theresa moved on, and soon the line ended with the arrival of the last guest.

"That went well. Thank you, Enid, for arranging this and introducing me to everyone."

"It's a pleasure. Now come; you can sample the cooking skills of our group. We have many talented cooks and bakers in our midst. Some notable for their skill, like Theresa, but everyone is good."

As they entered the music room, Enid led Gillian to the food tables, covered with hot and cold dishes and a large selection of desserts. Gillian whispered to Enid, "Everything looks good, but I won't be able to try them all. Show me the dishes I shouldn't miss trying."

Enid nodded. "Follow me and sample the ones I do. As I said, everyone here is a good cook, but some have special recipes we all look forward to."

Enid was like a mother hen and made sure Gillian had a good sampling of the top dishes. "Go sit with Sam and enjoy your food. There will be time for you to chat with everyone later."

Gillian obeyed Enid's order and found Sam sitting alone at one of the small tables. "Is that your first or second plate?"

With a look of guilt, Sam said, "Don't tell anybody, but it's my third. I can honestly say everything is delicious."

"What did you think of the service?" Gillian asked.

"It was good, excellent. I would say you chose a subject the pastor is passionate about. He had everyone's attention."

"I thought so too. Once I finish eating, I want to mingle and get to know as many as I can. Did you see Daniel?"

"Yes, I did. Guess where he is."

"I don't even need to look. Uncle Joe has him, doesn't he?"

Sam laughed. "Yes, he made sure Daniel sat at his table."

Gillian put her plate down. "That was all so delicious. If you will excuse me, I'll go mingle. I think you should too, that is, if you don't mind."

"I don't mind. I was thinking of doing just that. We can compare notes later."

"Sounds like a plan. Let's start at opposite ends of the room, so no one will be left waiting."

Everyone greeted Gillian with warmth and anticipation, as if they expected her to announce something. By the time she reached Theresa, she was ready to sit down. "Do you mind if I sit with you for a break?"

"I would love that. What do you think of our group?"

"Everyone has been so welcoming. I'm curious about one thing though. There doesn't seem to be any young people here. Not that those here are old but there are no young families."

"We had some, but with few jobs here, many of the young ones need to move for work. When they come back to visit family, they attend."

"But surely there are young families in the area. Are none of them helpers?"

"No, and it's a concern for us. It seems as if our younger helpers have all been pulled away to other areas. Even my children and their families live away from here. So many work with technology and there is none of that here."

Gillian felt an uneasy feeling in her stomach. Theresa's comments bothered her, more than they should have. *What is it about the young ones being pulled away from the area that has me feeling so uneasy?*

"Do you think they would return if something in their line of work opened here?"

"Oh my, yes. My children don't like being where they are and would love to come home, but they have families to provide for."

"Tell me about your children."

"My eldest, Douglas, is in research and works in biochemistry. He is married and has one child. My youngest,

Ariella, works in software design. She is married, with two children. I miss them, but I understand. Like so many families here, they must go where the work is. It's not like the old days."

"It sounds like you have wonderful children. Are they helpers too?"

"Yes, they and their spouses. They must have been needed in the areas they now live, or work would have been provided for them here. They wanted to move back after their father passed on, but I told them if they were meant to return, a way would be provided. We go where we are directed."

"How true. I need to continue meeting the others. I don't want to offend anyone. I'm sure I'll see you again before I leave. One more question, what's the secret ingredient in your Eccles Cakes?"

Theresa laughed. "Gillian, I'm shocked you would ask. If I told you it wouldn't be a secret, now would it?"

"Can't blame a girl for trying. They are the most delicious I've ever eaten," Gillian said before making her way to the next table.

Gillian continued around the room, spending a few minutes talking with each guest. Her eyes found Sam, he seemed relaxed, like when they were at Iona. His smile never left him, as he went from table to table, talking with the guests. *He seems to be enjoying the social interaction here.*

At the last two tables, she found Banks and Pastor Patrick at one and Uncle Joe and Daniel at the other.

"Pastor Patrick, thank you again for the wonderful sermon. How long have you been with this church?"

"Coming up on forty years and it has been a joy to serve."

"That's a long time. What is the denomination of the church?"

"We don't have one. We go by no rules, other than God's rules. It seems almost every day I hear of a new denomination, with their own set of rules. That is not how it was intended. In the beginning, the early Christians answered only to God. Each community had a teacher, a leader of the faith, to unite and guide them. Now, they have ministers, priests, bishops, archbishops, deacons, oh so many titles. We follow the rules laid out in the Bible, none other."

"Where did all the rules come from? I mean, these are all people who follow the Bible, so why so many different rules?"

"I can give you a brief answer. Interpretation. The full history and explanation you could get from Daniel. He's the expert on almost everything; he has an amazing mind."

"So I've heard. I look forward to talking with him. Something is bothering me; I don't understand why it's bothering me as much as it is, but I think there's a reason. Look around the room at your congregation. Is anyone under fifty?"

183

"I understand your concern, as I worry about it also. I have prayed for guidance on ways to keep some of the young helpers in our area, but they all leave. Not one, not one young helper has stayed."

"You would think there would be a balance; some would leave, some would stay. I think that's why it is troubling me. Who will carry on all the good work with no young ones to fill their shoes?"

"These are all things I have thought of, Gillian. I don't have the answer. If it's bothering you, perhaps an answer will be given. I can only pray."

"So will I, Pastor Patrick. I'll let you and Banks return to your conversation and see if I can talk with Daniel."

"I hope to see you again, Gillian. You have brought a new hope with you. If you need anything of me, you only need to ask."

"I am grateful for the opportunity to get to know you and these good people. It is not one, but many, that will make the difference."

At the last table, she said, "Uncle Joe, do you mind if I intrude and speak with Daniel?"

"Not at all Gillian, I'm sure he will welcome a new face. I tend to get carried away with my questions."

184

Gillian laughed. "I've heard that before. Daniel, thank you for coming this evening and agreeing to visit with us tomorrow. I have questions for you, but I don't want to tire you out. What time will you arrive tomorrow?"

"I will be here by nine o'clock. Would you like to meet with me before I meet with Joseph?"

"If it's all right with Uncle Joe, yes, that would be perfect."

"I have no objection," Uncle Joe said. "I can organize my notes and questions while you meet with Daniel. You will be amazed at his knowledge of not only this area but his knowledge of all history."

"I look forward to it. I'll let you get back to your discussion."

Gillian wandered to the food tables and found one lone Eccles cake. *I want it, but it would be selfish of me to take the last one.*

Sam interrupted Gillian's thoughts. "Your face is showing the struggle. You want it, but you don't want to take the last one. I'm here to rescue you. I have one for you at our table, along with a few other delicious sweets, all of which you must try at least a bite. I've sampled them, and I'm impressed by all the talent here."

"Oh Sam, thank you. I was struggling." They walked back to their table, and Gillian saw an Eccles cake on a plate and another plate with a selection of pastries and cakes.

"You've been busy. I don't think I would feel well if I tried to eat all of these."

"You don't have to eat them all, just a bite, and I will help finish them for you."

"How generous of you. I suggest we go for a run in the morning; you've overindulged this evening."

Sam groaned, "You're right, I did, but everything was so good. The talent in this area is amazing."

The knot formed in Gillian's stomach again. "Sam, something about the lack of young people bothers me. I keep getting an uneasy feeling."

"If it's bothering you, then there's a reason. Relax, it will come."

"I hope so, Sam." Gillian enjoyed a bite of each sweet on the plate. "They are all delicious, but I think I will save this Eccles cake for tomorrow. All the pastries are superior to any I've had before."

"I told you. It's like they all have a special talent. Everything we had here tonight was superior to anything I've ever eaten."

Enid joined them. "They are all in love with you two and are thrilled they got to chat with you."

"I enjoyed meeting them, and from what I observed, Sam did too."

"I did. I was impressed with the various trades represented here. If the tradespeople are half as talented as the bakers, I'm coming back here when I need anything."

"What trades, Sam? I didn't get into that when I spoke with them."

"There's a master carpenter, mechanic, mason, artist, author, tailor, hat maker, and cobbler. I can't remember them all, but basically all the trades I know of, and some old trades you seldom hear of now."

"Yes, we have an assortment who all help here from time to time. I don't know what we would do without them. They have taught Tom and me so much, but there are some things we just can't do."

There goes that knot in my stomach again. Young people and skilled workers, when either comes up, I get an uneasy feeling.

"I'm glad they could all come. Let me know when they're ready to leave. I would like to be by the door and personally thank everyone for coming."

Enid nodded. "They will like that. I think everyone has finished eating so I'll box the leftovers for Pastor Patrick."

"Let me help," Gillian said.

"Me too, I need to work off some of what I ate," Sam said.

Enid smiled. "Well then, you can go fetch another cart from the pantry, and we'll take everything in the kitchen to box."

Sam left to get the cart and Gillian looked over the table.

"There is not a great deal left. I'm glad their hard work was appreciated, but I hope that doesn't leave the needy hungry."

"I have other food in the kitchen prepared for Pastor Patrick to take. We make sure they don't go hungry."

The other ladies joined them, so it didn't take long with all the help to have everything put away and boxed for the needy.

Sam stood with Gillian at the door saying goodnight to all the guests. Each guest handed Gillian an envelope as they left, telling her not to open it until later. *Must be thank you cards. How sweet they came prepared.*

When the last guest left, Gillian held a bundle of envelopes.

Sam pointed to the envelopes in her hand. "Are you going to open them?"

"No, I'm too tired tonight. I think they are thank you cards and I need to make a list so I can reciprocate. I will take them to my room, and I'll be right back."

Once in her room, she placed the envelopes on the writing desk. *I'll look at them in the morning, or I'll get sidetracked and stay here too long.*

Gillian found everyone seated at the kitchen table when she returned.

"Are you ready for a cup of tea?" Enid asked.

"I am. Thank you all again for making this evening possible. I think everyone enjoyed it. I know I did."

"They enjoyed the evening and were delighted to meet you. Your ears will burn for days. They will all be talking about meeting you."

Gillian laughed at the idea. "I'm glad we had the opportunity to do this."

As she drank her tea, Gillian looked around the table. *What would I do without all these wonderful people in my life? Surrounded by goodness. Thank you, God.*

"I think I'll call it a night. Sam, I'll knock on your door at seven in the morning for our run."

Sam gave her a quizzical look. "Seven? Why so early?"

"I need to return and prepare for meeting Daniel at nine o'clock."

"All right, seven it is."

Climbing under the covers, the envelopes on the writing desk caught her eye. *I'll just take a peek at a few. I'm curious to see what they wrote.*

She opened the first one. It wasn't a thank you note but a recipe of the dish the sender had brought to the gathering. She opened several more and found recipes in each. *So that's why Theresa smiled and put her finger to her lips when she gave me her envelope. Does that mean...? Oh, I have to know.*

Opening each envelope, she continued until she found the one that left her the most curious, Theresa's. She jumped up and down with excitement. *Yes, yes!* The note included with the recipe read, "Gillian, I trust this will remain between us, and you won't reveal my secret." *My lips are sealed. I must thank her in private.*

CHAPTER TWENTY

True to her word, Gillian knocked on Sam's door at precisely seven o'clock.

Sam opened the door, dressed and ready for their run.

"Good morning, Sam. Are you ready to burn calories?"

"I am. Where do you want to run?"

"I thought we could run up the path by the greenhouse. I didn't go far on it the other day with Enid, but it looked like it went a distance."

"It does, Tom took us that way when we went to look at the cars."

"I still want to see the cars, but not this morning. I need to get back in time to shower and change before meeting with Daniel."

"Do you mind if I sit in on your talk with him?"

"I don't mind. If you have questions, feel free to ask them."

"I doubt Uncle Joe slept much last night; he's so excited with all the information he's gathering. He probably made notes until the early morning hours."

"I enjoy seeing his pleasure in learning. We have to expand our minds and keep learning…" It hit Gillian what she was missing, what she needed to do.

"What is it, Gillian?"

"I'll tell you later. I need to think about this on our run, but I have an idea."

They kept an even pace, in step with each other the entire way. Almost back at the house, they slowed to a brisk walk to cool off.

"That felt good. I miss my morning runs."

"It did feel good. Now I can indulge in Enid's cooking and not feel guilty."

"Sam, you're terrible."

"What? I like good, wholesome, natural food. It's my weakness. That's why I learned to cook."

"I can't fault you on that."

They found Enid cooking breakfast.

"I'm just going to take a quick shower." Gillian hurried to the back stairs.

"No rush, it will be here when you are ready," Enid called after her.

Gillian considered her idea while showering. *A way to instruct people in all the blessings… God intended for us is to teach them how to use what he gave us. We need to start classes on all the crafts and skills, not just for the faithful but nonbelievers too. They will soon see we were designed to be more than we are. Yes, I think I'm on track. Each generation*

passes on their skills to the next, not only through generational
memory but through teaching. Not everyone is blessed to have
someone who knows of these things.

Back in the kitchen, Gillian found Sam, showered and
changed, helping Enid. "What can I do to help?"

"The kettle just boiled. If you would like to make a pot of tea,
Sam's making toast, and everything else is ready."

Uncle Joe, Banks, and Tom entered just as they placed
everything on the table.

Gillian sensed someone watching her. Upon seeing Banks,
she tilted her head as if questioning him. He nodded. *So, I'm on*
the right track. Good.

They finished eating twenty minutes before Daniel's arrival.

"Before everyone leaves the table, I would like to discuss
something with all of you," Gillian said.

"Last evening, the lack of young people in the congregation
concerned me. Then I realized, ancient skills, some long since
lost to most, need to be kept alive. Not just by the helpers but by
everyone. When someone learns of the beauty of nature and how
God designed everything we need to survive, they will believe in
Him too. I want to start classes. If the congregation is willing,
we can find a place in, or near, town to create gardens and
workshops for all the crafts and trades. Plus, as a bonus, this
might entice some of the helpers' children back to the area. I

193

want to create a business plan, where sales of the products they make will provide income."

She looked around the table at their faces to determine if they approved of her plan, waiting for someone to say something.

Enid spoke first. "I think your idea is excellent. Why haven't we thought of it before? As helpers, we tend to close ourselves off to the outside world, only sharing our knowledge with those within our group. Showing others how we use what God provided for our survival will help change lives. I think it's exciting, and I doubt you will receive any objections."

"It's a tool we should have been using all along. I agree with Enid; it will be beneficial to all involved," Tom said.

Uncle Joe cleared his throat. "Gillian, I'm impressed with your line of thinking. For many years, I've thought it's a shame so many of the old ways have disappeared. Technology is useful, but basic survival skills need to be passed from generation to generation. The ancient crafts, which provided beautiful work, are almost lost. Everything is mass-produced now. Yes, your idea excites me, and I'm sure it will excite others also."

"Thank you. I need Joe's help in completing a business plan. He's the expert. If they agree, Maggie and Joe can stay here for a few weeks to help formulate the plan.

"Enid, could you arrange a meeting with the congregation after Sunday's service? If the weather stays nice, we can have a picnic on the grounds near the church. I want to meet with everyone, make a list of their skills, and learn their adult children's occupations. Perhaps we can use them as well."

"Gillian, they fell in love with you last night, and I have a feeling this idea of yours will fill their hearts with joy. They will do whatever you ask. What was it that made you think of this?" Enid asked.

"I kept getting an uneasy feeling, like a knot in my stomach. I realized no young helpers were present, no families with little children. I learned the young adults left to pursue careers because there was no local industry. The subject of God providing us with everything we need to survive kept needling me. The saying, we must know the past to succeed in the future, also came to mind again and again. Then all the pieces of the puzzle came together. Why weren't we sharing skills with people we want to learn of God and His wonders? This question produced the idea. This will be a pilot project, one we can tweak and improve before extending worldwide."

Tom returned to inform Gillian, Daniel had arrived and was waiting for her in the conservatory.

"Thank you, Tom. I would like input from all of you on this. If you would make a list of your ideas, we can discuss this over lunch."

Sam accompanied Gillian to the conservatory. "You never cease to amaze me. Does your mind work all the time?"

Gillian sighed. "I'm afraid so. I have always been a thinker, but lately, my head is full all the time." She paused. "Don't let me monopolize Daniel. If you have questions for him, please interrupt. I can get carried away sometimes."

Daniel stood at the window, looking out at the garden, when they entered. "Good morning, Gillian, Sam. I hope I can help you with your questions today."

"I'm sure you will, Daniel. Thank you for taking the time for us. Uncle Joe is excited to meet with you again. We'll try not to keep you too long. Can I offer you some tea or water before we begin?"

"Tea would be nice, but don't worry. Knowing Enid, I'm sure she will be in with a tray soon. She's a wonderful lady and always seems to anticipate the needs of her guests."

Before Gillian could respond, the door opened, and Enid entered with the tea and water on a tray.

"I thought you might like to have something to drink while you talk. Ring if you need anything else. You know where the button is." Not waiting for a response, Enid left the room, leaving them free to talk.

Gillian pulled a sheet of paper from her pocket. "I hope you don't mind, but I made a list of the most important questions I have for you."

"At least it's only one page." He chuckled and shook his head. "Joseph has a notebook." Then he nodded at Gillian. "Please begin."

"Are there any documents from the first century Christians who inhabited this area and other areas in Britain?"

"There are many. Some, we have in our archives. Others, we know of their existence but have not yet located. The early Christian writings were transcribed and taken to safety during the second and third centuries. Scholars who had access to the early writings have written of these. Are you familiar with the history of Polycarp?"

"I've heard of him."

"He studied under the Apostle John and traveled with him. Some scholars will debate this, but there is sufficient evidence from both early Christian writers and early historians to confirm this. We are aware he had access to the letters and writings of the Apostles and their followers. We have copies of some of his early writings. Prolific writers, the early Christians documented the smallest of details. In addition to details of the faithful, they documented local history, travelers who visited their area, births, marriages, deaths. They knew of the importance of keeping accurate records. With such extreme documentation, they also knew the danger of it falling into the wrong hands."

"Where are the documents we know of?" Gillian asked.

"That answer is a little more complicated. The writings of the early scholars are historical and can be found at various universities, libraries, and record archives; these are well known to the public and available for their viewing. The Vatican Library holds many of the early writings, but all are not accessible to the public. One you might find interesting is the Annales Ecclesiastici by a sixteenth century curator of the Vatican Library, Cardinal Baronius. Using documents stored in the Vatican Library, he wrote of Joseph of Arimathea and eleven or twelve others landing along the Somerset coast, at Glastonbury, to establish the first missionary base in the British Isles. He writes that the Apostle Philip directed Joseph and his group to travel to Briton because of Joseph's familiarity with traders there. He also writes of Peter visiting Briton and sojourning with Pudens, the son of Pudens and Claudia. In AD 179, King Lucius built a church and dedicated it to Saint Peter in commemoration of Peter's evangelizing labors in Briton. It is still known as St. Peter's of Cornhill. They excavated a stone in Whithorn, which measured four feet high by fifteen inches wide, with the Latin inscription, 'Locvs Sancti Petri Apvstoli, The place of Peter the Apostle.'

"Many early scholars wrote of the Apostles, drawing their information from the early writings of the followers. We have writings by these same scholars, and writings by those not as well known, in our archives. We also have ancient works written by the first Christians, which have not been available to the general public. As I mentioned, we have some of Polycarp's writings, which I think you might find interesting. Many of the early documents distributed for safekeeping have been lost. They are hidden in safe places, waiting to be found. Some we have found, others still wait. From public and private archives, I have discovered many historical documents were changed to suit the holder. For instance, we are in possession of a scroll that recorded the church in Glastonbury in the first century. The same document, translated and available in public archives, does not include the reference to the early church."

"Why did they want to hide so much? Why was it so important to deny Christianity was strong in Britain in the first century?"

"It was accepted and written of until about the fourth century. As time went on, it was realized the greater the history, they could attract the more wealth. The early church here cared not for power.

"I am sure you have noticed none of the helpers call themselves anything other than Christian. To us, there is no need to classify a denomination, because we should all be the same. There is but one God, which we all follow, so how could we differ? There should be no difference between any of the Christian faiths, yet there is. We all pray to one God and follow his law, yet beliefs among Christians still vary."

"I agree. I've struggled with why the denominations have animosity between them. The animosity amongst Christians turns people off. So, this difference started in the beginning? It's not a new thing?"

"Oh my, no, not new at all. If early Christians had stayed true, there would not be different denominations. It was intended there only be one church amongst Christians, God's church, followers of The Way. Wars have been fought between the denominations. This increased the struggle to bring nonbelievers into the fold. How can you preach 'God is love' when Christians disagree and defame one another?"

"How can scripture be changed? Do you mean they changed the word of God in the Bible?"

"That could never happen. It's all in the interpretation, Gillian. Are you aware of how many versions of the Bible are in print? The scripture is not changed per se, but the interpretation is. God's law and the teachings of Christ have not changed; the fundamentals of mankind remain constant. Denominations have been known to adjust their teachings based on the will of the people. It is not for me to judge nor denigrate any denomination. I would, however, challenge their interpretation."

"This bothers me, Daniel. How can we tell people of Christ while there is so much angst amongst Christians?"

"Truth, we only speak the true Word, no interpretation, no generalization, only the truth. It is not for us to say what we think scripture is telling us. It is up to each individual to open their hearts and minds to the Word. Those who insist on pushing their view will answer for it one day, but if we condemn or judge them, we do as they do. The truth stands firm. There are those who wish to make it complicated, but it is not. The basic rules of doing as God intended us to do are simple; man has made it complicated."

"Do you know what happened to the documents from the monastery at Iona?"

"The ones that are believed to have been destroyed in the fire?"

"Yes. I'm aware the Book of Kells was taken to safety, but what of all the other manuscripts? The monks there devoted time to transcribing scrolls of the apostles and scholars. I'm not sure why I think this, but I don't believe they were destroyed."

"Your instinct guides you on the correct course. The early Christians knew to trust no one. Their work was important, too important to keep the original document in their libraries. Every monastery, abbey, and house of worship kept scribes to create duplicates of everything they held. Correspondence, scrolls, manuscripts, journals, any form of writing documenting the life of Christians, the apostles, and Christian travelers from other countries. The letters from the disciples were copied and sent to all the churches they could reach. The originals and copies were then stored away for safe keeping. Through the years our group has recovered some of these, but many are still missing. They have not found the ones from the monastery on Iona, but we know they exist from the writings of a monk who went to another Abbey."

"Did he give any clue as to where they were hidden?"

"Not to my knowledge, though another pair of eyes might see something I missed. I can obtain a copy for you if you would like to read it. It is quite an interesting diary. He tells of his time on Iona and at the Abbey in Ireland, where he remained until he died."

"Yes, please, if it's not too much trouble, I would like to read it."

"No trouble at all. I will send for it and will have it for you in a day or so."

"Thank you, Daniel. I've taken enough of your time. You've answered many of my questions. Though some of your answers have raised more questions, they must wait for another time. I appreciate you sharing your vast knowledge with us. Sam, did you have any questions?"

"No. Daniel's given us a lot to consider. Should we send Uncle Joe in, or do you need to take a break?"

"I would like to take a small break and visit Enid in the kitchen. No doubt she will have something to fortify me until lunch."

CHAPTER TWENTY-ONE

After talking to Daniel, Gillian excused herself and went to the library near the schoolroom. She closed the book she was reading and rubbed her eyes.

The books I've looked at have answered many of my questions. But each question answered creates another. I now know more of my ancestors who lived here. They all worked hard but were joyful, even in the hardest of times.

Sam entered the library and looked at the books strewn at her feet. "Catching up on some reading or looking for something?"

"Both. I'm humbled to come from such a long line of hardworking, talented, and faithful people."

"I don't want to interrupt your progress, but Enid has lunch ready. She wanted to know if you would prefer a tray or to join everyone downstairs?"

"I was thinking of going back to my room and looking at the books there. If it's not too much trouble, I would like a tray in my room. I can get it; I don't need to be waited on."

"No need, I'll bring it up for you. Do you mind if I join you, or would you rather be alone?"

"I welcome your company. You can look at the books too. Sam, this is so exciting. It's like being alone in the manuscript room of a museum, able to look at anything you want, and there's so much information."

"I'll meet you in your room with lunch. Do you want me to help you put these books back?"

"No, some I want to read further. I'll return the ones I'm done with."

Gillian carried the books that held her interest to her room and went through the books in her bookcase. She pulled several from the shelves which caught her attention before Sam returned with a tray.

"I'll set this on the table. You can tell me what seized your interest while we eat."

"Let me wash my hands, and then I'll join you."

After eating, Gillian picked up one of the books from the school library. "This one might interest you. It's a daily record of one of my ancestors. They documented everything: what they did, who visited them, the smallest details of life. I feel like I know them."

Sam took the book she offered. "Thank you. You're sure you don't mind me sitting with you?"

"Not at all. I'm glad you're here."

Engrossed in reading, they lost track of time. When Sam stood to stretch, he looked at his watch. "Oh my, it's almost 5:30. I was completely absorbed in this book."

"I know. Me too. We should check in with the others. They will wonder what held our attention so long."

Banks and Enid looked up as they entered the kitchen.

"Did you think we got lost? We were absorbed in the books we found and lost track of time. I hope we haven't kept everyone waiting," Gillian said.

"No, you haven't. Tom and Uncle Joe are showing Daniel out, and Enid and I are enjoying a cup of tea."

Gillian helped herself to a cup of tea and poured one for Sam. "Daniel has been here all this time? Oh my, Uncle Joe must have asked a lot of questions."

"I think Daniel enjoys teaching as much as Joseph enjoys learning. They seemed happy with their day. Did you find something interesting?" Enid asked.

"There were several books; the most interesting was the Book of Logic. The writer used logic to answer doubts about the facts in the Bible. Well written, the logic used is hard to dispute. I was pleased to find it was written by one of my ancestors and to learn there is a place for logic in faith."

Banks nodded. "I understand how it would please you. Although I must admit, you are relying more on faith than logic these days."

"Yes, I am, but it was nice to learn some logical arguments for those who doubt."

"What about you, Sam? Did you learn anything?" Banks asked.

"As a matter of fact, I did. The book Gillian gave me to look at detailed, and I do mean detailed, the daily lives of those living here. It was interesting, educational, and inspiring. I'm amazed at how talented and creative they were. They not only lived off the land, they lived as one with the land. They wasted nothing. If they came across a fallen tree, they would use it to make furniture or build something; if it couldn't be used for those purposes, it served as firewood. They lived well, created beautiful things, and wasted nothing. Perhaps the noise in today's world clouds the mind and blocks the creative process."

"I agree." Banks said. "Sometimes you need to step back, quiet your mind and clarity comes. They lived simpler, less complicated lives than people of today. It was easier to stay in tune with nature and God. Today's world is full of noise: phone, television, computer, radio. Besides being hard on the spirit, hearing must suffer too."

Gillian remained quiet. Sam and Banks provided an answer. *They are both right. My mind is too noisy. Instead of quieting my mind, I'm always thinking. I need to return to Iona, to quiet my mind. I am trying to process too much information. I must start the project here, and then we will leave.*

After dinner, Gillian excused herself; she needed alone time. In her room, she let all her thoughts and feelings pour into her journal. She wrote of her fears, hopes, and questions. Putting the journal down, she went to the closet, reached for the satchel, and stopped. *No, not now. I am trying to absorb too much information. I will be guided to what I need to know. I must concentrate on starting the project here. Once that is started, I will look again.*

CHAPTER TWENTY-TWO

The group spent the next few days planning the organization of training programs. Gillian spoke with a local realtor and discovered an old factory outside of town with over three hundred acres, which had remained unused for years. The realtor promised to contact the owner to find out if they were interested in selling.

"Enid, would you and Tom like to ride with us to look at the property? I need your input on whether it would be suitable."

"I would love to, and I'm sure Tom would too. When?"

"This afternoon, if you're free. It shouldn't take too long."

"Let me check with Tom, but I think we can manage. I contacted everyone about the picnic after church tomorrow, and they are all excited. Everyone is bringing a dish. Pastor Patrick had some of the men set up picnic tables in the meadow near the church."

"Once I get a list of all the trades and crafts, I can complete the training plans. I hope they're agreeable to teaching others their skills."

"Don't worry, Gillian, they will not object. Many of us have worried about this subject for years. I am so glad you thought of this. You'll see, you will have more volunteers than you can use."

"I'll be upstairs in the school library if anyone needs me. Where is everyone anyway?"

"Joseph and Banks went for a walk, and Sam is helping Tom with repairs. They will all be back by lunch. You go do what you need to do, and I'll let you know when lunch is ready."

"Thank you, Enid, you're such a blessing. I'm grateful for all the hard work you and Tom do here."

"'Tis we who are blessed. Now, go take care of things, and we'll talk more at lunch."

Scanning the rows of books in the library, she knew what she needed and hoped the information was here. Sitting down on the floor to better see the bottom row, she pulled out books and scanned through them. One by one, she found exactly what was needed. *Miracles never cease. There are books here on almost every craft and trade. It's as though someone in the past knew we would need these.*

She piled the books in one corner, keeping a list of each subject she found. *I'm making progress; it must be meant for us to do this.*

Sam looked up as Gillian entered the kitchen. "Enid said you were busy plotting and planning. Did you make any progress?"

"I did. Once again, the information we need has been provided. There is a textbook on almost every craft and trade, skillfully detailed and complete with drawings. I found a book of herbs, which is illustrated, allowing identification of the herb with instructions on how to use it, when to use it, and when not to use it. I put the books needed for training in the schoolroom for now."

"Tom and I will join you to investigate the property. Odd, but neither of us can remember a factory around here. How far out is it?"

"I have a map the realtor emailed me. I'll show you after lunch. Who else would like to come?"

Uncle Joe shook his head. "I have reading to do, so I will stay here. I look forward to hearing what you find,"

"If you don't mind, I will remain here also," Banks said.

"The realtor is contacting the owner and asked that I call him after we look at the property. He may have an answer for us then. He didn't know much about it. He said he found it on the county property records, but that's all he knows. He said it must have been empty a long time because he couldn't remember any factories in this area. Even if the building doesn't work, the amount of land makes it a possibility."

"You might want to put your boots on if we're going to walk around an old abandoned property," Enid said.

"Right. I'll go get my boots." Pulling her phone out of her pocket, she opened the email attachment showing the map.

"Here Tom, you can look at the map while I get ready. I'll be right back," Gillian said.

When she returned, Enid said, "Tom and Sam are waiting for us out back."

Gillian smiled when she saw which vehicle they were taking, and Sam in the driver's seat held no surprise.

"Tom asked me to drive so he can follow the map."

"Are you familiar with the location, Tom?" Gillian asked.

"Well, I have passed the area before, but I've never been to where this map shows, nor did I know there was once a factory there."

"I'm intrigued that neither you nor Enid knew of it. I'm getting used to mysteries; maybe we can solve this one today."

Gillian gazed out the window at the green pastures and cottages they passed. *Everywhere around here is so vibrant. Even the empty pastures are a beautiful emerald green. I hope the property is not in too bad of shape. I want to get this project underway.*

They turned off the main road and traveled several minutes on a dirt road through a wooded area. The further they went, the rougher the road became. The woods thinned, and they entered a clearing. A three-story brick building stood before them. The area surrounding the building looked maintained.

"Interesting." Gillian could think of nothing else to say. She jumped out of the jeep when it came to a halt. The large, sturdy building looked in good repair.

Sam looked at the structure before them. "From the outside, it looks in good shape. Windows intact and roofline good, no sagging. Do you think it would work for what you have in mind?"

Gillian's face glowed as she took in every detail. "It looks perfect. It looks more like a school than a factory, and that's what we need it for. I'm eager to hear the details. The owner must have someone care for it."

"Enid and I will explore while you two look around. There looks to be a path into the woods over there." Tom pointed to a gap in the hedge.

"I've seen all I can without going inside, so Sam and I will tag along. Are you sure it's safe to walk into the woods here?"

Tom laughed. "You'll be safe luv, nothing in these woods will bother you."

The path led to another clearing. The group stopped in amazement at the scene before them.

Gillian counted. "There must be twenty-seven homes here."

"Aye, these are old terrace homes. It looks like there are nine to a row. I have no idea who lived here, but this makes me even more curious. How could a factory and this many people be hidden from our community? Granted, it's not in town, but it's not that far out. Perhaps the people in the next village knew of it." Tom seemed genuinely baffled by their finding.

"Now I'm even more eager to talk to the realtor. I wonder if he's aware of these homes and if they are part of the same property?"

"One way to find out. Call him," Sam said.

"Oh, sorry, I left your phone in the car. Let me go get it," Tom said.

"No Tom, it's okay. I'll wait until we get home. I need to make a list of questions for him. If the owner is willing to sell."

They wandered around the rows of homes before leaving. Each member of the group remained quiet in their own thoughts regarding the mysterious find.

CHAPTER TWENTY-THREE

On the drive home, Tom and Enid talked about the mysterious factory and houses. Both expressed confusion over their lack of knowledge.

A strange car parked in front of the manor made Gillian ask, "Are you expecting anyone, Enid?"

Enid looked at the car. "No, and I don't recognize the car. Do you, Tom?"

"Can't say as I do. Perhaps it's someone Joseph or Banks invited."

Gillian's heart rate increased. Something was about to happen. *Good or bad? Good, it's a good feeling I'm getting.*

They entered through the kitchen which was empty.

"I would think Banks would take them into the conservatory or parlor. You wait here while I check," Sam said.

"No need to worry, Sam. I have a good feeling about our guest. Whoever it is, they bring good news, not bad." Gillian followed Sam to the conservatory.

Banks stood as Gillian entered. Before he could speak Gillian saw the visitor sitting on the sofa. Her chest tightened. "Auntie Mary?"

The elderly lady stood and opened her arms to Gillian. "No child, I'm not Mary. Come, let me embrace you. I have waited so long to meet you."

Gillian walked over to the lady. *My eyes are playing tricks on me. She looks just like Auntie Mary, except for the clothing style. Same hair, complexion, eyes.*

She felt only love in the arms of this lady. "I'm sorry, please forgive me, but you bear a striking resemblance, almost identical."

"Sit, and I will tell you all. Banks, please excuse us. I would like to speak to Gillian alone."

"Of course. I will have Enid bring a tray," Banks said, as he led a confused Sam out of the room.

Gillian couldn't help staring. "Please don't say anything yet. Wait until Enid brings a tray. I don't want to be interrupted."

"As you wish."

They both gazed and smiled at one another, neither speaking, just taking in the other's appearance.

Enid stopped in her tracks upon seeing who sat with Gillian.

She composed herself and smiled. "If you need anything else, press the button." Without another word, she left them alone.

"Does Enid know you?"

"Oh yes, but don't get ahead of things, I will explain all. Do you want to pour or shall I?"

"I'll pour. Auntie Mary used to ask me the same thing. Your voice isn't like hers, but you look so much like her."

"Mary and I talked often of how you would react. Now, let me introduce myself to you. My name is Ruth, and I am Mary's cousin. People always mistook us for twin sisters because of our likeness. We grew up together. Her mother and my mother were sisters, and her father and my father were brothers, so you can see why we would look so much alike. There are a few differences in our features, but you must look hard to see them. If you saw us side by side, you would see the differences."

"If you were so close, why did I never hear of you? You never visited, and Auntie Mary never spoke of you."

"There are reasons for that. As you know, each helper has their own calling, their own set of gifts, and their own path they must travel. My path took me into darkness and danger. To protect all those dear to me, through my own decision, I kept away from anyone my work could bring harm to. Over the years, Mary and I met secretly and a few helpers, few, knew of my existence. Even some Chosen do not know of me."

"Enid knows you."

"Yes, she does. This is the secret place Mary, and I met. Enid can be trusted implicitly, with no reservation. She has no darkness within, nor has she ever. White light is the only light that emanates from her."

The Descendants Series: The Revelation

"You mention the darkness. Was your work like Sam's?"

"Similar, except darker. My work led me to the darkest of the dark. I do what I can to aid those who are trying to escape from them. I see the minutest darkness in anyone. It is both a blessing and a curse."

"You have endured this your entire life?"

"Only since adulthood. I had the opportunity in the past to be relieved of this gift, but I chose not to. The work is too important, and I am a stubborn old lady. I will fight against the darkness until my dying breath."

"You know Banks, Enid, and Tom. Do you know Sam also?"

"We've met, but he doesn't know of our connection. That I am Mary's cousin."

Gillian exhaled. She hoped there weren't other secrets Sam had been keeping from her. With the others, she could accept secrets, but she wanted none between her and Sam.

"You seem relieved Sam doesn't know. Is it because you don't want him to know, or because you don't want to think he was keeping something from you?"

"I have no problem with Sam knowing. He has become a strong shoulder for me, but I was hoping there weren't more secrets he was keeping from me. We have agreed to be open and honest with each other."

"You and Sam are more than friends."

218

"Oh, no, we're only friends, just very good friends." Gillian felt herself blush under Ruth's scrutiny.

Ruth patted Gillian's knee. "Oh, come now, you can't fool me. There are deeper feelings than that between you two. You may not want to admit it yet, but you will."

Gillian changed the subject. "Did Banks or Enid inform you I was here? Is that why you came?"

"No, you let me know."

"How's that? I didn't know of you, so how did I let you know?"

"Mary always said you were one to question everything. My attorney contacted me to let me know someone inquired about the property I own near here."

"The property with the factory and the houses?"

"The very same. Except it is not a factory. We listed it as one, but it is not."

"Did Auntie Mary know you owned it?"

"Yes, she did. I never had children; all the funds I acquired I had no need for. We needed a place we could bring those we rescued to allow healing. I found the land and had the facility built, with additional homes for helpers who worked with the rescued. It's been a while since it was fully staffed."

"Is it still used?"

"No. They now use another safe place for those in need. My role has decreased. Now, tell me, what makes you want to buy this property?"

Gillian told Ruth of what she had learned since coming to Glastonbury and her thoughts for the land's use. She laid out her plans for training and the sale of products from their work.

"It seems you have a well-thought-out plan and I applaud you. You are on the right track for bringing in new followers. I am proud of you. I have followed your life closely over the years, and you have done well.

"Mary fretted over the secrets she needed to keep from you. She loved you. She and I were very close, alike in looks but different in personality. I have had to harden myself over the years because of my work. She, on the other hand, was all love and softness. Like a kitten. When my burden became heavy, she would sense it and seek me out to comfort me. Don't let me get off track reminiscing; I could talk for hours about my times with Mary."

"That wouldn't bother me at all. I have many happy memories of her. She was a blessing to us all. Please tell me you will stay with us for a few days. I want to get to know you better."

"If you wish for me to stay, then I will stay. I will need to ask Enid to provide accommodation for my driver, but it will not be a problem. Enid and Tom keep the doors to this house of refuge open to all who are good."

Gillian pressed the button on the mantle. "Enid will be in soon, and we can arrange for you and your driver to stay. Do you mind if I hug you again? You've lifted my spirits today. I needed that. Since Auntie Mary passed, I've felt alone, no family. My best friend, Maggie, is like family, but it's not the same."

Ruth stood and embraced Gillian. "You can hug me whenever you wish. Now you have sought me out, we can visit more often."

"Well, it was by accident I sought you out."

"Nothing is by accident, Gillian. There has been a design in place all along. I knew one day you would summon me, and here we are."

Enid entered. "What can I do for you, Gillian?"

"Do we have accommodation for Ruth's driver and a room for her also? She has agreed to stay a few days."

"Already taken care of. The driver chose to stay in the guest house, and Ruth is in the room next to yours. The one she always uses when here." Enid's face revealed her pleasure at Ruth's arrival.

"Once again, you amaze me at how you perceive the need before someone requests it. Now, if there is no one else in the kitchen, I would like for the three of us to chat over a nice cup of tea."

Ruth and Enid laughed together.

"We laugh because Mary always insisted on the three of us gathering in the kitchen over tea whenever Ruth visited."

"Let's not break tradition then." Gillian took Ruth's and Enid's hands, and together they made their way to the kitchen.

They talked while they prepared dinner.

Gillian looked up from her task as someone entered. Sam stood in the doorway, smiling at the interaction between the ladies.

"Sam, let me introduce you to my Auntie Ruth. I don't know if the term is correct because she was cousin to Auntie Mary. But I will claim her as my Auntie."

"We've met before, but I had no idea you were related to Gillian. You've put the biggest smile I've ever seen on her face."

"Thank you, Sam. I do believe I'm not the only one to make this girl smile of late." Ruth giggled at the expression on Gillian's face and the broadening of Sam's smile.

Gillian changed the subject. "Enid, is there anything you would like Sam to do?"

"Dinner is ready. All I need is the dinner cart. You know where it is, Sam, if you wouldn't mind bringing it. Then you can tell everyone dinner is ready."

"Happy to." Sam brought the cart and left to find the others.

"Did I embarrass you, dear?" Ruth asked.

"Not at all, but you have the wrong impression. Sam and I are just good friends. He's been very supportive, and I enjoy his company. That's all," Gillian said, emphasizing *all*.

"So you say." Ruth tried to hide her smile behind her teacup.

CHAPTER TWENTY-FOUR

They talked late into the evening before Ruth declared she would like to go to her room.

"I'm still active but find I need to keep a regular sleep schedule to be at my best. Gillian, if you wouldn't mind escorting me to my room, I will say goodnight to everyone." Though in good shape for her advanced age, Ruth appeared tired.

"I'm sorry Auntie Ruth, I didn't mean to keep you up so late."

"I caused quite a stir for you today, and you needed answers to your questions. I hope I have clarified most of them. We will talk more in the morning. I'm an early riser and like to walk before breakfast. Will you join me?"

"I would love to. What time?"

"I will be ready at 6:30. Wear comfortable shoes because I walk a few miles on my morning walk."

"I'll be ready. Do you have everything you need for the night, or should I ask Enid to come up?"

"I'm sure Enid has taken care of everything. Good night dear, sleep well." Ruth kissed Gillian on the cheek before entering her room and closing the door.

As she prepared for bed, Gillian's thoughts were on Ruth. *I have a relative, a real flesh and blood relative. Another secret kept from me. They say it was all for my own good, safety. Did they not realize how alone I felt, especially after Auntie Mary died? I have two choices, be angry they kept this knowledge from me, or rejoice that I now have her in my life. My heart tells me to choose joy at finally meeting her.* After falling asleep with the conflicting feelings still on her mind, she dreamt of Auntie Mary.

Gillian woke early and prepared for her walk with Ruth.

Ruth's door stood open. "Come in, just putting my shoes on. I'm pleased you like to be on time. That is a good trait to have, being late without an excuse is inconsiderate."

"I always try to be on time, and I would not want to keep you waiting. After all this time of not knowing you existed, I don't want to waste a minute."

"Gillian, the world would be a better place if everyone remembered not to waste a minute. We are only given a certain amount of time on this earth, and no matter who comes into our lives, we should cherish each moment."

"I agree. I wish I had spent more time with Auntie Mary. I visited with her every chance I could, but not enough."

"No need for regrets, you were getting your education and starting your working life. She knew you were not careless with your time."

"Thank you for telling me that. She was the one constant in my life. My adoptive parents loved me and gave me a good life, but I could never talk to them like I could with her. Her guidance helped me so much."

They talked throughout their walk. The tales of Ruth and Mary growing up together lifted Gillian's spirits.

"We need to discuss the property. It's yours to do with as you wish. Your objective is to help people and bring them into the fold. That's the only thing I ask. I want it used for good."

"You don't have to give it to me. I can pay for it."

"I have no need of money. All my needs are provided for. I live a very comfortable life. The work you are doing is important, and you will need help."

"Thank you, Ruth. I know this will help people. I'm curious why Enid and Tom weren't aware of the buildings or their use?"

"Few knew of its existence. The ones we brought there for healing came from some very dark places. We could not risk exposing anyone to them until they were fully restored. We provided helpers from all over the world who specialized in cleansing and leading them into The Way."

"The Way, that's a term Rachel used in my vision when she spoke of the followers of Christ."

"It was the original term used and still fits today. Following The Way of our Lord is what we are about. We follow in The Way He intended, spreading hope and love. Those who lose hope and feel unloved are the most vulnerable. It matters not what walk of life someone comes from: rich, poor, believers, non-believers, educated or uneducated. When they have no hope and no love, they are easy to lead along the wrong path."

"I understand. Did you ever stay at the property?" Gillian asked.

"No, my job was to rescue those I could and take them to where they could get help. I kept in touch with their progress. Some we saved, some we lost. No one ever left the property to go into town. We had a continual rotation of helpers. When the rescued reached a good point in their healing, they sent them to other places for help in adapting back into society. Those we could not save were taken somewhere else."

"I can tell by your expression the lost ones bother you," Gillian said.

"Every single soul is important."

"True, but it sounds like your work has saved many. You can't save them all."

"You will see in time. Regardless how many you guide into The Way, it is the ones who get away that burden your heart. Enough talk of sadness. What can I do to help you get your project started?"

"I have a list of helpers who will assist with getting this implemented. I will need some who can sense the darkness. Not that we won't accept any students who have darkness in them, but they are the ones who will need special attention. I'm sure you understand what I'm saying."

"I do. I'm glad you realize your work is important, but protecting the followers is also important. I'm acquainted with many who sense the darkness and those who can aid in healing. I will contact them and arrange the help you will need. Do you know what classes you will offer and who will teach them?"

"I have a general idea. We're having a picnic at the chapel in the woods tomorrow after service. I should be able to complete the trades list and find out who is willing to teach."

"No one will turn down the opportunity to teach of the gifts given us. You have seen a need and are working to address it. I'm pleased. Mary always said how caring and smart you are. She was not wrong. Tell me of these visions you have experienced."

Gillian told her of the visions she experienced while in Iona and the ones here, at least those she could share.

"You have been blessed. It confirms you are open and ready to see, learn, and listen. Visions and visits from angels were commonplace in the beginning. Over time they diminished for most people but increased again during the time of Christ. As more and more have let the world control their thoughts and actions, they have again diminished. Even the faithful get bogged down in daily life and close themselves off."

"I am blessed. To see and hear the early Christians is amazing. In one of my visions I was told, 'what was will be again.' I hope I can make a difference. I realize I'm not the only one working toward this goal, but there are things I am to find that will help them."

"Each of us, has specific duties, all that is asked of us is that we do our best. Always remember, do what you can and know when to walk away."

They passed the greenhouse, their walk almost over. "I have enjoyed our long walk and talking with you. After we get this project underway, I'm to return to Iona. Will you join us?"

"I would love to, but I have something else I am directed to do. I will stay a few days with you here. Don't worry; we will see each other again soon."

"I hope so."

CHAPTER TWENTY-FIVE

The picnic after the service went better than Gillian could have hoped. She had a list of trades, with a teacher for each one. *It will be a wonderful program. Everyone was excited and eager to take part.*

"Where are your thoughts this morning Gillian?" Enid asked.

"Oh, sorry. I was thinking of how excited everyone had been about our new trade school. I have at least one teacher for each class; the cooking class has twelve instructors and the carpentry class has five. We have the location and the teachers. Now all we need is students."

"How do you plan on recruiting them?"

"I have something in mind, but I'm not sure yet. I will know soon though." Gillian sighed. "I wish Ruth didn't have to leave so soon. I have enjoyed her company."

"I know you have, luv, and she also enjoyed spending time with you. Her property came as a surprise; she never mentioned it during her visits. I thought I knew everything around here, but she kept this secret."

"She's coming with Sam and me to the property this morning. She arranged for us to meet the helpers we may need for security."

"Tom and I wondered about that. When you open something to the public, there are always risks. I shouldn't have worried though, it seems you have that covered. Tom and I will help you any way we can. You only have to ask."

"Thank you, Enid. I don't want to put any more on you than you already do. You work hard and provide for so many, but I do have you listed for classes. I hope you can teach one of the herbalist classes and Tom can teach a class on land management. We will offer more advanced classes later. Classes which will benefit the helpers as well as those who come to us and are fully committed."

"What kind of classes would that be?"

"Inherited memory, ancient languages, and early Christian writers. The helpers know of these things, but I sensed some have not opened themselves to the possibility."

"You could be right. We get so busy doing what's needed, we sometimes forget to take time for our own awakenings."

"It's in the thought stage, but it would be beneficial. Have you seen Uncle Joe this morning? I need to ask a favor of him."

"He's in the upstairs library. Would you like me to get him?"

"No. I have time before Ruth will be ready to go to the property. I'll find him."

Gillian found Uncle Joe and Sam in the school library. Engrossed in what they were reading, neither noticed her until she sat.

"Your reading must be interesting."

Uncle Joe placed a scrap of paper to mark his place before closing his book. "The information in this room is more than amazing. The writers included such detailed accounts of their lives, I feel I know them. Learning history is one thing, but to read first-hand accounts of daily lives is magnificent."

"I'm so glad you feel that way. What about you, Sam? Any interesting reading?"

"Yes, I echo Uncle Joe's sentiments. There's so much I thought I knew, but reading it on a more personal level provides a new, deeper understanding."

"Good, that reaffirms my thoughts on also offering classes for helpers. Sam, would you like to come with Ruth and me to the property this morning?"

"Yes. I need to talk with Banks about something I read, but then I'm free. I'll meet you in the kitchen when I'm done."

I wonder what he read that he needs to discuss with Banks?

"Uncle Joe, I have a favor to ask. First, no pressure. If you don't want to, don't hesitate to say no. Would you be able to stay here for a few months?"

"A few months? Well, I would need to speak with Joe to check if he needs me for anything, but otherwise, I don't think it would be a problem. Might I ask why?"

"I would like you to assist in the set up and oversight of the classes. I need someone I can communicate with to ensure we get off to a good start. If the project is as successful as I think it will be, we'll implement it in other places. If you agree, I think you would be the perfect person to oversee each start up."

"I'm flattered. My only hesitation is being away from Joe for any length of time. Since his mother passed, we've always been near one another."

"I understand. I would like Joe and Maggie to assist in the set up. Joe is a genius at business planning and will be able to implement and streamline it to the best advantage of all."

Uncle Joe's face broke into a huge smile. "It would be a wonderful opportunity for all of us. What of Joe's business and the shop?"

"I think I can arrange temporary help for both, with Joe and Maggie's approval, of course. Would you like to call Joe and ask him?"

"Yes, yes I would. Oh my, this is a blessing. Spending more time here and having Joe and Maggie with me, all while helping others. Who could ask for more? Thank you, Gillian."

"It is I who should thank you. Your vast knowledge of so many things will help ensure we start this project in the best possible way. This morning Ruth will introduce me to helpers gifted in sensing the darkness and some gifted in the healing process. We need them in place for the safety of all concerned. Once the darkness realizes the magnitude of what we are doing, they will try to destroy it any way they can."

"I agree. You are wise to provide the project with added security. You have come so far in these few short months. Samantha said you would amaze us all, and she was correct. Do you mind if I call Joe now? I must admit, I'm more than excited and eager to talk with him."

"Please do, explain as much as you can, but don't give any details of location or anything else until you see him face to face. Banks told me to be cautious of revealing anything over the phone."

"I understand. I will only say what I need to. When do you need them here?"

"I don't want to interrupt their honeymoon, but as soon as possible. After you talk to Joe, I'll have Banks arrange for their travel here. If they agree."

"Oh, I have no doubt they will agree. My son would not pass up an opportunity like this." Uncle Joe's smile had not diminished.

CHAPTER TWENTY-SIX

When they arrived at the property, Ruth handed Gillian a set of keys. "Here are the keys to your new project. I pray it will be as successful, if not more so, than the project I previously used it for."

"Thank you so much, Auntie Ruth. Which key is for the factory, or what was thought of as a factory? I would like to view it first."

"They are all numbered. The one with zero on it is the factory. Each house has a number and the key for it is numbered likewise. The caretakers also have sets of keys. They are trustworthy and loyal. Do you need me to get the keys back from them, or are you comfortable with them keeping keys?"

"If you trust them, I have no objection to them keeping their keys. I would like to meet them though. They may be able to help us here if they wish."

"I will arrange for them to meet with you. They would be honored to help with this new venture. The others you meet today should be here in about an hour. I wanted to allow time for you to look inside and get a grasp of what is here."

"Perfect. Sam, do you mind doing the honor of unlocking the door?"

Sam took the keys from her and found the one marked with a zero. Holding the door open, he motioned for Gillian and Ruth to enter.

The door led into a large room resembling a school cafeteria with long tables and chairs. Everything looked well maintained.

"This is fantastic; we can build partitions to separate the different classes and use the tables and chairs for the classrooms." Gillian made a note of the number of tables and chairs.

There were two hallways leading off the large room. They entered the hall on the left, which had several smaller rooms.

"These will be perfect for office space and smaller classes, ones that don't require work areas." She made notes of the contents of each room.

At the end of the hallway, they passed through another door leading into a large kitchen. *Plenty of counter space, center island, and lots of storage cabinets. We will need to add another stove, maybe two, a commercial oven, and a commercial refrigerator. This will work well. I'll ask Enid for her input on stocking the kitchen.*

"This is perfect. The only thing I don't see are restrooms."

"Follow me." Ruth led them through a door leading into another hallway.

Ruth opened a door to reveal a large bathroom with cubicles, sinks, and showers. "The room next door is identical to this one. We used one for the ladies and one for the men."

Further down the hall, Ruth opened a door to the stairway.

They followed her to the next floor, where Gillian couldn't believe her eyes. A large fireplace was at the far end of the room with several sofas and chairs grouped around it. The walls on each side sported built-in bookcases. Reading tables, like those used in a library, stood in front of the bookcases. She looked at the area near the stairs and saw another staircase leading to the top floor. A small kitchen area adjacent to the stairs completed the second floor.

"This is amazing, Auntie Ruth. What's on the top floor?"

"Storage. Furniture and a lot of junk you will want to throw away. Come, I'll show you."

Gillian gasped as they reached the top of the stairs. They opened to a room crammed with furniture, boxes, several old trunks, some large old mirrors propped against the walls, and two vintage sewing machines.

"We were blessed to receive many donations. Some we used in this building, some we used in the helper's houses, and the rest we stored. I couldn't tell you what's in the boxes and trunks. You are welcome to return and explore to your heart's content, but we need to move on if we are to keep on schedule."

Gillian hugged Auntie Ruth. "This is amazing. I imagined a lot of work would be required before we started, but this is better than I expected. We only need to build a few partitions in the main room to separate work areas and add additional stoves to the kitchen."

Sam nodded. "I agree. From what you told me you envisioned, this building is perfect."

"I should draw a layout of the building to determine what classes we can fit."

"No need for that. I will have the caretakers bring a copy of the building plans." Ruth pulled her phone out and started texting.

"You text?" Gillian was surprised at Ruth's use of such a modern form of communication.

Ruth laughed. "I may be old, but I can manage with most of the new technology. You are used to Mary's ways; I never could convince her to text. I did finally get her to email so we could stay in touch."

"She hated the new technology. When I bought her a new phone for the cottage, she hated it. She said she had used a rotary phone forever and didn't understand why she needed to learn to use a push-button phone." Gillian laughed at the memory. "I think she kept the rotary phone and only used the new phone when I was there."

"The caretakers will be here in two hours with the plans. That will give you enough time to view at least one of the homes before meeting with the others."

"Perfect, let's head over to the homes. I'm excited to see inside."

Entering the first home, she sensed peace and love. "This feels nice."

The small entryway contained a narrow table, placed under a mirror. A coat stand was in the corner by the door. Stairs faced her to the left and a hallway to the right. Down the hallway she entered the first room. Two comfortable chairs flanked the fireplace, a sofa on the back wall and a love seat on the wall nearest the door. A large bay window, complete with a window seat, faced the street. A small drop leaf tea cart sat in one corner and a china cabinet in another. The furniture was old but in good condition.

The next room, a dining room, included a round pedestal table with four chairs, which graced the center of the room. An antique buffet lined the wall nearest the door, and storage cabinets flanked the fireplace. French doors led to a small garden area.

The kitchen reminded Gillian of the kitchen in Auntie Mary's cottage. A deep farm sink with counter space covered one wall. Behind a door, a nice sized pantry with a stone floor included shelving sufficient to hold dishes and food. Bucket sized enamel containers marked with the contents sat on the floor.

"I can't believe how well maintained it is. It's ready to move into with no modifications or work," Gillian said.

Sam led the way up the stairs to the bedrooms and bathroom.

Each room included furnishings. The smallest bedroom, over the entry hall, housed a twin bed and a small dresser. The large room next to it boasted a four-poster bed and vanity. Built-in wardrobes stood on either side of the fireplace. The bay window mirrored the one below, complete with a window seat. The smaller bedroom at the back of the house contained a double bed, vanity, and wardrobes on either side of the fireplace.

A clawfoot tub, pedestal sink, and toilet left plenty of room in the bathroom for a floor to ceiling cabinet, which housed the water heater with shelving above it for linens and towels.

"Are all the homes like this one?" Gillian asked.

"They are all identical, furnishings differ, but the layout is the same. Each home is furnished and ready for occupancy. When you are ready, they can bring linens and dishware from storage." Ruth looked at her watch. "We need to return to the main building. Now you have the keys, you can explore the other homes whenever you like."

"Auntie Ruth, I can't thank you enough. This is better than I could have imagined."

"No need to thank me. I'm glad it will continue to do the work for which it was designed: teaching others of all the blessings available and how wonderful we were all created to be."

CHAPTER TWENTY-SEVEN

Gillian made notes until the others arrived. She guessed the three men and one woman to be about forty to forty-five years old.

She stood to greet them. Sam greeted them by name. *He knows them. Good, he will be able to tell me about them.*

"Sam, I'll let you manage introductions while I make a phone call," Ruth said. "Sorry dears, don't mean to be rude, we'll chat after my call." She excused herself and disappeared down one of the hallways.

"Gillian, we couldn't have asked for a finer group to help with this. I am very familiar with all of them. They are diligent and accurate in their assessment of people." One by one he introduced her to the group. "This is Mark, Lucas, Brian, and Gabriella."

The one called Mark, a short, lean man, extended his hand toward Gillian. "Pleased to meet you. I'm interested to hear about your project. Ruth told us a little, but we would like to learn more."

"Of course. Please, be seated, and I'll tell you of our plans so far. The idea is new, and we're still working out all the details, but I can tell you the basics."

Gillian went over the plans and the desired goal. She watched their faces to gauge their reaction but could not read them. "So, that's the basics. What do you think?"

Mark seemed outgoing and served as spokesperson for the group. "It is a fantastic idea. You understand you're opening it to risks though. The times have become more turbulent, and the darkness grows more cunning. Some escape detection even by the gifted. Have no fear though; we have not yet found one who can hide their ways from us."

"I understand. It's a concern, but Ruth tells me you four are what we need. That alone gives me total confidence to proceed. Will all of you be able to live on-site at the same time, or will you take turns? How does that work?"

"Two and two. Two of us will remain here for a three-month period, and then the other two will take over for three months. We will continue that rotation until we are either no longer needed, or directed to do something else."

Gillian nodded, satisfied with what the answers. "That sounds fair. Sam, is there anything we need to mention?"

"What will your intake process be? Will one of you be in on the interview process for prospective students? Or will you be more behind the scenes?" Sam asked.

"Every person entering the premises will be screened by one of us. No one will slip through."

"That's all we can ask, protection of all concerned. I've known all of you for a long time and am confident you will do whatever is necessary to protect everyone."

"Thank you, thank you all. I'm not sure how big this project will be or how it will be received, but I'm hopeful it will be successful."

Gabriella stood, signaling the conclusion of the meeting.

"Gillian, from what you have told us, I think it will be very successful. Many of the lost are not bad people. They are just looking for something more; they feel an emptiness and are desperate for something to fill it. This will enlighten them to all that was given to everyone in the beginning. I've heard a lot about you in the past few months. You're doing well and are on the right track."

"Thank you, Gabriella, for your kind words."

Ruth emerged from the hallway. "Sorry for my absence, important call. Gillian, if you and Sam would excuse us, I need a moment alone with my colleagues."

"It was nice to meet all of you, and we'll see each other again soon," Gillian said.

After they had said goodbye to the group, they went outside.

"What's on your mind, besides a million things? I sense something is troubling you," Sam said.

"There is something, but I'm not sure what it is. I have an uneasy feeling."

"About the project?"

"No. I think the project will go over well. You know how sometimes you feel something is not right, but you can't put your finger on what it is? That's the feeling."

"Understandable. These are difficult times; there's a lot of anger and hate in the world. You're trying to show the good, and you know you'll meet obstacles. The darkness will try to stop you. Perhaps that's it."

"Could be. You're probably right. I want the world to know life was meant to be easier. So many wonderful things await them, they just need to open themselves to goodness and receive all that God intended."

The group came out of the building. Not stopping to speak, they waved and went on their way.

"They're not much for conversation, are they? They remind me of how you were when we first met."

"The job is difficult. Your guard is always up, and you look for the darkness in everyone you meet. We are taught to trust no one until we're sure. It doesn't leave room for congeniality. They are a fun bunch when they get away from the outside world."

"I'll take your word for it. Let's go back in and talk to Ruth while we wait for the caretakers."

Ruth sat at one of the long conference tables. She hung up from a call as they entered.

Gillian sat next to her and studied her face. "Would you like to share what has you concerned?"

Ruth shook her head. "I can't give you details. There are suspicions of some within our fold, and that troubles me. I have the best team working on it and I hope our concerns are unfounded."

"You say you have the best team working on it. Are you, like, a supervisor?" Gillian asked.

"You could say that. In my advanced years, it was determined it would be better for me to organize and evaluate than go into the Devil's den myself. I disagree. I may be old, but I can still defend myself. They tell me my role is important, and I know better than to question what we are directed to do. I miss the action though."

Gillian stifled a giggle. "You surprise me. Judging by your nature now, I can only imagine the fear you put into the hearts of those who came against you."

Sam laughed. "Oh Gillian, she could tell you some stories. She is a legend within our group. She was, and is, a force to be reckoned with."

"Sam, you make me blush at your flattery, but thank you. One day, when we have more time, I will tell you some of these tales Sam speaks of."

The door opened, and five people entered. Three women and two men.

"Ah, here are our caretakers. I believe you've met some of them, Pastor Patrick, Nathaniel, Miriam, Dolores, and Clarice."

"Pastor Patrick, nice to see you again so soon. Nathaniel, how is that wayward boy who taunted you?"

"Thanks to you, he is doing well. I hired him for odd jobs, and he and his friends are volunteering to do yardwork at the church in town. I have high hopes for him."

"That's wonderful news. He needed someone to care and guide him. Now he has you. Miriam, Dolores, Clarice, I don't believe we've met. No, wait, you were at the supper we had after the church service. My apologies, I met so many that night."

Miriam hugged Gillian. "No worries, lass, we can be a little overwhelming. I think I speak for all of us when I say you have brought new hope to our area."

Dolores and Clarice nodded in agreement and each, in turn, hugged Gillian.

"I have the blueprints you requested in my car. I'll get them before we leave," Pastor Patrick said.

"Tell me a little about how you came to be one of the caretakers here, Pastor Patrick," Gillian said.

"My father was one of the original caretakers, and I took over from him. There was such good work taking place here, I've been happy to be a part of it. Once this is in use again, we will need help. I think we can use volunteers from the church, now that the other helpers will be aware of it. We had to be careful before because no one local, except for us, knew of this place. Once you decide what changes you would like to make, I will arrange for a crew to start."

"Thank you. I'll go over the plans to determine how we can best utilize the space. I couldn't have asked for a better facility."

Gillian spent time talking with the ladies. When it was time for them to leave, Sam walked them out and returned with the plans.

"If you two are done, I'm in need of a cup of tea. I think it's time we head back," Ruth said.

"Of course. We can go over the plans later. I'm sorry I kept you here so long. You must be tired."

"Don't apologize, child. I wouldn't miss the opportunity of spending time with you. It's invigorating."

CHAPTER TWENTY-EIGHT

Maggie and Joe will arrive today. I can't wait to see them. The past two weeks since Auntie Ruth left have been so busy I have had little time to think. Everything is going as planned, better than planned. The remodeling and setup at the property is almost finished. Tom has a crew completing the new greenhouse, and the homes are ready. It is all in good hands.

"Deep in thought again."

Gillian hadn't heard Sam enter the conservatory, brought out of her thoughts at the sound of his voice. "Sam, I was thinking of all we have accomplished in the past two weeks. Pastor Patrick is bringing by a list of prospective students for the team to interview. I feel so…"

"Blessed?"

"Yes. It's all gone so well. I keep pinching myself."

"When it's meant to be, it's surprising how it all falls into place. Enid said Theresa's daughter and her family are moving into one of the houses this week. I'm sure that made Theresa happy."

"She is. I think she's a little disappointed her son hasn't decided yet. He would be an asset in the lab where we will make the natural essential oil products. From what I gathered, he has been helping someone, and he's worried they are not at a point he could leave them. If he's meant to come, someone will take over for him, but I admire his commitment."

"I agree. So, what's on the agenda for today?"

"Other than Pastor Patrick coming by, we are free. Everything is in place, and we have a good team. No, not good, they are fantastic. We'll be free to enjoy Maggie and Joe's company when they arrive."

"I know you're excited about that. Are we still planning to leave for Iona tomorrow?"

"Yes. My work here is done, for now anyway. Maggie and Joe will be here for a few weeks, longer if needed, then they will return home. I would like to spend more time here, but I am feeling a pull toward Iona. It's time, and Banks agrees."

Enid rushed in. "Sorry to interrupt, but Pastor Patrick is here to see you. He's in the kitchen when you are ready." She left as quickly as she entered.

Gillian shook her head. "She never stops working, and she never seems to tire. Let's go to the kitchen and see what Pastor Patrick has for us."

Gillian wasn't surprised to find Pastor Patrick enjoying a piece of pie.

"Gillian, Sam. Nice to see you both again. I hope you don't mind meeting me in the kitchen. Enid enticed me with her pie, and I couldn't say no."

Gillian nodded. "None of us can. It's nice to see you again too. I'm told you have a list of prospective students for our project."

"That I do. I put out the word to all the churches in the surrounding area, and we received a good response. I have met almost all the applicants, and I think you will be pleased."

"I'm hoping we have at least twenty to start. Are we anywhere near that number?" Gillian asked.

When he shook his head, Gillian's disappointment showed in her expression.

"Oh sorry, you misunderstand. We have considerably more than twenty."

"What? Oh, that's wonderful. Sam, isn't that exciting?"

"It is. How many are there?"

"This list contains 127 applicants. Your team will be busy."

Unable to restrain herself, Gillian hugged Pastor Patrick and grabbed Enid's hands as she danced around. "This is amazing. I had hoped within a year we would be over one hundred, but this many to start!"

Sam cleared his throat. "Gillian, I don't want to dampen your spirits, but they must be approved. Remember?"

"I know, but I have a feeling your friends will find nothing to deny their entry. Just a feeling, but we'll see."

"I agree with Gillian. As I said, I met almost every applicant myself and sensed nothing untoward. Some may not be living a good life, but I sensed nothing dark."

"You sense the darkness too, Pastor?" Gillian asked.

"Not in the same way Sam and Ruth do, but, let's just say, I have a gift."

"He's being modest." Enid said. "He has more than one gift, but that's his story to tell. We are blessed to have him in our little church."

Gillian shook her head. "I must admit, I had no idea how many gifted people I had around me. I'm learning new things every day, and I hope others are too. How can one doubt when so many gifts and blessings are bestowed on mere humans?"

"I believe that is the true purpose of your project, and I think we are all going to rejoice in its success. Sam, before I leave, I must ask a favor of you."

"Anything, Pastor, I'll be glad to help."

"This list contains the names and contact information along with the class or classes they are interested in. Can you pass it on to whoever is setting up the appointments with the team? I would do it myself, but I have some urgent matters to take care of."

"No problem, Gillian arranged an orientation session which includes the interviews. I believe they are holding the orientation at one of the churches in town. Is that right Gillian?"

"Yes, I have arranged a student processing team who will contact the students and inform them of the time and place of the orientation. We'll hold as many orientation sessions as needed to accommodate this number."

"I'll fill the team in on what Pastor Patrick has pulled together for us. They will be busy."

"Thank you, Sam. I must be on my way. Enid tells me you will leave tomorrow?"

"Yes. My friend Maggie and her husband Joe, will be here soon. They will assist with implementing the project. Joe is Uncle Joe's son. I'm sure you'll have the opportunity to get to know them while they are here."

"I look forward to meeting them. Take care on your journey, Gillian. Each thing you do, put in place, is sending a ripple effect around the world. The blessings are multiplying."

Gillian watched the pastor leave. "He's a good man. If a news channel existed that only reported on good things done by good people, they would have more than enough stories."

"True. Many think there are more bad than good, but that's not true. The bad gets more publicity because people think bad news sells. Most people would rather hear the good stories."

Uncle Joe came in all smiles. "Look who I found."

Gillian looked up to see her best friend charging towards her with open arms.

"Gilli! I've missed you. It seems like forever. I know it's only been a few weeks, well, almost a month. Iona is amazing! You were right; I loved Moyra and Abe. They are super. Wait until you see how close the new guest house is to completion."

Gillian laughed. "Okay Maggie, take a breath. I missed you too. We will have the rest of today and tomorrow morning to catch up before I leave. Where's Joe?"

"He's helping Tom take the bags to our room."

Gillian studied her friend. *Married life suits her. She is positively glowing. She's always been beautiful but now even more so.*

"Why are you looking at me like that? Do I look a mess? Are my clothes okay?"

"You look perfect. I was just thinking how happy you look, and how beautiful you are."

Maggie's smile grew even bigger. "I am happy. I'm married to the most wonderful man in the world, I have visited the most peaceful place and I'm with my best friend. What more could a girl ask?"

Sam cleared his throat. "If I might interrupt for just a second. I'm going to find Joe. It seems you two have a lot to catch up on."

"Tell Joe I'm going to take Maggie on a walk. We won't be long. We just need a little girl time. Enid, forgive my rudeness. Let me introduce you to my best friend, former business partner, and the closest thing to a sister I've ever had."

"Pleased to meet you, Maggie. I won't intrude on your time. Might I fix you a pot of tea before your walk?"

Maggie hugged Enid. "It's so nice to meet you too. I had a drink on the plane right before we landed. I think I'll wait for the tea until we come back from our walk."

Enid smiled as she watched the two girls leave for their walk, with Maggie chatting all the while.

CHAPTER TWENTY-NINE

"Mrs. Somerhurst, tell me of your trip to Iona," Gillian said as they descended the steps to the garden.

"Gilli, it was amazing. It's so beautiful and peaceful there. I like the sound of my new name, Mrs. Somerhurst. My face should hurt; I don't think I've stopped smiling since the wedding. Well, I did at one point, Gilli." She stopped and grabbed her friend's arms. "What happened at my wedding? No, don't say 'nothing' because I know something occurred, but everyone tried to protect me. You better tell me, or I won't talk to you."

Gillian laughed. "Oh Maggie, there's no way you could quit talking. There was a small problem, but Banks and Sam helped resolve it. That's all you need to know. I only want your memories of your wedding day to be happy ones."

"Something happened to you though. Didn't it? I felt, sensed, whatever, you were in trouble. It happened right after our vows, I looked around for you but couldn't find you. Everyone kept telling me everything was fine, but I knew better. I knew you were okay once I saw you, but you had a sadness in your eyes that was, well, haunting."

Gillian sighed. "Yes Maggie, there was an incident, and it wasn't pleasant, but it's over. Now, tell me what you think of

Moyra and Abe."

"You're not going to give me the details, are you? You're supposed to be able to tell me anything. Best friends, remember? All right then, as long as no harm came to you and whatever the problem was is gone, I'll leave it alone, for now."

"Thank you. Now tell me of Iona."

"Moyra was like the big sister I never had. I have a surprise for you. You will not believe it! Joe is so happy."

Gillian stopped. "This soon? You're having a baby!"

Maggie laughed so hard she was crying. "Oh no, I'm sorry, I understand why you would think that, but no, not yet. Not that we don't want children soon, we do, but we want to give ourselves time to adjust and enjoy it being just the two of us for a little while. Not long though. Think of something else I could do which would make Joe almost as happy as news of a baby."

Gillian thought for a moment. "Oh, I know! Moyra taught you to cook."

"Yes, she did. I'm still learning, but I'm capable of the basics. Joe is thrilled."

"Good news for Joe; you can continue your training here. Enid is a marvelous cook and knows everything about your favorite topic. She has an herb garden you will fall in love with."

"Wonderful, I love herbs. We went home for a few days after leaving Iona. Everything is going well at the shop. Beth and her sister Cass help the Rennie sisters when needed. Both girls said they could use the money. Such hard working, sweet girls. Cass is quiet unless talking about animals. She thinks Joe and I should get a dog, but I don't know how Banks would feel about that."

"I don't think he would mind, but you should ask him. How's Joe's business?"

"Abe put him in touch with a classmate who's struggling and needing work. He's a really nice guy. Joe said he had a nasty experience in his last job. Anyway, Joe talked to him on the phone and arranged for them to meet while we were home. He'll work for Joe while we're here, and if it works out, Joe may hire him full time."

"Sounds like everything is falling into place for you and Joe."

"It is. Everyone has been amazing. Moyra and Abe are excited about their new baby. It's sweet to watch the two of them together."

"Come on, let's head back so we don't keep everyone waiting. I want to show you and Joe the property before dinner."

Sam, Joe, Uncle Joe, Banks, and Tom were in the kitchen with Enid when they returned.

Joe greeted Gillian with a hug. "Good to see you, Gillian.

Dad filled me in on your project. At first, it sounded like a monumental undertaking, but I see everything is progressing and you only need my input to streamline, organize, and track."

"That's still a lot of work for you. I hope you don't mind, but I knew you were the best one for the job. I want it online, so anyone involved can check on students, classes, supplies, projects. I'd like you to set up an online store, for the products the students make."

"Not a problem. Between Dad and I, we can put together what you need."

"Oh, by the way, congratulations."

Everyone stopped talking and gaped at Maggie and Joe.

Gillian laughed. "I can tell you all had the same thought I did. No, it's not a baby but the next best thing. Maggie is learning to cook!"

Maggie blushed at the laughter and applause that followed. "All right, all right. You'll see how much I've learned, and Gilli tells me I can continue my studies with Enid."

"I will be pleased as punch to help you. We have many experienced cooks and bakers in our community, and all of us would be glad to pitch in."

"Thank you. I look forward to learning from you. Now, if you will point me toward the tea, I will start by making a pot."

CHAPTER THIRTY

During dinner the main topic of discussion centered on the property. The main building, the new greenhouse, and homes impressed Maggie and Joe.

"Gilli, from what you told me you envisioned, it's all just so perfect. How did you find it?"

"That's another interesting story. A local realtor I was working with contacted the owner's agent to ask if they would be interested in selling. The realtor had never seen the property but found it listed as a factory on the tax rolls, with sufficient property for our needs. While we were waiting to hear a response, we had an interesting visitor. It seems Auntie Mary had a cousin, more like a twin. Although they have different personalities, they looked like identical twins. Her name is Ruth, and she is, was, the owner of the property. Anyway, to make a long story short, we enjoyed a few wonderful days together before she needed to leave. The property now belongs to this estate."

"Really? Just like that, some unknown relative pops out of the blue, who just happens to own the perfect property for your project? Forgive me for saying the obvious, but it's a miracle. But I don't understand why you didn't know she existed?"

"In her line of work, she keeps a low profile, even from other helpers. Only a few people knew of her existence, and most who did, had no clue of her relation to Auntie Mary. When Auntie Mary stayed here, they would connect if Ruth was free."

"What do you mean by her line of work?" Maggie asked.

"She works with those taken in by the darkness."

"I'm impressed. You just spoke of miracles and spiritual things in a very matter-of-fact manner, not raising so much as an eyebrow. A few months ago, you would have reacted in a very different manner."

"Yes, that's so true. I've come to accept the wonders that were there all along. I still struggle with some things, but I'm adapting."

"Gilli, I'm so proud of you and happy to find you so relaxed. I was worried."

"Now you can ease your mind. I'm fine. If your husband doesn't object, I would like to steal you away for a little more girl time."

"Joe won't mind; I overheard Sam telling him about the building with all the old cars earlier, and I'm sure it will give them plenty to talk about. I'm eager to hear more about the cars, but I won't pass up time with my very best friend."

"You have a lot to catch up on, so no objections from me," Joe said.

Gillian led Maggie to the third floor.

"Gilli, this house has the strangest layout I've ever seen. I told Joe we need to keep our cell phones with us in case we get lost."

"I know what you mean. My first few days here were confusing, but Enid insists they haven't lost anyone yet."

"That's reassuring. Where are you taking me?"

"This floor includes the old school room, school library, and other guest rooms. Not as big or as elegant as the guest rooms on the other floor but still comfortable and adequate. A book I found up here gave me the idea for the project you and Joe will help set up."

"I wondered where you got the idea. It's marvelous, by the way. It will be a success, just one of my feelings."

"For once, I can honestly say, I understand what you mean by 'feelings.' I've learned to acknowledge and explore different ideas that pop into my thoughts for no apparent reason. Some lead me where I need to be, others don't, at least not yet. I have learned, my dear friend, although I hesitate to admit it, you have been right all along."

Maggie gathered Gillian into a tight embrace. "I'm so happy for you. Though you've always been a wonderful person, you were so, um, closed up. If it didn't seem logical, you refused to acknowledge it. Now that you know and accept the little voices and ideas that pop in your head, it will open up so much for you."

"I can't argue with you. As I said before, you were right. I have always appreciated the world God created for us. I just didn't know there was so much more He wanted us to share in and grow from. It's all so amazing and beautiful."

Gillian opened the door to the schoolroom and motioned for Maggie to enter.

Maggie wandered around the room, touching the desks, exploring the bookcases. "I feel love and happiness in the room."

"I felt the same thing. The children must have been like little sponges. The more they learned, the more they wanted to learn. There are some classes at the project you might be interested in taking while you are here."

"Hmm, you mean the cooking class?"

Gillian giggled. "Well, that too, but there will be classes on herbs and all their uses. How to identify, when and how to use them for cooking as well as other uses. I know you're a firm believer in herbal remedies, and this will increase your knowledge. Almost every craft will be taught. Some almost extinct crafts will be revived. The whole idea is to teach all the wonders God placed here for us and how to use them. The trend toward self- sufficiency and off-the-grid living will help bring a lot of interest."

"Is there another goal in mind?" Maggie asked.

"Most definitely. In learning of all His wonders, they will become curious to know more of God. This will serve the dual purpose of helping people learn and bringing them into the fold."

"You realize not everyone will? I mean, I don't want to sound negative, but some people have a wall so thick, nothing can penetrate it. I'm excited, I think your idea is wonderful, but I don't want you to feel responsible for those who choose to ignore what is right in front of them."

"I know. I've worried about that, but I'm learning we can only guide; the choice is theirs. I'm committed to this program, which offers them every opportunity to see, to know, and to understand. I'm just one of many tools in use at this crucial time. It's not all on me."

"Good, you have always sought perfection in what you do. I worried you would take it too personal for the ones who can't be reached. I don't want you feeling guilty. Now, show me this library Joe's dad has been raving about."

Gillian led Maggie into the library and waited in silence while Maggie looked at the contents of the shelves.

"Wow, some of these books are really old. Joe will love exploring in here."

Maggie sat in the chair opposite Gillian, leaning forward and taking Gillian's hands in hers. "We've always been honest with one another; now it's time for you to let me in on what happened at my wedding."

Gillian squirmed in her seat. "I told you earlier; it was nothing, just me having a silly moment, that's all."

"No, it wasn't just a silly moment. I need you to tell me. I knew right away something horrible was going on with you. Joe tried to distract me, but I was determined to find you. Uncle George stopped me. He said, 'She's in good hands and what is happening will not harm her. Everything happens for a reason. You will cause her more upset if she knows you're panicked. Leave it be for now; let her do what she must.'"

Gillian looked puzzled. "Maggie, how did he know? Is he a helper?"

Maggie's face lit up. "Yes, I didn't know either until that day; he kept it secret. I contacted him while we were in Iona because it kept playing on my mind. He told me my father's family have been helpers for centuries. It was all so bizarre. I haven't talked to my Mom about it; I'm not even sure she knows."

"She probably does. You need to talk to her; it may help explain things you've wondered about. Well, that's a twist. I'm not the only one learning new things about my heritage."

"I thought the same thing. Back to what we were discussing and don't change the subject. Uncle George calmed me down and prevented me from chasing after you. At the reception, you seemed different, but okay. I struggled to let it go that day, but Uncle George insisted, and when he gets that stern voice, I know to listen."

"It's strange Banks never mentioned anything about your Uncle George. Everything was a little chaotic at that time, but still, I would have thought he would have told us."

"No, Banks wouldn't do that. He would know it would be up to Uncle George to reveal himself. Everything happens when the time is right. Keep trying to change the subject all you want, but neither of us is leaving this room until you tell me." Maggie's firm tone indicated she wouldn't let up.

"All right, I'll tell you." Gillian went over all that happened leading up to and including her horrible experience at the wedding, leaving Maggie in tears.

"See, now you're upset. I didn't want to do this to you," she said, embracing her friend.

Maggie sniffed and pulled back. "No, I needed to know. I'm so sorry none of us saw what was happening. I'm your best friend; I should have sensed it. I'm so annoyed with Sam. How could he be so cold as to ignore you? He's not getting away with that; I'll tell him what I think."

"Maggie, no, no you won't. It wasn't his fault. He pulled back from me for a reason."

"What reason?"

"I can't say, but something happened that worried him. Something that made him think he wasn't being observant enough."

"Why can't you say? Does anyone else know?"

"Maggie, it doesn't matter now. Please let it rest."

"Was it the man in the restaurant? The one you were all hush-hush about? The one giving off dark vibes that everyone thought they were being so protective of me about? That one?"

Gillian gaped. "You knew?"

"Of course. You have known me long enough to know how I pick up on things. You all thought I didn't notice. I only kept quiet because Joe was in such a state. I finally made him tell me about it while we were away. I may be flighty and a little off the wall, but I am not, and you should know this, a delicate flower who needs protecting."

"Oh Maggie, I'm sorry. With the wedding approaching, we didn't want you worried and upset. I know you don't need protecting, and I know how sensitive you are. I should have known we didn't fool you. Please don't blame Sam though. He did what he thought best. Sometimes when we try to protect someone, we end up hurting them."

"Touché."

Gillian squeezed Maggie's hand. "I promise to be as open as I can be from now on. Enough about me, I want to hear about your honeymoon."

"It was fabulous. Joe is just..."

Gillian's eyes widened. "Okay, we can skip that part. I meant what you thought of Iona."

Maggie blushed. "I wasn't going to go into the details of, well, you know." She giggled. "But I never thought married life could be such a wonderful thing. On a serious note, I found Iona to be a special place. A place of renewal and blessings. I've never been anywhere that felt so peaceful. Moyra and Abe were wonderful hosts. Everything was wonderful."

"It's a special place. I'm looking forward to going back. I know I have work to do, but I will still enjoy my time there."

"I wish you didn't have to leave so soon. I'm looking forward to helping set up this project in any way I can. I don't know what use I will be, but Joe will have it all organized and running smoothly before we leave."

"You have more talents than you realize, Maggie, and you will be very useful. You have a way of connecting people and helping them on their path. Look what you've done for me."

"It's nice of you to say, but I know my limitations. Who's teaching the herb class?"

"Enid is teaching the basic class, and I am working on getting someone to teach the advanced blending class. Not that Enid isn't an expert, she knows everything about herbs, but I have something in mind that takes it to a new level."

"Care to share?"

"I want to get a biochemist on board who will know the chemical makeup to safely blend them for market."

"That would be great! Do you have someone in mind?"

"Yes, but they can't come yet. I have an idea that might help convince them. I think it will work out, at least I'm hopeful."

"You're amazing. Who would have thought that day we met Samantha that all this would come about?"

"It's all so wonderful. I understand about the importance of timing now. I mean, if I had learned all this earlier, I wouldn't have been as well equipped to accomplish what I'm doing now. My formative years, my education, work experience, both good and bad, all prepared me for now. It's almost as if a script was written of my life, and now I'm able and prepared to do what I can."

"Hmm, seems like I might have said similar words to you in the past. At which time, I believed you scoffed at me about 'things that were meant to be,' but now you see."

"Yes, Maggie, once again, as much as I can't bear to admit it, you were right. Anyway, I've kept you long enough. I must finish packing. I plan an early run. Want to join me?"

"I would love to. Joe and I resumed our running routine while on Iona. Do you mind if he tags along?"

"Not at all, Joe is always welcome. Sam will probably join us too. He needed to get back to exercising because he can't resist the delicious cooking here. He and Joe are alike in some ways. Neither can resist dessert."

"Still trying to claim you and Sam are just friends?"

"Yes, so don't start. Come on, let's go downstairs and let them know the plan."

CHAPTER THIRTY-ONE

Gillian's silence since they said their goodbyes and boarded the plane, did not escape Banks. "You seem troubled. Anything you would like to talk about?"

"No. I'll be glad when we get to Iona, so I can clear my head. I have so much running through my mind I can't think."

"You have had a lot to consider over the past months. Too much on your mind makes it difficult to sort and clear away the jumble. In a few short months, you have learned of your true family, traveled to new places, met new people, and still managed to think of new possibilities. You have done well. Relax, once we are on Iona, I want you to take a few days to clear your mind of all intrusion, and open yourself to what might come next. Don't dwell on what you might need to do, just wait, and it will come."

"You always calm me. Did you give Samantha pep talks too?"

"You've read some of her journal. What do you think?"

Gillian nodded. "Yes, she was quite a handful for you in the beginning. One of her biggest fears was that one day she wouldn't have you to help her."

Banks seemed to consider her words before responding. "It took a long time for her to have the faith you already have. She knew I would always be with her, yet she let 'what if?' play on her mind. When she finally put her worries aside, she committed her life to helping the suffering and the lost. She was a wonderful, strong-minded woman. Once she accepted her role, she went at it full force, but she remained troubled to some degree. Not surprising, considering what she entered into. You, however, and correct me if I'm wrong, seem to have an inner faith that I will always be by your side."

"Well, of course I do. I don't think I would still have my sanity if I thought otherwise. You have given me no reason to doubt anything you have told me. Besides, I couldn't stand to think otherwise. You are the only one on earth I have complete faith in."

"I am flattered, but you have others you can trust."

"Trust yes, I do have many I trust, but I also know they are human, and humans can and will let you down from time to time."

"Are your reservations connected with the secrets that were kept from you?"

Gillian paused before replying. "No, it's not that. It's common sense. The original disciples were dedicated to Christ and loved Him. Yet, their humanity got in the way, and they let Him down. I would be silly to think any human could garner complete loyalty."

"Yes, in the beginning, some were doubters. Remember, they did not really know and accept who He was in the beginning. As they witnessed His teachings and miracles, their faith grew. Their belief and faith solidified with the resurrection. After that, their dedication was strong in doing what He had directed them to do. They dispersed around the world to teach of Him. The rest, as they say, is history."

"Ah, history. That wonderful knowledge we crave. I have learned history takes on a new light when you read first-hand daily accounts. My time spent in Glastonbury was not wasted. I learned so much. The struggles and achievements of the early followers were inspiring. Until then, I gave little thought to how far we have strayed from using what God placed here for us to survive and thrive. When I have time, I want to return and take some classes."

"Gillian, you have wasted no time since we first met. No one could ever accuse you of that. This school will be successful, and I believe it will do as you envision. There are many wonders in this world, waiting to be revealed."

"Banks, I shouldn't ask, but I'm curious. What's your history? How long have you been in this role?

"I understand your curiosity, but that information is not for now. One day, all will be revealed to you. Until that time arises, know I am here for you."

273

Gillian chewed her lip. "Sorry, I should have known when I asked what your response would be. Can't blame a girl for asking."

Banks laughed. "No, but the time is not now. You have more important things with which to concern yourself."

"Speaking of important concerns. Auntie Ruth has a team working on an issue within the group. Is that something I need to worry about?"

"We must all worry about that, but for now all you need to do is relax and enjoy all Iona offers. Ruth has excellent help and will let us know if we are needed. We will spend the night with Mirabelle before leaving for Iona in the morning. I am sure that meets with your approval."

"Oh good. I enjoyed spending time with Mirabelle."

Banks stood. "We should land soon. I took the liberty of acquiring a warmer coat for you. It will be considerably colder when we land, and you will need the extra warmth. You will find it in a box under your seat. There is also a book, which Enid said Daniel dropped off for you."

"It must be the one written by one of the monks who had been at the monastery on Iona. Daniel mentioned I might like to read it."

She watched Banks walk to the front of the plane. *What would I do without him?*

274

Reaching under her seat, she pulled the box out. Inside the box, she found a sheepskin, hooded, knee-length coat like the one she borrowed from Moyra, so she knew it would be warm. From the bottom of the box, she pulled out a pair of matching gloves, a cable knit scarf, and the book from Daniel. *These will keep me nice and warm for the many walks I plan to take.*

Sam left his seat and sat down beside Gillian. "It looks like I need not worry about you getting cold on this trip."

"Banks chose well, I love them. What about you, Sam? Do you have a warm coat or jacket?"

"I do. Mirabelle is kind enough to keep some things there for me."

"Do you have a box of forgotten things there?"

"I have a box there. However, rather than forgotten things, they are things I need only when there. I have clothing spread around the world, which frees me to travel light."

"Hmm, if you keep eating like you have been, you might need to go shopping."

"Oh! That was rather mean. Are you implying I'm getting fat?"

"Of course not, just that you will if you don't curb your appetite."

"Point taken. I'm fortunate to have a good metabolism. There may come a day when it slows, but until then, I will enjoy all the treats our wonderful group of helpers provide."

"You are incorrigible. I plan to take long walks while on Iona. You can join me if you like."

"I would love to. Nice, brisk walks and a beautiful lady by my side. How could I decline?"

Gillian felt her face grow warm at Sam's words. She was relieved Banks chose that moment to reappear.

"Does the coat meet your approval?".

"It's perfect, as are the gloves and scarf. Where did you find them? I know you didn't go into town while we were in Glastonbury. None of them have a label. Were they handmade?"

"They were all made on the estate. Enid made the scarf from wool spun there, and the gloves and coat were made by one of the artisans who helps there."

Gillian shook her head. "I shouldn't be surprised, but I am. These are beautiful. I want these classes added to our list."

Banks smiled. "Enid said you would and has already arranged for that to happen. The pilot is preparing for landing. You will be able to try out your new clothing items."

They secured their lap belts and within minutes the pilot made another smooth landing.

Sam led Gillian to a car parked on the side of the airfield.

"I'll start the car so you can get warm while I go back and get our luggage."

My goodness, it's cold. I'm glad Banks had the foresight to get this coat for me. I would freeze in my jacket. It was cool last time we were here, but this is a little too cold. Her thoughts were interrupted as Banks and Sam got into the car.

Banks turned to her. "Are you glad you have the coat?"

"Yes, I am. Thank you. It's much colder this time. I didn't realize how cold it would be."

"This is only the beginning. The winters here can be severe, especially for those not accustomed to them."

"At least the sun is shining, that helps." She gazed at the sun glinting off the hills and lochs during their drive to Mirabelle's. In the heated car, with the sun shining in, warmth soon enveloped her.

Gillian spotted a small stone building with a sign advertising locally sourced wool products. "Oh, I wish I'd seen that sooner. I would like to purchase a few sweaters. I don't think I packed enough warm clothes."

"I can turn around and go back. We're not on a time schedule today." Sam made a quick U-turn and parked outside the stone building.

"Anyone else want to come in?" Gillian asked.

"We will wait for you here. It doesn't look big enough to hold many people. Besides, it's warmer in the car. You will be safe here," Banks said.

"I'll hurry." Gillian scurried out of the car and ran into the building.

As promised, she returned within five minutes. "Did you find what you needed?" Banks asked.

"I did, more than I needed. I knew what type of sweater I wanted, but I had no idea how many colors they would have. I have cream, brown, black, blue and burgundy.

Sam laughed. "Did you get every color they had?"

"No. They had several shades of green too, but I've never cared for green, at least on me."

CHAPTER THIRTY-TWO

Mirabelle was waiting at the door of her cottage when they arrived.

"Come inside, all of ye. It is too cold to be standing on the doorstep. Let me take your coats. I have a nice warm fire ready to take the chill off. Make yourselves comfortable, and I'll be back in a jiff." Mirabelle was a whirlwind of smiles and chatter.

Gillian settled into a large, comfortable chair near the roaring fire. "Ooh, this feels nice."

"Ye haven't seen anything yet. The winters here get bitter cold," Mirabelle said, rolling a tea cart into the room. "Now help yourselves and don't be shy. There's plenty more where that came from."

"This all looks nice, Mirabelle. What do we have here?" Gillian said pointing at a plate of sandwiches.

"These on the left are salmon and on the right are cheese and onion. This little pot here has some pickled chutney if you like to add a bit of spice to the cheese, and I have some fresh dill sauce, if you like, for the salmon. Don't worry Sam; there are plenty of tea cakes and pastries in the kitchen to satisfy your sweet tooth once you've had a sandwich or two."

"Mirabelle, you're a gem. I didn't think for a minute you would let me down," Sam said.

Mirabelle sat opposite Gillian. "I'm hearing wonderful things about a new project you are getting underway. Once you've had a bite to eat, I want to hear all about it."

After they indulged in the sandwiches and a selection of pastries, Gillian stifled a yawn. "My goodness, I'm sorry. The food and warmth in the room have made me sleepy."

"No doubt you also had an early start to your day as well. Why don't you take a nap? We can catch up once you're rested."

"Mirabelle, thank you. A nap sounds wonderful. We were up early for a run with Maggie and Joe before we left. I don't normally nap, but it's been a busy few weeks. Same room as before?"

"Yes love, you should have everything you need."

"Please, don't let me sleep too long, or I won't sleep tonight."

"Just you rest now, I'll be up to check on you soon," Mirabelle guided Gillian out the door and toward the stairs.

She made her way upstairs and lay down on the comfortable bed, pulling a blanket over her. *I'm so sleepy.*

A man in a long robe knelt on the edge of the cliff. As she watched him, she saw both joy and pain play over his features. She walked toward him, feeling a need to connect with him.

He needs me, and I need him.

Standing, he turned to her. "You have come."

"Yes."

"Do you feel it? The gathering of all that is good? Equally, all that is bad is gathering also. The battle has been fought through all time. Now the final battle approaches."

"Is it the end?"

"The end will not come until God knows there is no longer hope. When all have been taught. Given the choice. Only then. We serve a merciful God. He has faith in us all."

"We have time? Time to reach more people?"

"You will have time as long as there is hope. Do you feel there is hope?"

"Oh, yes. Many know of Him but don't know Him. Does that make sense?"

"It makes perfect sense. You are right, many know of Him but are ignorant of all He truly offers. There are some who serve Him, yet they deny His wonders. Yes, I understand what you mean. Ways will be provided to change these thoughts. All who doubt, believe, or disbelieve will see and experience wonders beyond description. The choice will be theirs. Do what you can, my child, to keep the hope alive. You will be guided and instructed. Keep your heart and mind open to receive."

"Who are you?"

The man smiled at her. "I am one who walked with Him, and saw the wonders and miracles. It was a beautiful time and shall be again."

"I don't know your name though. You have come to me before. I saw you in the chapel on Iona. I've dreamt of you. Can I not learn your name?"

"One day, not today. Be blessed."

He was gone. She ran along the cliff looking to see where he went. Distraught over not finding him, she sank to the ground and lay on the damp grass, staring at the sky.

Gillian jerked awake. *Looking up, she saw only the ceiling of the small bedroom. Another mysterious dream. It's odd, although he didn't tell me anything, his words comforted me. This man with no name, I feel so connected to him. He gave hope, and hope is what he said is needed.*

The dream filled her thoughts as she washed her face and combed her hair. She felt rested, relaxed, and hopeful.

Gillian found Mirabelle busy in the kitchen.

"Did you have a nice nap?"

"I did, just what I needed."

"I made a fresh pot of tea. Let's have a cup while you catch me up on this new project of yours."

Mirabelle listened and nodded as Gillian explained about the project. She told of meeting Ruth and how everything was falling into place.

"You've had a busy time since I last saw you. This is wonderful news. I'm glad you met Ruth. Quite a character that one."

"Mirabelle, I wanted to ask you something. Remember how Elizabeth acted last time I was here?"

Mirabelle's face darkened. "How could I forget?"

"Well, I was wondering if you had ever seen her act that way before?"

"No lass, can't say I have. She's uppity for sure, and has been known to be difficult. The way she acted toward you, I have never seen her act that way. Why do you ask?"

"I'm not sure. It's just something that has been playing on my mind."

"Don't let petty things fill your mind. Sam and Banks are in the front parlor. Why don't you join them while I finish preparing dinner?"

"I'd rather help you."

"As you wish. You like to keep busy, and I won't fault you for that."

Gillian helped Mirabelle prepare the dinner.

Something's off. Other than to give me instructions on what she needed done, she has hardly spoken. She's not her usual cheerful self. Her thoughts remained focused on Mirabelle's mood as she studied her face. *She seems troubled.*

"Mirabelle."

"Yes?"

"What's wrong?"

"Nothing to worry your head about."

She grasped Mirabelle's hands. "Come on. I may not know you well, but something is off. You're not your usual chatty, cheerful self. If you don't tell me, I will imagine all sorts of terrible, disastrous things and stress myself. You don't want that, do you?"

"No lass, I wouldn't want you to worry or stress. There was something, but there is nothing gained by adding to your burdens."

"I'm not taking no for an answer. I will sit here at this table all night if needed. I'm not budging until you tell me."

Mirabelle nervously wiped her hands on her apron. Her knuckles were white as she gripped it. "Let me ask Banks if I should tell you."

"No, I want you to tell me. I value his opinion, but he's overprotective. I'm a big girl. Maybe I can help."

Banks entered the kitchen. Gillian watched the wordless interaction between him and Mirabelle. At first, he shook his head, then he saw Gillian's face.

"Very well then. She will not rest until we tell her. Go ahead, Mirabelle."

"Oh dear. Can we wait until after dinner?" Mirabelle asked.

Now I feel bad. She's nervous and upset. I'll wait until after dinner. Gillian studied Mirabelle. *No, she will be like this throughout dinner, we might as well get it over with.*

"No, I will make us a cup of tea, and we will sit here and talk. I don't want whatever this is, looming over dinner. I'm sorry this is upsetting you, but it's best to get it out in the open."

Mirabelle paced the kitchen while Gillian made the tea. Banks, had left the room but returned with Sam.

"Sam, just in time. Would you like a cup of tea?" Gillian didn't wait for an answer and got two more cups.

While she poured, Sam and Banks coaxed Mirabelle into a chair. *She's so distraught. Whatever it is, we'll deal with it like everything else. After all, it can't be that bad.*

"Banks, I don't think I can. I've been so worried. She will feel the same." Mirabelle dabbed her eyes, waiting for a response.

Banks looked toward the ceiling before he spoke. "Mirabelle, we must. Yes, it will be distressing, but she needs to know. We do as we are guided. Now we are guided to tell her. Go ahead."

"Earlier, while you were napping. I had an uneasy feeling. No, not uneasy, more like a feeling of dread, which wouldn't go away. I prayed for guidance and protection. I was compelled to open the front door. On the step was…"

They waited while she composed herself.

"I'm sorry. You must think me silly. My word, I've seen horrible things in my time, but this hit me hard."

Gillian held Mirabelle's hand. "Please go on."

"A dead dove lay on the step with an envelope attached to it. I couldn't touch it at first. When I recovered from the initial shock, I fetched a box to put the poor thing in and put the envelope to one side. After taking care of the dove, I came back inside. The envelope had your name on it. I showed it to Banks, and he told me to open it and read it."

Mirabelle paused, dabbed her eyes, and struggled to compose herself.

"What did it say?" Gillian asked.

The silence was overpowering. Gillian heard a clock ticking somewhere in the house. Her stomach knotted, palms sweating, she took a deep breath, waiting for Mirabelle to continue.

Banks cleared his throat. "Mirabelle. I will continue for you. I do not think I need to include all the vile words it contained, so I will summarize. It said that just as the dove of peace died, so too, will you and all whom you love."

Gillian shuddered. "Do you have any idea who left it?"

Banks shook his head. "No, they were cloaked in darkness. I can tell you it was evil, pure evil."

Gillian hugged Mirabelle. "I'm so sorry you had to be the one to find that. Now, you stop worrying. It has no power over me or those whom I love. A silly threat."

"Oh no, lass. It's not just a threat. Banks, tell her."

Gillian looked at Banks. "Tell me what?"

"Your parents received the same thing, delivered in the same way, written in the same hand."

"Was it just before they died?"

Mirabelle sobbed. "Yes, it was their last trip here."

"May I see the note?" Sam asked.

"No, I burned it. It was evil."

"I don't understand. My parents were killed because they trusted someone they shouldn't. I haven't done that. The list of people I trust is small. How could this be the same?"

"You are correct; it is different, but it is the same evil. We had hoped to find the source, but it is cunning and has evaded even me."

"I'm not happy you wanted to keep this from me. How can I be prepared if things are kept from me?"

"You have had so much to deal with, Gillian. We didn't want to add to your concerns. Please don't be angry," Mirabelle said.

"I'm not angry. I understand your reasoning, but you couldn't hide it. I sensed something was off. I need to know everything. No surprises. Are we clear on that?"

Banks and Mirabelle nodded.

Sam looked annoyed. "I'm upset that neither of you chose to share this information with me."

Banks nodded. "I understand your displeasure. I did not want to give you information you could not share with Gillian. I felt it best not to tell you. This is no one's fault but mine. I told Mirabelle to keep it quiet, and I chose not to tell you or Gillian."

Tension filled the room.

Banks was just trying to ease our burdens. He meant no harm. Time to change the subject and get everyone in a brighter mood.

"All right. Enough talk of this. We agreed to be open and honest with one another, so let us put it to rest. I want to share a dream I had while napping. It was wonderful."

Mirabelle's face lit up. "Oh, please do."

The three listened while Gillian told them all the details of her dream. When finished she looked at their faces and saw all three relaxed and smiling back at her.

"Keeping hope alive. That's wonderful, Gillian. I feel much better now. Thank you for sharing with us. Now, if you would all like to help me finish dinner, we can eat and celebrate hope for the world."

During dinner, a thought kept playing on Gillian's mind. *Of all the places my parents visited that I have been recently, why here? Why did both birds and notes appear here?*

"Something troubling you, Gillian?" Sam asked.

"Yes, there is. Why here? Of all the places my parents traveled, and all the places I have been in the past few months, why here? Both notes left here, on this doorstep."

"I wondered the same thing," Mirabelle said.

"Banks, what are your thoughts?" Gillian asked.

"The same thought ran through my mind. I wish I had the answer, but I do not."

"Is Mirabelle safe here? What of the other helpers who stay here? Are they safe?"

"One never knows for sure, but I would say yes. The threat is directed toward you. It is of no surprise you have gotten the attention of the darkness. The work you are doing is bringing forth good, and they dislike that. Their goal is to create division, anger, and hate. Those who bring people together in harmony are obstacles to their goal."

"There are a lot of people who bring harmony. Why single me out?"

"Remember your dream. You are putting plans in place to bring hope back to the hopeless."

"Me and a billion others. There is still something I feel you're not telling me." Gillian didn't wait for a reply. "I'm going to bed." She hurried upstairs before saying something she would regret.

She tossed and turned most of the night. *Something is going on. An underlying vibe of... What?*

She prayed for guidance as she drifted off to sleep and slept dreamlessly for those few hours.

Mirabelle looked up from the stove when Gillian entered the kitchen.

"You're up bright and early this morning. Eager to get to Iona?"

Gillian sighed. "Yes. More than anything though, I wanted to talk to you before leaving. I want to apologize for my irritable behavior last evening. The frustration of not knowing all I want to know does not give me the right to take it out on those around me."

Mirabelle turned the stove down and joined Gillian at the table. "Lass, you have no need to apologize. I understand your frustrations. You have learned a great deal in a short time, but there is still so much more. Sometimes we know things but cannot tell what we know, even if it provides help for another."

"Sorry, Mirabelle, but that just isn't sensible. If you know something that will help someone, it is your duty to tell them."

"There is a time and a place for everything. Let me give you an example. A teacher giving a test knows all the answers, but providing the answers to help the students would be wrong."

"Of course, that would be cheating."

"Exactly. Life is like a test, and we have many teachers along the way who guide and provide resources for us to learn and pass the test. What I'm trying to say is, take all you have learned and apply it to your questions. You may find you already know the answer."

Gillian rubbed her forehead as she remembered how many times Auntie Mary had said, "You have the answer you need, find it. If I tell you, it may not be all you need or maybe too much. The path is there for you to discover."

Mirabelle watched Gillian. She smiled, as if she knew her words had made the point.

"I understand. If I seek answers from others, I may not find what I really need."

"That's it, lass. The answers mean different things to different people. Interpretation can be a funny thing, but God will always guide you to what you need. Many times I wanted to provide information to help someone, but I was directed not to. If I had disobeyed and given them the information, it might have sent them on a path not intended for them. I don't have all the answers, but there is a reason for everything. We are like a pebble on a pond, sending ripples to the shore. Everything we do in some way affects another."

"I understand most of what you say. What I don't understand is why no one could intervene and save my parents. Why did they have to die? I'm sure Banks, you, or someone knew and could have saved them. They should never allow evil to take the life of the good just because of a mistake in judgment."

Gillian immediately regretted her words when she saw the pain on Mirabelle's face. "I'm so sorry. I had no right to…"

"No, you have every right. I have felt the same way myself. I don't have all the answers. None of us do. I do know God has a plan in place and sometimes innocents get taken from us. The question of why God allowed that to happen has troubled many since time began. We can only trust and have faith that one day all will be revealed. One day, sadness and evil will not exist. It may seem evil wins sometimes, but not for long. Every evil act is countered with a multitude of good. The light overtakes the darkness every time. Keep that thought in your heart."

Gillian hugged Mirabelle. "I should not have put that on you. You are a blessing in my life and my parents' lives. I could tell from their journals they trusted you implicitly. Whatever this person or thing is who left the dove and note, they will not win. I wish you were coming with us to Iona."

"Not this time lass, but I will go there soon to help Moyra when she has the baby. Now, would you like to help me finish this breakfast and put it on the table? Banks and Sam will be down soon and will want to be on their way."

An air of tension permeated the room while they ate. Banks and Sam remained quiet and distracted.

What's going on with these two? Neither one seems to want to talk this morning. No point in asking. It's probably another of those things that I don't need to know, right now anyway.

"All right, you two. It seems Mirabelle and I are the only ones interested in conversation this morning. Whatever has you both so deep in thought will not ruin my mood," Gillian said, with an air of sarcasm.

Banks nodded. Sam made no pretense of acknowledgment.

"Right. I'll help Mirabelle clear the breakfast dishes while you two load our bags into the car. Mine are packed and in the hall. Let me know when we're ready to leave. Until then, I will enjoy Mirabelle's cheerful company."

Sam and Banks left the table without a word. "I wonder what's wrong with those two," Gillian muttered under her breath as she cleared the table.

"Don't worry your head over their silence. They most likely have the journey on their mind. Today's weather is not good for travel; perhaps that is what has them so quiet."

"If that's so, we can travel another day; it's not urgent we leave today. I look forward to Iona, but if they are worried about the weather, we can wait." She put down the dishcloth and went to find Banks. When she found him in the front parlor, he was on his knees, head bowed. She quietly backed out of the room and returned to the kitchen.

"I can finish here. You've been a big help. Now put your warm coat on; you'll need it. I've made a flask of tea for you to take. It'll help to keep you warm. Be safe and remember to listen to your instincts. I will see you on your return."

Mirabelle left the room without waiting for a reply from Gillian.

That's odd. She usually stays right with me until we are out the door. Something is going on, and my instincts are telling me to shut up, watch, and listen.

Gillian looked back several times as they drove away, expecting to see Mirabelle waving and smiling, but the door remained closed. *I don't like this.*

CHAPTER THIRTY-THREE

Gillian waited in the car while Sam bought tickets for the ferry. She didn't attempt conversation with Banks. She felt her mood souring, and the silence was now irritating.

I will not let their silence destroy my mood. We are going to a beautiful, peaceful place. Maybe they are worried about the note left with the dove? Silent because they are on guard?

The weather was terrible. The first ferry ride over to Mull was rocky; several passengers vomited. Gillian's stomach resisted as the boat rocked from side to side. *Please don't let me be sick. Breathe deeply and slowly; focus on something. It's mind over matter.*

On dry land, a sip of the tea Mirabelle sent settled her stomach. They didn't have to wait long for the bus taking them to Fionnphort.

Sliding into a window seat, Banks shocked her by taking a seat in the row in front of her while Sam sat in the row behind her. *They really don't want to communicate with me. I showered this morning, so it's not hygiene. Unless I have bad breath, oh no, what if I do have bad breath? For heaven's sake, why am I thinking such stupid things? I'm thinking like an insecure adolescent.*

Sam leaned over the seat and whispered in her ear. "You're not alone. There are reasons for our silence. I'm right here."

A wave of relief swept over her. *That makes me feel better. I wonder what the reason is? Am I in danger? Are they keeping guard?* Deep in her thoughts, chastising herself for her reaction to the silence, she didn't notice someone settle into the seat beside her.

"Hello. Are you going all the way to Fionnphort?"

She jumped. Sitting next to her was a man who must have fallen off the cover of a magazine. *Those eyes, they are almost silver.* She struggled to regain her composure. "Sorry, I was lost in my thoughts. Yes, I'm going to Fionnphort."

"Excellent. It will be nice to have pleasant company for the hours ride."

Gillian politely smiled and turned to look out of the window. *This man is not nice. His appearance is pleasing, but there's something that gives me the creeps.*

Her silence did not deter him.

"My name is Mark. I'm on a sabbatical; I teach history at a university. I've been wanting to explore the ancient history in this area. It should be interesting."

"That's nice."

He ignored the hint. As his voice droned on, she felt a coldness creeping over her. His voice was eerily hypnotic but repulsed her at the same time. Realization gripped her. *I know what he is. His good looks and charm don't fool me.*

She turned to him and smiled, catching a fleeting, smug look on his face. He thought he had won her over.

"Mark, you need to find another seat. I don't want you sitting by me."

When he smiled back at her, pure evil radiated from him. "Gillian, you are weak, you can't possibly think you will succeed."

She laughed. "Interesting that you know my name. I didn't tell you. It validates my instincts. If you insist on sitting here, I will be happy to share with you the wonders of my God. He is a loving and forgiving God. So many people are turning to Him. Turning from the darkness to the light. Perhaps you would like to hear more of Him?"

The hateful look he gave her as he leapt from his seat made her laugh even more. She didn't turn to see where he sat next.

When the bus arrived at Fionnphort, she remained seated while the other passengers disembarked. Banks and Sam remained seated as well. The line of passengers filed past. A chill ran up her spine as she saw a young woman smiling and talking with Mark. *Oh no, I sent him away, and he found another victim. I must do something. She may not realize the depth of his evil.*

As she stood to follow them, something Mirabelle had told her stopped her. "We can't try to influence their decisions. We can only guide and pray they see."

Stepping off the bus, she watched the woman. *What can I do or say to help? I can't cross a line. The decision must be hers.*

She noticed a similarity in the woman's accent to Moyra's, thinking she might be a local, she seized the opportunity.

"Excuse me, sorry to intrude. I'm not from around here. Do you know of anywhere I can get a great cup of hot chocolate? Not the fake stuff."

"Aye, I do. My friend's mom has a tea shop just down the road, and she makes it with real chocolate. Not the powdered stuff. I planned to stop by on my way home if you'd like to tag along."

"I would love to. I don't want to take you away from your friend though." She smiled at Mark, who glared at her and failed to hide his annoyance.

"Oh, he's not my friend. I just met him."

"But I thought you agreed to show me around?" Mark's voice dripped with anger.

The young woman sensed it too. "I told you I would show you where you could pick up a local map. It's right there." She pointed to a newsstand. "I'm not in the habit of wandering about with strangers." She took Gillian by the arm. "Come on, luv; hot chocolate's on me."

"I hope it wasn't because of me you dumped Mr. GQ," Gillian said.

"Not at all. I saw right through him on the bus. I sensed he might get ugly if I told him to get lost, so I waited until we got here. He was eye candy for sure, but something about him gave me the creeps. My mam taught me to go with my instincts."

"My auntie told me the same thing. She said, 'God equipped us with warning sensors; we need to listen and use them.'"

"Your auntie and my mam must have gone to the same school, because those were Mam's words exactly."

Gillian looked back to find Banks and Sam following at a distance. Mark was nowhere to be seen.

"I should introduce myself; my name is Gillian."

"Pleased to meet you, Gillian. I'm Andria. I've lived on this island most of my life. I left for a while to go to university but now I'm back. I live with my mam, that's what I call my grandmother. I started my own business when I came back. I put all my money into the business, which left nothing for lodging, so I moved in with Mam. She likes the company, and I enjoy being spoiled with all her delicious home-cooked meals. Mom and Dad died in a plane crash when I was just a wee thing.

Sorry, I'm giving way too much information. I tend to ramble on."

"I was just thinking you remind me of my best friend. She never meets a stranger and is at ease making conversation. I like learning about other people and their stories, but I'm more of a listener, so you're not rambling."

"Are you staying on the island or traveling on?"

"Going to Iona on the ferry. I have friends there."

"Lovely place, been there many times. It's so peaceful. Mam likes me to take her there. You may not get a ferry over today though. The water between here and Iona can be a beast in this weather."

"I didn't know that. Is there a hotel or B & B you would recommend? Just in case."

"Aye, there is a perfect B & B near the ferry. Homey atmosphere and the owners are fantastic. Here's the shop for the hot chocolate. My treat. I like you. You have a nice aura."

Gillian laughed. "You are like Maggie. She told me the same thing when we first met at university. We've been friends ever since."

Andria chatted while they drank their hot chocolate. Gillian watched the door, wishing Banks and Sam would come in, but they didn't. *I hope they aren't waiting outside in this cold. I'd better hurry.*

Gillian stood to leave. "Thank you Andria, I'm so glad we met." She handed Andria a card with her email on it. "Stay in touch and watch out for creepy guys on buses."

Andria laughed. "That I will. Something about him gave me the chills. I hope he's not preying on some innocent, young thing."

"Me too. Thanks for the hot chocolate. I hope we meet again. I'll be on Iona for a few days, maybe longer. Come visit if you can. Tell your Mam she taught you well."

She stepped outside into the cold wind. *My goodness, it's so cold, and the wind is bitter.* Looking around, she caught sight of Banks, as he and Sam came out of a shop.

"Your timing is perfect, Gillian. We were just enquiring about lodging. It seems the ferry will not run due to rough seas. There is a B & B near the ferry they recommended," Banks said.

"Andria said the same thing. Let's find out if they have room for us, and then we can grab lunch somewhere. I just want to get inside by a fire. It's so cold the wind blows right through me."

Sam smiled and nodded but remained silent. *Somehow, I feel like I am being tested. I may be wrong, but I think they are keeping their distance to test how I handle situations. Or is it because I'm in danger and they are keeping me safe? Did they know Mr. Creepy would be on the bus? That I would meet Andria? At least I made a new friend. Someone I wouldn't have*

met if they had been sitting with me. Everything happens for a
reason.

Banks arranged for two rooms. He and Sam took the bags to
the rooms while the host showed Gillian into the parlor,
complete with a roaring fire.

"This is perfect, nice and cozy in here. Thank you."

"No problem. Make yourself at home. We like our guests to
use this room as they would their own living rooms. There will
be other guests in later. This room makes friends of strangers. It
never fails; they come in not knowing one another, and before
they leave, they're like best friends. We enjoy watching new
friendships made. After all, the more friends we have, the fewer
enemies."

"I couldn't agree more."

She had thawed out and was relaxing in the glow of the fire
when Banks and Sam came in.

"You look comfortable. Your bags are in your room. Sam and
I will share a room. The host was very accommodating and has
recommended a place near here where we can get lunch. Are
you ready to brave the cold again?"

"No, but I'm hungry. I'll bundle up first." Taking her coat,
Sam held it in front of the fire.

She slid her arms in while he held it for her. "Oh. That feels
good. Thank you for warming it for me."

"No problem. Don't want you getting chilled."

After a light lunch, they made their way back to the B & B and went to their rooms.

Removing her coat and boots, she lay on the bed and pulled the blanket over her. *I may as well take a nap. It's too cold to do any sightseeing.*

"They tried to distract you, but they failed. Well done Gillian. There will be more. They won't give up that easy. Be on your guard and trust your instincts. There is danger around you. No matter how it looks, see through the cover."

She rubbed her eyes. "What? Who are you?" Sitting up in bed, she looked around the room. *Alone. Was I dreaming? Who was that? It was a man's voice. The incident on the bus must have created the dream. Or was it a dream?*

Gillian found Banks and Sam relaxing in the parlor with other guests.

"Did you have a nice nap?" Banks asked.

"I did. The room's warm and the bed's comfortable. I could have stayed there longer, but then I wouldn't sleep tonight."

The lady Sam had been speaking to stood to shake Gillian's hand.

"You must be Gillian. I'm Margaret; this is Stan, my husband. We're marooned here as well. We had planned on taking the ferry over to Iona, but the weather decided otherwise. Our daughter, Stephanie, is out braving the cold and exploring the island."

"Nice to meet you, Margaret, Stan. Where are you staying on Iona?"

"We are meeting our church group there. I'm told they have something similar to a hostel they stay in while on retreat. We've wanted to make this trip for a long time. I hope the weather improves tomorrow. They say Iona is a healing place."

"It is. You will notice the feeling as soon as you step off the ferry. Your daughter is brave, sight-seeing in this bitter wind."

"She's young and foolish. Sorry, I didn't mean it to come out that way. She's at an age where if asked not to do something, that is precisely what she will do. She is part of the reason for the trip here."

Stan's irritation showed on his face and in his tone. "Margaret, really? We have just met these people. You want to air our problems with strangers?"

Margaret looked down at her hands. "Sorry, Stan. Gillian, I'm sorry for speaking out. It's been a difficult year. You must think me a horrible mother."

"Not at all. I think you're a caring mother trying to guide her child. Nothing wrong with that. How old is she?"

"Seventeen, almost eighteen. She has never been a problem until this year."

"Margaret!" Stan's tone was firm.

"Stan, please don't feel uncomfortable around us. The three of us have seen the problems facing the young in today's world. It's a difficult time. None of us will think bad of Stephanie, nor Margaret."

Stan's shoulders relaxed. "You're very kind, Gillian. I apologize for my discomfort. It's a difficult situation when a minister's child becomes a problem. There are those who look upon us as failures. If we cannot guide our child, how can we guide the congregation?"

"I understand. Everything you've taught her is still in her. She knows right from wrong, but she's at the age where she wants to find herself."

"It's more than that." Margaret wiped her eyes before continuing. "We had another child, a son. He was in his first year at university. Such a wonderful person, kind hearted, always willing to help someone. Helping someone got him killed." She paused, trying to compose herself. "On his way home one weekend, he stopped to help a stranded motorist with a flat tire. The person he stopped to help, shot him and stole his car. Left him dying on the side of the road."

Stan cradled his sobbing wife to his shoulder. "It was hard for us to keep the faith after that. Stephanie took it hard. She says there's no point trying to be good and doing the right thing. You will die anyway."

"I'm so sorry. I can't imagine your pain." Gillian wanted to cry herself. She glanced at Banks, pleading with her eyes.

Banks stood. "Stan, why don't you join Sam and I. We want to find a place that sells pastries. Sam has a weakness for them, and if we find a bakery, we can bring some back to have later."

"Sounds like a wonderful idea. I have a bit of a sweet tooth myself. Margaret, will you be okay if I go with them?"

"Yes, I have Gillian to keep me company."

After the men had left, Gillian took Margaret's hand. "Why don't we go up to my room. There are two nice chairs in there and something to make tea and coffee. It will be more private."

"That sounds nice, but Stephanie might come back and won't know where I'm at."

"I'll let the owner know. If she comes in, he can show her to my room."

"All right."

In the room, she made a cup of tea for each of them.

"Please, feel free to talk. That's what I'm here for. I can't do much, but sometimes just being able to speak of your troubles helps."

She listened while Margaret poured it all out. Her pain, anger, fear. It was all so tragic. *How does one explain a good person being taken so young? Especially in the act of a good deed.*

Margaret was exhausted from her emotions. "Why don't you lay down on my bed and rest. I'll let Stan know. Margaret, someone wise told me something that might help. It's always important to keep hope alive. As long as there is hope in this world, God will hear us."

Gillian found Stan, Banks, and Sam in the parlor. "Margaret is exhausted and is napping in my room. Has your daughter returned yet?"

"No. I'm getting concerned. I think I'll go look for her."

Sam stood. "I'll go with you. It's too cold for her to be out this long. She may be in the shops, but they will close soon. Banks, would you like to join us?"

"Yes, good idea. Gillian, stay here. Margaret may need you."

"Okay. While you're out, check if there's a nice restaurant close by. I don't want to go far for our evening meal."

She quietly let herself into her room. Margaret was still sleeping. She pulled her journal out of her bag and settled into a chair to write.

After writing several pages, she sensed, rather than heard, Margaret stir.

"I needed that nap more than I realized. Thank you for the use of your room and for listening. The pain will never go away, but you've given me what I needed. Hope for the future. I need to check on Stan and Stephanie."

"Stan went with Banks and Sam to look for Stephanie. They were concerned as the temperature has dropped even more. I'll go find out if they are back yet."

"Thank you. I'll freshen up in our room, and then I'll be down."

Sam and Banks were sitting by the fire. "Did you find Stephanie?"

"We did, Stan's with her. They went up to their room to talk. He has his work cut out for him. She's an angry young lady," Sam replied.

"It's understandable. I'm sure she was close to her brother. It's a difficult thing to process, even for those more mature."

"I invited them to join us for dinner, but Stan said he would rather have a family dinner, to talk in private. Our host recommended a place just a few minutes from here. Are you ready to brave the cold?" Banks asked.

"No, but I have a nice warm coat, thanks to you."

After dinner, they grouped around the cozy fireplace in the lounge, where they met several of the other guests and learned the weather forecast predicted improvement in the morning.

Before retiring for the night, she let Banks know of her thoughts. "This delay was for a reason. Just as the silence from you and Sam served a purpose. I'm learning to look for the reasons instead of reacting in frustration or anger."

"You did well. Very well. Goodnight, Gillian. We will continue our journey in the morning."

CHAPTER THIRTY-FOUR

Jumping out of bed and opening the curtains, she saw sunshine. *Yay, it doesn't look windy today, so maybe the ferry will run. The delay served a purpose. Was it for me to meet Andria? Margaret and Stan? Or to send Mr. GQ on his way? Maybe all the above. I think I handled everything well. If not, I'm sure I'll find out what I should have done or still need to do.*

She was ready to start the day in record time.

Sam waited downstairs. "Good morning. You look like you slept well and are eager to get going."

"Is it that obvious, Sam? Not that I wouldn't mind exploring this area, but I'm eager to get to Iona."

"You don't want to say farewell to Mr. GQ?"

"Hilarious, he was a creep. He thought he could lull me into letting my guard down, but he thought wrong. I hope you would have rescued me if I hadn't seen through him."

"You know we would have rescued you. We knew you could handle it though. He was sly, but we had every confidence in you. Sadly, not everyone slipped his grasp."

"What? Did he hurt someone?"

"Not physically, but he got into the head of a young impressionable mind. Margaret and Stan will need our help when we get to Iona. Stephanie met him and fell for his charms."

"Oh no. That's not surprising. From what Margaret told me the family has been in turmoil since their son died."

"They're struggling. They're scheduled to stay in a hostel with other church members, but we think they need more privacy to work through their problems. Banks is working on getting a private location for them."

"I'll do whatever is needed to help them. What if Mr. GQ shows up on Iona?"

"He won't."

"How can you be sure?"

"Because he couldn't tolerate the love and peace there. There is too much light and hope there. Darkness can't survive when surrounded by love."

"I sensed the darkness in him. Is he one of the terrible ones?"

"Not the worst, but he has considerable experience in disrupting lives. He targets those in turmoil. He knew he was out of his depth with you, but his ego made him try."

Gillian shuddered. "I hope we can help Margaret and her family. They've suffered enough."

"Here's Banks now. I'm starving, let's see if the breakfast lives up to its reputation."

The breakfast was magnificent as promised. A traditional English breakfast. Bacon, sausage, egg, grilled tomatoes and mushrooms. Too much for Gillian to eat, but she managed to taste everything.

"Our host told me everything they prepare for breakfast is from local farms. That's what I want to encourage with our training school. Self-sufficient communities able to provide for all the needs of the residents. It's so much better than processed foods. The big chain stores and suppliers won't like it, but they have provided sub-standard food far too long. They need to get with the program by sponsoring local farmers," Gillian said.

"The big companies will fight you on that. They put many of the farmers out of business, with the support of government, by enforcing use of genetically modified seeds and passing laws that made it too costly for the small farmer."

Sam's reality check didn't deter her. "Banks, are you ready to go to the ferry?"

"Sam, take Gillian and our bags to the ferry, then come back here. We need to accompany Stan and his family. They had a difficult night. I have arranged a cottage for their stay on Iona. I need you to assist me. We will stay with them. Gillian will stay with Moyra and Abe. Sadness is felt in heaven when a person of God loses their faith. The death of their son has shaken them to their core."

"Oh Banks, I'm so sorry. I knew they were in trouble, but I didn't realize it was that bad. What can I do to help?" Gillian asked.

"You will know when the time comes. Follow your instincts as you did yesterday. We were impressed with how you handled yourself. I will meet you on the ferry."

"If it's operating. I hope the condition of the sea has improved. We'll check before we take the bags with us."

"No need to leave the bags. It will operate today," Banks said with conviction as he walked away.

Banks was correct as always. The ferry was in and ready to board.

After Gillian and their baggage were on board, Sam said, "I'll help Banks and be right back. I don't like leaving you alone. Will you be okay while I'm gone?"

"Yes. Go help Banks. I'll be fine."

Several passengers boarded as she waited for Sam and Banks. *The ferry appears to have a full load this morning. There must be quite a few like us unable to make the trip yesterday. I wonder if they will run extra ferries to pick up the excess.*

The engines made a loud noise, and the ferry shuddered.

What on earth? Oh no, they can't leave yet. Banks and Sam aren't back. Pushing her way through the crowd to the stern of the ferry, she could see a panicked Sam running toward the departing ferry.

Smiling and waving, she yelled, "I'm okay." Could he hear her above the sound of the engine? *This boat is packed. Iona must be a popular place this week.* She looked around. *I wonder where Banks is? He's not with Sam. Maybe something happened with Margaret and Stan, and Banks is staying with them. Whatever the reason I'm sure we'll be reunited soon.*

She tried to make her way back to the main area of the ferry, but the congestion prevented passage, so she stayed near the rear, leaning against the railing on the side.

The water looks calm today. I hope Sam isn't too worried. Banks will let him know all is well. I'm not sure how I'll manage all the bags myself though. I must find them first. Sam put them toward the front and pushing my way through this crowd won't be easy. Oh well, I'll figure it out. No worries once I get to Iona.

The houses dotting the shoreline of Iona came into view. A cold feeling of dread swept over her, and a darkness surrounded her. A sensation of raw fear, something she had never before experienced. She felt herself being lifted and then falling. Thoughts of Sam filled her mind. The last thing she saw before she lost consciousness was the water, crystal clear and so very cold. *I can't breathe. Am I dead? Dying? Oh God, help me.*

Warm arms enveloped her, lifting her. *I'm safe now*. She thought before again losing consciousness.

.

CHAPTER THIRTY-FIVE

Oh, that hurts, everything hurts. Where am I? Struggling to sit up and focus her eyes. It was dark with only a glimmer of light, which offered little help in determining her surroundings. Too dim to see further than her immediate surroundings.

The surface was hard, damp, and cold. Trying to stand proved useless; she was too weak.

"Rest child. You are safe. Perhaps not comfortable, but you are safe."

Turning toward the sound of the voice, the man from the cliff, was beside her. The one in her dreams.

"Where am I?"

"You are in a cave."

"On Iona?"

"No, but near."

"How did I get here?"

"Angels. Angels from heaven lifted you from the water and brought you here."

"I felt them. I didn't see them, but I felt warm, loving arms surrounding me. Just at the point I thought I was dying. Something, someone threw me overboard. I remember a feeling of complete fear and darkness and then being lifted, then falling.

I must have been knocked out when I hit the water because I remember nothing until just before the arms surrounded me."

"Do you remember asking God for help?"

Gillian paused and then nodded. "Yes, yes, I remember that. I couldn't breathe, it was so cold. I asked God to help me. I thought I was dying."

"You were, but you knew; you had faith God would answer your prayer."

Her stomach tightened. "You mean, He wouldn't have saved me if I hadn't asked?"

"You must ask to receive."

"But what if I remained unconscious? What if I couldn't call out? He would have let the darkness win? I find that hard to believe."

"You called out. Whether consciously or unconsciously, because of your faith, it is within you to call to Him. Why do you concern yourself with 'what if'?"

She shook her head. "I'm sorry, my thoughts are jumbled. Why was I brought here? It's cold, dark, and wet."

"You seek answers."

"Yes. Again, I'm sorry. I'm asking too many ridiculous questions instead of showing my gratitude for being alive."

"No. I understand your questions. I know of your gratitude. You spoke while you slept. You thanked Him for helping you. I meant the answers you seek are here."

Her heart rate increased. "Here, here in this cave?"

"Somewhere here."

"Will you help me find them?"

"Yes. Not yet. First, you must rest. Warmth will be provided for you. You will not perish. Not this day."

He vanished, leaving her alone. Drifting back to sleep, she felt the warmth of arms surround her. Like a warm blanket on a cold night.

Dreams of Sam and Banks tormented her sleep. They were distraught, searching for her but unable to find her. She hovered above them in her dream. She heard them talking.

"Banks, how could this happen? Why were we directed to leave her alone? We must find her!" Sam said as he paced up and down the shoreline.

"I know not why this has happened. I only know He had a reason. It is not for us to question. I have never been directed to leave one I protect, nor have I been blocked from them. I know it is not the darkness that is blocking me. Only God possesses that power. Wherever she is, I believe her to be safe, in good hands. We must hold true to our faith."

"But why? Why were we separated? I failed her. She trusted I would look after her. What if she's hurt? Scared and alone?"

She couldn't take it anymore; watching the anguish on Sam's face hurt her. In her dream she reached down to Sam and stroked his cheek, whispering, "I'm okay. Don't worry. You will see me again soon."

Waking on the cold, hard stone, she gained comfort from her dream. *Was it a dream? Or did I receive answers to some of my questions? Banks said he would always be there to protect me. Yet, in the dream he said he was blocked. Am I to take this journey on my own? Without them?*

She could hear water running over rocks somewhere near her. She tried to stand but couldn't. *Hitting the water must have bruised every part of me. I feel like someone beat me.*

She crawled toward the sound of the water. A small stream trickled over the rocks on the wall. Cupping her hand, she let the water fill her palm and drank the cold liquid.

The man from her dreams reappeared. "Are you well enough to walk with me?"

"I think so. I'm sore, but otherwise okay." She tried to stand but to no avail. Her legs would not cooperate.

"I will carry you."

The man from her dreams seemed to emit his own light source as the faint light stayed with them as they traveled further back into the cave. They seemed to be walking uphill. The path was narrow, and the sound of water became distant.

"You do not look well."

"Maybe it's because someone threw me into freezing water and I've been sleeping in a cold cave for…" She looked into his dark brown eyes. "How long have I been here?"

"Time is insignificant."

After what seemed like hours they came to a doorway which opened into a large room filled with clay jars, barrels, and leather satchels. Torches lining the walls ignited as they entered. She noticed another doorway on the other side of the room with what looked to be an iron door sealing it.

"Is this what I think it is?"

"I do not know what you think. It is what you seek."

"The documents, early writings from the first followers?"

"Yes. There are many hidden around the world. Fragile writings from the first followers, copied over and over for many centuries."

"Can I touch them?"

"You may do as you wish. Remember, their safety is vital. They have been protected for those who seek."

The warmth from the torches filled the room. "I'm exhausted." The room spun as he eased her down onto the floor.

"You need rest. You are not well. Rest now; I will return."

Her dreams tormented her. Darkness, reliving being thrown overboard, laughter, evil laughter, echoed in her mind as she hit the water.

When she woke, she felt fevered. Hot but cold at the same time. *I must find my way out of here. My lungs are probably full of water. I need help. God, what is it you want me to do? Help me, guide me.* As she prayed, she drifted back to sleep.

This time she dreamt of the other Chosen she met at Samantha's. They were with Banks. No, not all, Elizabeth was not there. As in her previous dream, she appeared to float over Sam and Banks. They looked concerned. *I need to hear what they are saying. Maybe I can get closer to them.* Her dream-self floated closer to the group.

"Everyone on Iona and the surrounding isles with boats are out searching for her. They are concentrating on the shorelines, because if she is still in the water…" Jacob swallowed. "She could not survive. The water is too cold to sustain life."

I remember him; he's the oldest Chosen one. He gave me the key to the trunk. They all look distraught.

"Yes, Jacob, we are aware. I refuse to think she could still be in the water. I am hopeful she will be found soon," Banks said.

Another man spoke, then hesitated. He looked around the room as if sensing something, and then he gazed upwards.

Can he see me? Sense me? Tell them to have hope. Don't lose faith. Somehow, this is a test for all of us. We must keep hope alive! She screamed at the man in her dreams.

Banks stared intently at the man. "Yes, Ben? Is there something you wanted to share with us?"

"Well, I was going to say we should put search groups on all the islands around here. Just in case she is injured and confused. Perhaps wandering around or maybe taken shelter somewhere. But then, as I was about to speak, I had a thought."

"Yes, go on," Banks and Jacob said in unison.

"We must not give up hope. It is important to keep hope and faith."

Banks demeanor transformed, a small, faint smile appeared on his face. "We will find her soon. She is alive."

She woke with an incredible thirst. *My mouth is so dry. I need water. Need to try to make it back to the water I found earlier.*

She struggled to stand but slipped back down against the wall.

"You are ill."

"Oh, you're back. I admit I don't feel well. I need water, so thirsty."

"It is your fever. I must get you to someone who can help."

"No, no. Not yet. I need to see the writings."

"You have found what you were seeking. You know their location. When you heal, you will find your way with the proper tools to protect and preserve them. Now it is important to heal your body."

"Will these documents help save people? Bring them to The Way?"

"They add clarity for those who believe and validate truth for those who doubt. These writings tell many stories of the miracles and teachings of the first followers. With this knowledge, the true Word cannot be questioned or disputed. The Bible offers the fundamental teachings. The way all should live. The darkness uses the lack of details to create doubt. The details in the early writings give vast knowledge of the paths of the Christ as He ministered, His disciples as they continued His work, the conversations they had with Him and amongst themselves. The details will fill hearts with renewed faith and hope for a better world. A world of peace and harmony."

"You are sure I will find my way here again?"

"Yes, you will be guided to return, when your body is healed. You have the keys to enter. You have done well. You have kept your faith and hope. The darkness, which has taken so many from us, lost this battle. Faith will be renewed from the miracle of your return. You will see."

"Why did these writings bother the darkness so much they would kill to keep them secret?"

"In the details, all will see that direction comes only from God. The details give harmony in the clarity of knowing each and every person, with the goodness and love of God, can do what Christ empowered His disciples to do. To teach of His love and perform miracles through Him. To love the land He gave us and nurture the fallen. Man is capable of so much. Weakened by looking to man to answer their questions, but only God has the answers they seek. A true prophet will direct those questioning to prayer for answers. The truth takes all power from the darkness."

"I think I understand. Thank you for sharing this with me."

"I must go now. You know what you need to do to find the help you need. We will talk again, soon."

Gillian smiled. A sense of peace came over her as she stared at the space the man had been. *Yes. I know what I need to do.*

Fading in and out of consciousness, she prayed for God to save her, to get her back to safety where she could be healed.

She dreamt angels were once again carrying her. Their arms felt soft like a feather bed. Like the bed at Mirabelle's. Soft, warm, enveloping her sore body in warmth and love.

CHAPTER THIRTY-SIX

"Come now, lass, let's see if you can manage a sip of this broth."

Gillian struggled to open her eyes. They felt sore, matted. She opened them enough to peer up at a beautiful face. The face of an angel.

"Mirabelle, you don't know how happy I am to see you. You came to Iona, after all."

"No lass. You are at my house, where you've been for over a week. You gave us a scare, but you're on the mend."

"What happened? I remember strange dreams. Falling overboard on the ferry. No, no. I didn't fall, I was thrown."

"Enough questions. I dare say you've had some strange dreams. Your fever was high for days. We will talk more about your dreams after you take some of this broth."

Gillian did as instructed and sipped the broth. It felt good against her sore throat.

Mirabelle washed Gillian's face with a cloth and covered her as she drifted off to sleep once again.

The sound of someone opening the curtains woke her.

"Mirabelle, is it morning already?"

"Yes lass, it is morning again. Do you feel up to getting up for a bath?"

"Yes, that would be great. I feel grubby, and I can't imagine what my hair must look like."

Mirabelle laughed. "I've seen it look better. We'll have you fixed up in no time. I've been giving you bed baths for the past few weeks, but I thought this morning you might be ready to take a real bath. I had a tub brought in here, so we can ease you out of bed into it. We can wash your hair too."

"Good. Wait a minute, did you say the past few weeks?"

"Yes. It's been just over two weeks since they brought you to me. You were delirious the first week. Raging with fever and rambling, you were. Then you were so weak you've been sleeping the better part of another week."

"How long has it been since I left here?"

"Oh, it's been about three weeks."

Gillian struggled to grasp how much time had passed. It took quite a bit of effort by both Mirabelle and Gillian to move her from the bed to the tub, but they managed. She remained silent during her bath. She gathered enough strength to wash, but needed Mirabelle's help washing her hair. Once settled back in bed, feeling fresh with a clean nightgown and hair combed back into a ponytail, she felt more like herself.

"I'll get your breakfast tray. This will be your first solid food in quite a while, so go easy."

Weeks? How long was I in the cave? Was I even in the cave?
Were they all just crazy dreams, or did I find the documents?
The man from my dreams, I've talked to him a lot lately. Or did
I? The dreams of Banks and Sam. Were they real? Did I witness
them or experience the result of a high fever? She remained
deep in thought until Mirabelle returned.

Setting the tray over Gillian's legs, Mirabelle sat by the bed.
"Do you think you can feed yourself, or do you need my help?"

"I think I can manage. Don't go though. I have questions."

"I'm sure you do. I'll answer what I can."

"Where are Sam and Banks?"

"Sam is resting. He remained by your bedside almost the
entire time. I made him go to bed last night and get a good
night's sleep. I'll not wake him yet. Poor thing has been worried
sick. After witnessing how he watched over you, no one can tell
me you're just friends. You kept calling out for him when you
were so fevered. Admit it or not, young lady, you are both in
love."

Gillian blushed. "We are close, Mirabelle, but I, well I can't
think about that right now. And Banks, is he here?"

"Yes. He's been by your side as well. He wasn't worried
though. He said you sent him a message to keep hope, and he
would not let you down."

Gillian gasped. "So it was real. I dreamt I was hovering over Banks and the Chosen ones, and I yelled at them to keep hope and faith alive. Ben repeated what I said, and Banks smiled in my dream. It must have been real. I've had so many strange dreams; it's hard to separate real from delusion."

"That's understandable. It will all become clear in time. I think it best if you start with the broth and then try the oatmeal."

Gillian obeyed and sipped the broth. She struggled to get the oatmeal down but knew she must regain her strength. Eating exhausted her, and she drifted back to sleep.

The man from her dreams, the one from the cave, appeared. "You are well."

"Yes, I'm feeling much better. Was I really in the cave with you or was it just a dream?"

"You were there."

"How will I find my way there again? Will you help me?"

"You will find it. You have the map and the keys, and you will be guided. You must take scribes with you; the writings must stay where they are for now. Scribes can help you write them."

"Could we photograph them?"

He tilted his head. "What do you mean?"

"Take pictures. We have the ability now to copy things with an exact image of them on paper."

"It would be exact? No changes?"

"Better than copying by hand, it recreates the document with no changes."

"Yes, you may. They must stay with the faithful for now. There is still work to be done. You will find, within the cave room, letters my brothers and I sent to all the faithful. I think you will be enlightened by how simple the Word is."

"Simple?"

"Yes. We taught of His love and told them of witnessing the miracles He performed. Then we told how to follow Him and do as He did. They must know and accept Christ as Savior. They must love one another as He loved us and follow the laws of God. Once their hearts are given to Him, He will guide them on their path of faith."

"You still haven't told me your name. I keep referring to you in my mind as Cave Man."

The man smiled. "The time is near. Rest, soon all will be revealed."

She awoke disoriented. *Was everything a dream? Like the dream I just had? Is my mind giving me answers I want, or is all this real?*

She felt a shadow pass over her and opened her eyes. *At last, Sam.*

As soon as he saw her eyes were open, he sat on the side of the bed and took her hand. "I have prayed for this moment for weeks. To once again see those beautiful brown eyes. How are you feeling?"

"Much better now I've seen you."

"Mirabelle will help you bathe, and then we'll try to get you up walking. You'll need physical therapy to help you regain your strength."

"I had a bath before I fell asleep."

"That was yesterday. You're very weak, and the rest has helped you, but now we must rebuild you."

"I'm so confused."

"You will be. Enid is here to help with your recovery. She has experience in physical therapy."

"Sorry I caused everyone to worry."

Sam's face darkened. "It's not your fault. I blame myself for leaving you alone."

"But you had to."

"How did you know?"

"I had a dream, I think it was a dream. You were talking with Banks, saying you were ordered to do as you did. It was planned."

He gazed at his feet for what seemed like minutes before he answered. "Yes, we were directed to do as we did. I questioned it, and I was angry. I still don't know why it was to happen as it did. To leave you unprotected against the evil still seems wrong. Banks said once you are well, the story you tell will make everything clear. At first, even he was confused. Then he insisted you were in good hands and we were not to lose hope."

She smiled. "I sent a message, at least in my dream I did. I hovered over all of you. You were meeting with the other Chosen, not all of them though, one was missing. Ben was talking. I kept screaming for all of you to keep hope and faith. Ben picked up on it and told Banks."

A flicker of pain flashed across his face. "I should have been more open, then I would have too. I was so angry and questioning everything, I must have blocked it out."

"Don't be hard on yourself. It's understandable. You and Banks have served as my protectors from the beginning."

"We didn't do a very good job that day."

"What delayed you? Why didn't you make it to the ferry?"

"That's for another time. I don't want to tire you. We will have time to talk about everything while you recover."

Mirabelle entered the room carrying clean sheets over her arm. "That's right, now off you go, and I will help her bathe. Then we will see if we can get her walking around a bit."

Sam leaned down and placed a gentle kiss on Gillian's forehead. "I'll be back."

"We'll get you in the bath and let you soak while I change your sheets. Enid is here, and she prepared an herbal mixture in the bath to help your sore muscles."

Enid appeared as Mirabelle helped Gillian sit up. In silence, they helped her stand, each taking an arm, supporting her as they made the slow walk to the bathroom.

As she sank into the water, the aroma of the herbs surrounded her. "This feels nice. Enid, thank you for coming. Who's looking after Tom while you're here?"

"Theresa's helping, and of course Maggie, Joe, and Joseph are there. He'll be well looked after while I'm here. Maggie wanted to come too, but we convinced her to stay. It wasn't easy though."

"I miss them."

"They miss you too. Now, quiet your mind, lay back and enjoy the aroma of the herbs and the warmth of the water. I have a cream to rub on you after your bath. It will relax the muscles so they won't cramp while we get you exercising."

Gillian closed her eyes and inhaled the aromas, enjoying the sensation of the warm water. Enid helped wash her hair and put something on it to remove the tangles. She was surprised to feel invigorated when done.

"Now, to get you dressed. Sam will be in soon, and we'll have you walk around a bit. Then we will increase your exercise each day until you are fit and well again. If you tire, let us know and we'll put you back to bed. Your mind plays a large role in your recovery, so no talking or questions yet of all that happened. Concentrate on healing your body."

"If you say so. I have many questions."

"I'm sure you do, but first we must get you well."

I'm on day three now of the physical therapy and treatments. Enid and Mirabelle are providing the care I need. I'm feeling stronger every day.

"You look beautiful today. A calmness surrounds you. Have you found peace with some of your struggles?" Sam asked, interrupting her thoughts.

"I think I have. Who would have thought facing death would bring such clarity? It's all so amazing. I feel stronger: physically, mentally, and spiritually."

"It shows. It's a beautiful day outside. Still cold, but not as bitter as it was. The sun is shining. Are you up for a short walk? I think the fresh air would do you good, and Enid agrees."

"Yes, I would like that."

"Let me grab your coat, and we'll get you bundled up."

"Sam, you're fussing. I can get my own coat. Let me start doing some things myself. I need to; it's part of my recovery."

Sam started to protest but stopped. "You're right. I'm being overprotective. Let's get ready for our walk."

As she stepped outside, the brightness of the sun blinded her.

"I've been inside too long. I think I had better take your arm for guidance while my eyes adjust to the outside light."

Sam pulled a pair of sunglasses from his pocket. "I thought you might need these."

Slipping the sunglasses on did the trick. "I can see!"

Sam laughed. "Good. Don't let go of my arm though; you're still a little unsteady. We don't want any falls to complicate things. Besides, I like having you close."

"And I like being close to you."

"There was one time while you were missing I thought I felt you near me."

"When was that?"

"We searched the shoreline, along with so many others. On our way back I ranted about my guilt at leaving you alone. I thought I felt you stroke my cheek and say something, but I couldn't make out the soft-spoken words."

Gillian nodded. "I remember that. You were upset, and it hurt to see you in such a state. I stroked your cheek and told you not to worry, you would see me soon. I thought it was a dream, but I guess it wasn't. It's odd how you experienced that, but not when I spoke to all the Chosen ones."

"I think it was because, well, I'm ashamed to admit it, but I still had hope then. As each day that came and went without finding you, I lost more hope."

"Never lose hope, Sam. Even if I had died, you must always keep hope alive. Hope feeds our faith."

"I've said the same thing to so many who suffer a loss. When it got personal, it was different. I learned that when you love someone, as I love you, it blinds you. If you let it, and I did."

Gillian stopped walking and looked at Sam. "Did you just say what I thought you said?"

The color rose in Sam's cheeks. "Yes. It's not the way I wanted to tell you, but there it is. I am completely and hopelessly in love with you."

She touched his face. "That's the best news I've heard in a long time. When I thought I was dying, one regret plagued my mind. I didn't want to die without telling you I loved you."

Sam encircled Gillian in his arms. "You have made me very happy, more than happy." Stepping back, he grasped her hands and kneeled in the snow. "Gillian, will you marry me?"

Her smile grew, even though hot tears trickled down her cheeks. "Logic would tell me to wait, that I have experienced too much to have a clear mind. My heart tells me yes. I would love to be your wife. I want us to be hand in hand in everything we do, experiencing His blessings and miracles together."

His face mirrored hers, radiating pure joy and happiness. "I wasn't prepared for this. I don't have a ring to give you. I will get you one though."

"I don't want anything fancy. I'm not into a lot of bling. Just a simple ring that speaks of the love and the commitment we share."

"Would you like to help me choose it?"

"That would be nice. If you don't mind, I would like to wait a few more days before we tell anyone. Just until I finish my recovery. They'll want to celebrate, and I want to have the strength to celebrate too."

"I understand. It's our secret, for now."

They laughed and talked throughout the rest of their walk.

Gillian didn't notice the cold, and she didn't think Sam did either.

CHAPTER THIRTY-SEVEN

"Enid, thank you so much for spending the last ten days here helping me. I feel strong and well. Please thank Tom also, for insisting you come."

"It was my pleasure. Tom will be glad to hear how well you are now. Everyone will. A large group prayed for your recovery."

"I know. I'm humbled by all the concern and well wishes that have come my way. Thanks to you and Mirabelle, I'm ready to continue what I started a month ago."

"That's what we prayed for. Keep using the creams and the herbal mixture for the bath. It will help you maintain your strength, now we have you built back up."

Gillian held tears back as she watched Enid depart. *I will miss her.*

Banks came to her side. "It is time we talked."

Linking her arm in his, she nodded. "Yes, it is. We will wait until Sam returns from taking Enid to the plane. I want you, Sam, and Mirabelle to hear my story, and then I want to hear what you knew."

"I will have Mirabelle prepare tea. We will meet you in the parlor. It won't take Sam long."

She read through her journal while she waited. As soon as she was well enough, she had written every dream and memory she could remember. She didn't want to forget any detail.

Mirabelle entered with the tea cart, followed by Banks and Sam.

Looking at the wonderful people who had cared for her over the past weeks, her heart felt full.

"This will be a conversation we have all waited for. I want to start with telling you how grateful I am for your care during my recovery. I'll share all I remember, and then perhaps you can fill in the blanks."

She saw different emotions play across their faces as she recalled every detail of the ferry and her time in the cave, including the many dreams she experienced during her recovery. When she finished, silence filled the room. She studied their faces, trying to gauge their reaction to her story. Sam's expression revealed a mixture of anguish and awe, a serene smile graced Banks face, and Mirabelle glowed.

"So, that's my story. Which of you would like to start with yours?"

Banks cleared his throat. "I will tell you all I know. I received direction never before given. In my role as guardian and protector of the seventh generation Chosen, I have always been dedicated to them, seldom called away to aid or assist others and never in time of danger. I admit, I was conflicted when directed to remain with Stan and Margaret to help Stephanie. She needed help, but others could have filled the role. Not only did I receive this direction, but Sam received it also. I knew it would leave you defenseless, but I also knew you would be on Iona and therefore safe. I failed to consider the danger in the journey there. When I questioned my direction, I was told you must endure this journey alone, without my help. The outcome would be your choice. For the most part, I felt confident your faith would keep you safe. However, you are young and new to all this, so I admit, I had some doubt."

"I don't mean to interrupt, but what was the problem with Stephanie? What happened?"

"A sad story of a broken family with broken faith. Stephanie lost her way after her brother died. She opened herself to the darkness and accepted it completely, with the belief that being good helped no one. The darkness consumed her in the worst possible way. Her father, a man of the faith, had lost his faith. Only Margaret retained some faith, not all, but some. We helped them through the difficult night and turned their care over to those experienced in recovery."

"Are they okay now?"

"Somewhat. They still have work to do, but the darkness is gone from Stephanie, and she is being cared for. Stan and

Margaret are receiving the help they need, and their faith is being restored. You played a part in that."

"Me? How?"

"When they heard about you going overboard and missing, they both prayed for you. They felt responsible for you being alone. Though they admitted they weren't sure if prayer would help, your recovery restored their faith in the power of prayer and miracles. Almost everyone had given up hope of finding you. The water was so cold, too cold to sustain life for more than minutes. They maintained if you were washed to shore, you would die of exposure. Your accident and recovery restored the faith of many. It is being hailed as a miracle. There have been news crews interviewing people from the ferry and in Fionnphort."

"I am happy to hear that. I was told news of this miracle would bring back some who had lost hope and faith."

"Gillian, I must admit, as much as it shames me, until Ben told us of the message of hope and faith, I questioned the outcome. Not that I doubted God. I am sorry to say, I doubted you. I was not sure your faith was strong enough. I knew as soon as I heard Ben's words, you were alive."

"I have a question though, Banks. I thought, as my protector, you always sensed my presence, my needs. Why didn't you then?"

"It has never happened before, but I was blocked from you. He knew I would have intervened. He wanted no intervention. You had to take the journey without my aid or assistance."

"Yes, it was my journey. Surprising even to me, I understand. At the time, it confused me, but it needed to play out just the way it did. I was never alone; that I knew. Another question. Who threw me overboard?"

"We do not know. The ferry was crowded, but no one saw anything until it was too late. One man did not leave the ferry at Iona. He stayed on and returned to Fionnphort. I suspect it was he."

"You had angels with you the entire time," Mirabelle said. "They brought you to me."

Gillian sat up in her chair. "So that wasn't a dream. I thought I was dreaming I was being lifted up in soft angel arms and I remember thinking the arms felt like the bed at your house."

Mirabelle smiled, "Probably because you lay in the bed. They took you to a place that I and a few others were told to find you."

"So, they didn't bring me here?"

"No, they lifted you to safety in a place you could be found."

"I don't remember that part."

"You were unconscious and fevered. The first week you talked of God and angels in your sleep. From what you have told us of your dreams, I understand more of what you were saying. Gillian, you experienced something few on this earth have. You walked with the apostles, angels carried you, and you conversed with God. Those weren't dreams; they were real."

"I am blessed, but it's not just me. They told me everyone is born able to talk with Him, not just in prayer."

All remained silent. Gillian, Banks, and Mirabelle had told their stories.

"Sam, I think it's your turn," Gillian said.

"I know. I'm struggling. I will be completely honest about everything. All the emotions and events experienced."

"That's what I want."

"Banks and I were with Stan and Margaret as he has already said. I was getting nervous because I knew we would be late for the ferry. Like Banks, I received direction to remain with them, and although I was blocked from you, I still felt something. I can't describe it, but I knew something was happening, so I ran to the ferry. When I saw the ferry leaving, I panicked. I saw you wave and smile, and I knew it was your way of telling me it was okay. But that fear grew. I'm not proud of how I behaved. My faith should have been stronger. In anger, I shut everything out. Had I maintained my faith, I would have understood the message from Ben, as Banks did. Until I saw you, I could not escape the feeling of fear. Fear of losing you."

"Sam, we all learned a lesson from this experience. I am the newest member of the group. I would like to share with you what I think we all learned from this." Gillian looked at each of her friends. "Yes, it was a catastrophic event, but it provided a remarkable blessing. For me, I spent hours in conversation with someone who had walked with Christ. I still have no idea who he is, but he assures me one day I will. The location of some early writings of the faithful has been revealed to me. They will change nothing we know of God or Christ but will offer clarity. Clarity needed to build, renew, and instill faith and goodness in the world. What took place was a learning event for all of us. It also tricked the darkness into thinking they had won a great battle. I am told, in their rejoicing of their victory, they let their guard down and many were lost to them. Those who believed my rescue was a miracle turned from the darkness into the light. Sam, you learned fear and anger can block the message we need to hear. Regardless of the outcome, we must hold faith. Even in times of peril and tragedy, there is a blessing to be found."

As Gillian sipped her tea, she watched different emotions play across the faces of her dearest friends. Banks smiled, his eyes bright. Mirabelle also wore a big smile. Only Sam still struggled. His face appeared happy but his eyes still held a sadness.

Banks spoke first. "You are correct in all you say."

Sam sighed, shaking his head. "In my work, I have often told those who suffer that there is a reason for everything. I thought I believed that. But, when it became personal, I lost that belief. This experience has enlightened me to the knowledge that sometimes we must face hardship to receive the miracles and blessings He provides for us. I should never have doubted, but I have grown from this. My understanding has grown."

Gillian had been waiting to ask a question that had been on her mind. "When the Chosen got together, I noticed one missing. Where was Elizabeth?"

A shadow passed over Banks' face, "She declined to come. She said she was too busy, and she was sure we had sufficient help to handle the situation."

"Interesting. I think it deserves further questioning, but for now, we have more important things to deal with. I want you to read my journal. Samantha told me it was for my eyes only. However, I have it on good authority I am to share it with you. It is a recount of what happened, but in more detail, including more of my thoughts and emotions."

"I do not wish to intrude on your intimate thoughts, Gillian. Are you sure you want us to read it?" Banks asked.

"Yes. I'm sure. We'll be working together, and we have much to do. A better understanding of one another will help. We have grown closer during this, and I want to share everything."

"Thank you, Gillian. I, we, are honored. You have included me in your journey like none before you. May our joint work bless all we come across." Banks' voice contained a slight catch as he spoke.

"There is one more thing I haven't shared. Sam, I believe now would be a good time. Though I think it would be more appropriate for you to tell them."

Sam grinned at her. "I would love to. Gillian and I have had a special connection since we first met. If you remember, she chastised the group for not including me in the dinner. I was taken aback by her actions. Through everything, she has endured with faith and grace. During her recovery process, we bonded further. I have asked her to marry me. To my amazement and joy, she accepted. We don't have the ring yet, but it will come."

Mirabelle hugged them both. "I knew you were meant to be together. I'm so happy for you both. I... Oh yes! I'll be right back."

A puzzled look passed between the couple as they watched Mirabelle dart out of the room. "Is she all right?" Sam asked.

Gillian shrugged. "I'm not sure. It seemed like she remembered something important."

Banks nodded. "Yes, I think you are right, Gillian. She remembered something important."

Within minutes, Mirabelle bustled back into the room and sat on the arm of Gillian's chair.

"The last day your mother and father were here, your mother was so distraught poor thing. They had taken you to safety, to live with Mary. She missed you so. Anyway, I digress. She gave me this to give to you. Though she planned to leave it with Mary, something told her I would know the right moment to give it to you." Reaching in her pocket, she pulled out a small box and handed it to Gillian.

She opened the box, her tears fell unheeded as she saw what it contained. A small white-gold ring with three delicate stones: ruby, emerald, and sapphire. She struggled to speak. "This was my mother's?"

"Yes, and if you and Sam want, I think she would want you to have it as your engagement ring."

"Sam, you don't mind, do you? This way my mother will be a part of our union."

"I don't mind at all. It's beautiful, and I couldn't have picked better myself. I would like to put it on your finger though."

"I would like that."

Sam knelt on one knee, took the ring, and slid it onto her finger. "Now we are official."

Gillian noticed Banks' emotional expression and the moisture building in his eyes.

347

"Banks, do you know anything about the ring? Do the stones hold special meaning?"

He nodded. "Yes. They are the birthstones of your mother, father, and you."

Even though tears streamed down Gillian's face, her smile grew. "This gives even more meaning to this happy occasion."

"Have you decided where and when the wedding will be?" Mirabelle asked.

"Yes, Glastonbury. We made so many wonderful friends there, and the little church on our property will be perfect. Though it may seem rushed, we would like to get married before Christmas. Our work must continue, but I'm still recovering, so now is the perfect time."

"I am happy for you both," Banks said. "It would be wise if you spent the next week on Iona. It will be a healing time for you. I will contact Enid, and she will make all the wedding arrangements. You and Sam just need to decide on the date."

"Thank you, Banks. I need to call Maggie first. If she hears it from anyone but me, I'll be in trouble."

Banks laughed. "Yes, you would. I will wait until tomorrow to call Enid. That gives her time to get home and settled."

"Mirabelle, I know you dislike leaving here and traveling, but would you please come to the wedding? It would make us both very happy."

Mirabelle dabbed at her eyes with the corner of her apron. "Oh my, yes. I wouldn't miss it for the world."

Gillian slipped her hand into Sam's. "I was told that he who shared my light would make me stronger. That together we would achieve all we are destined to. I'm happy to know Sam will be by my side as we continue the work started by the disciples."

Banks nodded. "Your strength and faith will increase in your support of one another. I am incredibly blessed to take this journey with both of you."

CHAPTER THIRTY-EIGHT

Gillian waited until bedtime to call Maggie. Taking a deep breath, she waited for Maggie to answer the phone.

"Gilli? Is everything okay?"

"Yes, Maggie, everything's fine. I miss you and wanted to chat."

"We just talked yesterday, so I wondered. You rarely call for no reason. I mean, you know, you're not much of a talker."

"Maggie, pause for breath." Gillian laughed at her friend's never-ending chatter.

"Sorry, you know me. When are you going to be well enough to come back to Glastonbury? I want to see you before we leave. I so wanted to come to you, but everyone seems to think you need quiet for your recovery. Like I'm noisy or something. I mean…"

"Maggie, hush. I'll be there in just over a week. I'm leaving for Iona tomorrow and will rest there for a week, then return to Glastonbury. Will you and Joe still be there?"

"Yes, this program is growing so quick that Joe needed to expand your website and tweak the performance plans. He said we might as well spend Christmas here and then go home. His business at home is good, and the shop is doing well. It's amazing how wonderful everything is. It's all falling into place."

"That's wonderful. I can't wait to see you. I wanted to tell you something important. Sam asked me to marry him, and I said yes."

The squeal penetrated through the phone. "Gilli, I knew it. Oh, wait until I tell Joe. He knew it too. Oh, this is so exciting. Details, I need details."

"We are planning on a small wedding in Glastonbury just before Christmas. Banks will contact Enid with all the arrangements, and he assures me I won't need to worry about a thing."

"You won't. We'll take care of everything. Enid and I will arrange everything." Maggie laughed one minute and cried the next.

"Oh Maggie, don't cry."

"I'm not sad; its happy tears. The best kind. Gilli, I love you, and I'm so happy for you."

"Thank you, Maggie. I'll leave it all up to you and Enid then. I'll see you in about a week, we'll talk more then."

"Love you, Gilli. I'm going right now to tell Joe. Oh, and tell Sam I love him too!"

Smiling, Gillian shook her head as she put the phone down. *Where would I be without my wonderful, crazy friend?*

Getting ready for bed, her thoughts were full of all who loved her. *I am blessed to have so many who love me. It's hard to*

351

believe, not that long ago, I thought I was alone. God's love has opened my eyes to all the surrounding love. I don't want to waste a day. I want to share this outpouring of love with everyone. Thoughts of love lulled her into a peaceful sleep.

"You must tell the world of your experience."

"Ah, my friend from the cave. You are back. What should I tell?"

"Tell of all that happened, except the location of the writings. You may reveal that soon; proof will be found, proof that will end any doubt. Tell of the miracle and tell them more miracles will come. Tell of the love, hope, and faith which will bring such joy."

"You want me to tell the world? Everyone?"

"Yes. You know how to do it. Let it be. Follow your heart to spread the word."

She woke from her dream with a smile. *Yes, I think I know just how to do what is asked.*

She hurried through her morning ritual and went to find Banks.

She found him with Sam at the kitchen table.

"Good morning, fellow travelers. Today we leave for Iona; this time the journey will be a peaceful one. I need help to arrange something." She told them of her dream.

"If your direction is to tell the world, then that is what you need to do. How do you plan on doing this?" asked Banks.

"I want the word to get out we will be at the ferry in Fionnphort today. The news crews will show up, and I'll let them interview me."

Sam shook his head. "Do you think it's wise to let everyone know you will be on the ferry? I mean, what if…?"

"No need to worry this time. I will have you and Banks by my side. There will be no problems. I've heard many faithful are visiting there, the site of the miracle. I don't think anything dark will want to be around such love."

"Gillian's right, Sam. She will be safe." Banks pulled a piece of paper from his pocket. "Mirabelle, have someone contact this lady. She is a celebrity in the news world. She will spread the word. Tell her Gillian is willing to be interviewed."

"I'll take care of that right now. Gillian, eat your breakfast before you go. I've included all the foods Enid said would help in your healing." Mirabelle hurried off to do as Banks instructed.

She could tell by Sam's expression he was worried. "Please relax. Everything will be fine. Have faith."

"Sorry, the memory of what happened is still too fresh. I know you'll be fine, and I do have faith, but I still worry."

Banks patted his shoulder. "It is only natural you feel as you do. If you will take the bags to the car, I will look after some minor details, and then we can leave."

Once they were alone, Gillian took Sam's hand. "I need your faith to be as strong as mine. I would not have been guided to do this if there were any chance of something bad happening. You know that."

Sam hugged her. "You're right. I'll do as you ask. Are your bags ready for the car?"

"Yes, they're at the bottom of the stairs."

As Gillian put on her coat, Mirabelle entered. "Stay warm; we don't want you catching cold. Here's a flask of herbal tea for you to take with you. I will see you on your return. Be safe, my little one."

"Thank you for everything, Mirabelle. I am so grateful to have you in my life."

Sam and Banks waited in the car for her. She slid into the back seat and waved to Mirabelle. Relief flooded her when she saw Mirabelle standing in the open doorway, smiling and waving.

Yes, it's different this time. All is well.

The ferry from Oban to Craignure was a smooth ride as was the bus to Fionnphort. When they arrived at Fionnphort, Gillian felt anxious.

I hope I get the words out I need to say. I've never been good at public speaking.

Sam took her hand and helped her off the bus. She waited while they retrieved their bags and they started toward the ferry. She heard her name being called and looked for the source. She saw Andria running toward her.

"Gillian, I'm so glad to see you. We only met the one time, but I felt connected to you somehow. News of your accident and the miracle of finding you has lifted us all," Andria said, all in one breath.

She is so like Maggie. "Thank you, Andria. I'm glad to see you too."

"Is it true you are going to Iona, on the ferry? The entire area near the ferry is covered with news crews and vans. Do you need help to get through?"

"We'll be fine. I have agreed to an interview, to reveal what I experienced. I hope you can come. I think you will be enlightened."

"I plan on it. Mam will want to come too. I need to run and get her. She wants to meet you."

"We will see you there. I would love to meet your grandmother."

First, they went to the B&B. "What are we doing here? Gillian asked.

"Sam will take the bags to the ferry and get the tickets," Banks said. "Then we will make our way through the crowd of reporters to the ferry. They have agreed to hold the ferry while you give your interview."

"I hope I get this right." She could feel the palms of her hands start to sweat even though it was cold.

The host of the B & B greeted them with warm drinks.

"Glad you're recovering well. You caused quite the sensation in our little area. With all the news coverage, we are booked until next fall."

"That's wonderful news." Gillian sipped her tea, waiting for Sam to return.

As soon as he entered, she hurried to him. "Come on, let's get this over with. The more I wait, the more nervous I get."

"You'll be fine, don't worry. Have faith, remember?" he said, with a smile.

Sam and Banks supported her as they made their way through the crowd. Multiple questions came from every direction. The crowd of reporters pushed and shoved to get to her.

Banks did a good job blocking them.

When they arrived at the ferry, an area had been blocked off for her. A woman approached her with a microphone. Gillian recognized the woman from a news program. She didn't wait for the woman to speak. "I will not be taking any questions. I will only tell of what happened. I'm still recovering, so I hope you understand."

The woman seemed taken aback, at having someone tell her how to conduct the interview. "Very well. If that is what you wish. I will introduce you, and then you may speak."

"Yes, thank you."

The woman motioned to the cameraman; he held up three fingers, then two, then one and pointed for the news person to begin. "I have the pleasure of introducing Gillian Snyder. As you are aware, she experienced a harrowing event and wishes to share her story of what happened that day. Ms. Snyder, can you tell us what happened after you fell off the ferry?"

She cleared her throat as she took the microphone. "I did not fall off the ferry." She paused. "I was thrown off." A calm descended upon Gillian. "There is evil in this world. An evil so dark it will stop at nothing to put an end to good. I lost consciousness soon after hitting the water. My last thoughts were that I was dying, and I called out to God to help me. Angels came and lifted me. They carried me to a safe place. I'm unsure how long I remained there. During that time, I had many visions. I was blessed and comforted by angels the entire time. They kept me safe until someone could rescue me. In my visions, I spoke with one who had walked with Christ. He told me of the love Christ taught, how simple it would be for each and every person to turn to Him, to the light, accepting Him as our Savior and honoring the laws of God. The most important law is to love one another. Not to condemn or judge, but to guide through love and understanding. In doing these simple things, our hearts guide us to follow in His path. Empowered, as He empowered His Disciples to work wonders in His name. It is by a miracle I stand here today. You know what can happen to someone falling in these waters at this time of year. Yet, I stand before you, a testament of His love. I received instruction to share this with you, and to tell you this is a time of miracles. For all who believe, let your faith light the way for those in darkness. For those who are lost, know faith in God can lift you and carry you through the darkest times. Hope and faith must be kept alive. More and more people will turn to Him, and more and more miracles will be seen, not just by one or two but many. I will close by asking you to look within your own hearts, address your own failings, and reach out to those suffering. God bless you."

Gillian turned to walk away. People screamed questions at her. Then she caught sight of Andrea, with a frail, petite, elderly lady at her side. "Banks, can you help Andrea and her grandmother through the crowd? I promised I would meet her."

Without a word, he made his way through and brought Andrea and her mam to Gillian.

"Gillian, I don't know what to say. All that happened to you? I want to hear more. Sorry, that was rude of me. This is my grandmother. Mam, this is Gillian."

The little lady took Gillian's hands in hers. "I have seen the angels too. You are blessed. How long will you be on Iona?"

"We plan to stay a week. Please visit us there. I want to hear of your experience with the angels. We will stay with our friends, Moyra and Abe."

"Yes, I know of Moyra. I knew her family well. I will have Andrea bring me to you in a few days. You rest and heal more first."

"I would like that. Banks will help you back through the crowd. We must leave now. We have delayed the ferry long enough. They prohibited other passengers from taking this trip, so we may go undisturbed."

Waving goodbye to them, she asked Sam, "How did I do?"

Sam tilted his head to one side, and a smile grew. "Amazing. One simple word. You said so much in so few words. It will broadcast around the world. Many will want to know more of God. A time of miracles and blessings for all."

"Thank you, Sam. That is all we can hope for."

With Banks' return, the ferry pulled out, and they were on their way, across the narrow body of water that held many mysteries.

Banks put his arm around her shoulder. "How do you feel?"

"Hopeful, blessed, and ready to get to work."

He laughed. "I think you need to enjoy the peace of this beautiful island for a few days. Then we will talk about what's next. The information you revealed to the world will have many wanting to learn of Christ. That is all we can do, bring them to the point of wanting to learn more, then lead them on the path of learning and love. The rest is up to them. Your revelation will ripple around the world. We received blessings from God this day."

"Will the darkness fight back?"

"They always do. I think the promise of a loving God, goodness, and miracles far outweighs anything the darkness can offer. Don't you?"

"I couldn't agree more. Judging by the expressions on some in the crowd, they were in awe. Do you think it came close to the impact the early followers had on people when they spoke and taught of Christ's love and miracles?"

"Very much so. A look of hunger to know more."

Gillian walked to the side of the boat when Sam grabbed her and drew her back. "Oh, no you don't. You're not getting anywhere near the railing. I never want to be apart from you again."

"Nor I, you. I'm safe now."

The ferry engines whined as they maneuvered into the landing point at Iona.

"We arrive at last. I wonder what I will learn here on this trip?"

"Gillian, this is a resting, healing time for you. Remember you must rest and be well for our wedding."

"Oh, I know. I just have a feeling I'll learn more and meet my friend from the cave again. Just a feeling."

Thank you for reading

The Revelation, Book 3 of The Descendants Series.

Where will Gillian and her team be led in Book 4?

Stay tuned for updates.

Visit my website at http://www.susanabushell.com for updates and my blog.

Facebook: http://www.facebook.com/authorsabushell

Twitter: http://twitter.com/susan_bushell

Made in the USA
Coppell, TX
29 May 2020